RECKONING

CreateSpace ISBN: 1-4750-0921-6

www.bluespikepublishing.com

Printed in the United States of America

To My Family

OTHER BOOKS FROM DAVID LENNON

The Quarter Boys

Echoes

Second Chance

Blue's Bayou

Fierce
(Available April 2013...or sooner)

Author's Notes

One of the challenges of writing a series is that there's no guarantee people will start reading it from the beginning. That means each book has to provide enough detail from previous books that new readers can easily understand the characters, the relationships you've established, and so forth. When you write mysteries, that can be tricky, because you have to be careful not to give so much detail that you reveal key plot twists from previous books.

Up until now, I've been very careful, and each book has been written to stand on its own. There's been an overall progression in the characters' *personal* lives, but each mystery has been discrete, starting and finishing in the span of a single book, and it hasn't been necessary to read the earlier books to understand what's going on. This book is different, because it was originally intended as the series' finale. This time, I liberally brought back characters and referenced major plot points from the other books, because I viewed this one as the payoff for the faithful. In other words, IF YOU HAVEN'T READ ANY OF THE PREVIOUS BOOKS, DON'T START HERE! (And no, that's not just a shameless ploy to sell my other books.)

Though I work on a computer, I'm not technologically very savvy (like I don't know how to get my email unless I'm on my home computer, and I can't text). I know how to do only what I *need* to do, and beyond that, I really don't have much interest. For *Reckoning,* I had to do a little research...and by little, I mean just enough to get the gist of how some things work before my eyes glazed over. I hope I got it all more or less correct. I think it's fair to say, I've striven for plausibility, but don't guarantee accuracy.

I'm very lucky to have a great support team of family and friends. I'm not a brooding writer, but I do have occasional fits of insecurity while I'm writing, and I spend a lot of time lost in my own head. My husband, Brian, and friends Bob Mitchell and Vion DeCew have to bear the majority of that on a daily basis, and I'm thankful to them for putting up with me, and for their unflagging support.

Thanks to Esme McTighe, my eagle-eyed proofreader since *Second Chance* (so don't blame her for the typos I'm sure still exist in the first two books).

Thanks to all my family (Lennons, Lowries, Hugheses, Shaughnesseys, Nills, Scofields, Streeters, Laings, Falls, Bellinis, and more).

And finally, thanks to Michelle McCarthy, Paul Saltzman, Ernie Gaudreau, Ed Makuta, Kim Buchanan, Ken Dixon, Randy Stephens, Joel Fortner, Drewey Wayne Gunn, and Amos Lassen (among many others) for being fantastic cheerleaders, and for encouraging me to continue doing what I do.

One last thing: you may have noticed I said this book was *intended* to be the series' finale, and that I've listed a sixth book, *Fierce*, as coming in April 2013. I'll explain more about that next time.

D.L.

RECKONING

A Novel

DAVID LENNON

Chapter 1

As he drifted toward consciousness, Michel Doucette realized he was having trouble breathing. A heavy weight pressed down on his chest. He took a deep breath, held it for a few seconds, then exhaled loudly.

"Good morning, Blue," he said, without opening his eyes.

He heard a sound like the beating of huge butterfly wings, and felt the mattress vibrate. He knew the dog's tail was beating out a quick cadence somewhere near his feet. He opened his eyes and stared into the light brown-and-yellow speckled eyes only a few inches away. As always, Blue's expression looked slightly anxious, as though she'd been afraid he might not wake up.

"How are you?" he asked gently. "Did you have a good sleepy-sleep?"

The dog responded by jabbing her nose against his and darting her tongue quickly into his right nostril, then she pulled her head back and continued staring at him.

"Thanks," Michel replied with a combination of mock revulsion and genuine affection. "I'll take that as a yes."

He pulled his right arm from under the blanket and began rubbing the scruff on the left side of the dog's neck. She responded as she always did—turning her head away from him as though she didn't welcome his affection, while at the same time pressing into his hand more heavily.

"Okay, Greta Garbo," he said after a minute. "I suppose you want to go outside?"

Blue responded by increasing the rhythm of her tail, which now thumped loudly against the comforter.

"Well, I can't get up with you lying on me," Michel replied.

The dog gave him another quick lick on the nose, then jumped up excitedly and bounded from the bed toward the door. She paused for a moment and looked back at him expectantly.

"I'm coming," Michel said, rolling his eyes. "Why didn't you just have Joel let you out if you're in such a hurry?"

"Because you open the door so much better than I do," Joel's voice called from down the hall. "Besides, it's about time you got your lazy ass out of bed."

Michel smiled and threw back the comforter.

"Give me a second," he said to Blue. "I have to take care of some business."

He pushed himself up and shuffled into the bathroom, straightening the waistband of his boxer shorts as he went, and wondering for the thousandth time how they got so twisted while he slept. He closed the bathroom door and stood in front of the toilet. He could hear Blue pacing in the bedroom while he emptied his bladder, her nails lightly clicking on the cypress floor.

"Okay, okay," he said as he shook off and flushed the toilet. "I'm coming."

As soon as he opened the bathroom door, Blue bolted from the bedroom and down the hall. Michel followed her at a more leisurely pace.

"Good morning, sunshine," Joel said with a faux sincere, morning-TV-anchor smile.

He was standing in the entrance to the kitchen, dressed only in a pair of low slung, baggy gray sweatpants, and holding out a mug of coffee.

"Morning," Michel replied with exaggerated grumpiness, despite the fact that seeing Joel made him want to smile.

2

He took the coffee and gave Joel a light kiss.

"What time is it, anyway?" he asked.

"Almost eight," Joel replied.

"What time did you get up?" Michel asked as he headed for the back of the house.

Blue was standing inside the French doors, her body taut with excitement. Michel opened the far left door and she charged outside.

"About six," Joel replied as he came up behind Michel.

"Why so early on a Saturday?" Michel asked.

"I wanted to go for a run before it got too hot," Joel replied.

"That explains that stink," Michel said with an impish smirk as he walked out to the patio.

"Very funny," Joel replied. "I already showered. You're probably smelling yourself."

Michel made a show of lifting both arms and sniffing.

"Not me," he said, shaking his head. "I smell like sunshine and lollipops, just like always."

He dropped down into one of the wrought iron chairs and immediately felt the craving for a cigarette. It had been six months since his last one, and while he didn't think about smoking most of the time, he still longed for a cigarette with his first cup of coffee every morning. He took a deep breath to remind himself how much better he felt since he quit.

Blue finished patrolling the walled perimeter of the garden, and settled down in front of the fountain.

"Good girl," Michel said. "Did you scare away all those dangerous killer squirrels?"

Blue looked at him and seemed to smile proudly, then lowered her head between her front paws and blew out a loud sigh that stirred the dust in front of her nose.

Michel felt a surge of affection and smiled. It continually amazed him how much his life had changed in the six months since his cousin Verle had died. At the time he'd been living alone, his relationship with Joel had been stuck in a seemingly perpetual state of limbo, his professional life was in transition after leaving the New Orleans Police Department, he thought he'd lost his last living relative, and at best he could have said that he wasn't unhappy with his life.

Since then everything had changed. Since then he'd been on a roll: he'd become a "father" to Blue, Verle's dog; his relationship with Joel was thriving; the private investigation firm he'd started with his former police partner and best friend, Sassy, was turning a profit; he'd met his father and begun building a tenuous relationship with him; and he'd inherited a substantial fortune. Most importantly, though, he felt happy and contented. Still, even at his happiest moments, like now, he couldn't help but worry that the other shoe was about to drop.

Maybe the other shoe will just be that I'll become a fat, boring, middle aged man, he thought.

"So what do you want to do today?" Joel asked.

Michel looked at him and raised his eyebrows mischievously.

"Guess," he replied.

"Gee, would it have anything to do with real estate?" Joel replied sarcastically.

Michel had been on an obsessive quest to find a new house with a larger yard since Blue had come to live with him.

"Ding, ding, ding," Michel replied in a sharp, nasal voice like a cartoon carnival barker. "We have a winner, folks."

Joel gave him a deadpan look.

"And apparently a great big loser, too," he said.

Michel gave a self-satisfied smile.

"You really want to look at houses again?" Joel asked with a mild note of protest. "We have to have seen every house in New Orleans by now."

He was leaving the next morning for a three-day seminar on antisocial personality disorder in Orlando, and didn't relish the idea of spending the day house hunting.

"Not quite," Michel replied. "There's one more. Though technically it's not really a house. I swear it'll only take an hour."

Joel gave a resigned sigh.

"This is a sickness, you know," he said, shaking his head tolerantly. "You really need to get some help."

"Well, that'll give you something to talk about at the conference," Michel replied.

*****

"So what do you think?" Michel asked.

The overly solicitous realtor had just stepped outside.

"It's kind of...gothic...don't you think?" Joel replied.

"Of course it's gothic," Michel replied. "It was a church. But just picture it without the bench-thingies and the stained glass windows."

"You can't get rid of the windows," Joel protested.

"Why not?"

"Because they're probably historic."

"So we can donate them to a museum," Michel replied. "And we can get rid of the big cross, though Jesus does look kind of sexy..."

"You're just not right," Joel said, shaking his head.

"...and we could have a big living room over here," Michel continued excitedly, ignoring him, "with a pool table over there. Then we could put the dining room back there on the left, and the kitchen on the right, and we could build a half wall and put our bedroom up there."

"In the sanctuary?" Joel replied with disbelief.

Michel shrugged innocently.

"What?"

"You want to put our bedroom in the sanctuary?" Joel replied. "The place where we'll be having sex, in the same place where they performed marriages and baptisms and funerals?"

"So?" Michel replied.

"So that's sacrilegious," Joel replied.

"Not any more it isn't," Michel replied. "The whole place has been desanctified, or whatever you call it."

Joel just stared at him in reply.

"Okay, fine," Michel replied, turning around. "Then we can put our bedroom up there where the band played."

"The choir loft," Joel interjected.

"The *choir loft*," Michel corrected himself, "and we could put the dining room in the sanctuary since that would go with the whole 'this is my body, eat it, this is my blood, drink it' thing. Then we could turn the priests' dressing room into a guest room."

"It's called a vestry," Joel replied, sighing.

"Okay, altar boy," Michel replied. "So what do you think?"

"I think it would be a lot of work to make it seem like a home," Joel replied.

"But it could be fun," Michel countered, "and we could work on it together. You've got a month before school."

Joel had started at Tulane University the previous fall, pursuing a degree in criminal psychology, but had been forced to miss the spring semester to help care for his grandfather back home in Natchez. He was starting classes again in September.

He shook his head slowly.

"I don't know."

"The location is great," Michel replied, not ready to give up his sales pitch yet, "and it's got a huge yard that's already walled in for Blue. Plus we could dig up the parking area and put in a patio and pool."

Joel's eyes lit up a little, but he kept his expression neutral.

"And you're sure that yard isn't an old graveyard?" he asked. "I can just imagine Blue coming to the door with someone's arm in her mouth."

"I'm sure," Michel replied, laughing.

Joel looked around at the bare stone walls and up at the high vaulted ceiling. He had to admit it really was quite striking, though he couldn't imagine how they were ever going to make the space seem intimate.

"I think before you make an offer, you should bring in a contractor to find out how much it would all cost," he said.

"Fine," Michel replied. "I can do it while you're in Orlando. And I was thinking about asking Ray to draw up some plans."

Ray Nassir was an architect who had been dating Joel's best friend, Chance, for the past seven months.

"I wouldn't mention that to Chance just now," Joel replied.

"Why not?"

"He just dumped Ray's ass. Apparently Ray didn't consider things to be quite as monogamous as Chance did."

Michel frowned. Although his relationship with Chance had been somewhat contentious in the beginning, and still had a fair amount of competitive antagonism, he was actually liked Chance quite a bit.

"That sucks," he said, "though I wasn't actually planning to mention it to Chance anyway."

Joel gave him a look that was both curious and suspicious.

"And why's that?" he asked.

Michel averted his eyes for a moment, then looked up sheepishly.

"Well, because I think that maybe he was planning to buy this place and convert it to apartments," he said in a small voice.

In addition to managing the office and finances for Michel and Sassy, Chance had used money he'd inherited from his grandfather to start a property development company that specialized in renovating old buildings for affordable housing.

"Michel!" Joel exclaimed.

"I don't know that he was definitely planning it," Michel replied defensively. "I just happened to notice the listing on his desk while he was at lunch yesterday."

Joel shook his head and gave Michel a chastening look.

"You need to talk to him," he said.

Michel looked at the ground for a moment, then nodded reluctantly.

"Fine," he said. "I'll call him this afternoon."

Joel had to fight the urge to laugh at Michel's sullen expression. He looked like a kid who'd just been told he had to tell the cranky neighbor that he'd broken his window.

"Okay, you can wait until Monday," Joel said. "I suppose he's already got enough to be pissed off about right now."

"Thanks," Michel replied without enthusiasm.

"By the way," Joel said, "I hope you don't mind, but I made plans with him tonight. I figured he needed a girls' night out."

"No, that's fine," Michel said. "Maybe I'll call Sassy and see if she wants to play."

Chapter 2

Michel arrived at Good Friends Bar on Dauphine Street a little before 7:30 PM. He had a half hour to kill before he met Sassy for dinner at Bayona, a few blocks away. He headed up the stairs to the Queen's Head Pub, and settled in at the nearly empty bar.

"Jack on the rocks?" Mitchell the bartender asked.

"Yeah, thanks," Michel replied.

He pulled out his wallet and put a ten on the bar, then reflexively patted the breast and side pockets of his jacket, checking for cigarettes. He shook his head and smiled to himself when he realized what he was doing.

Out of the corner of his left eye, he saw someone moving unsteadily toward him. He fought the impulse to look, hoping it was just a drunk on the way to the stairs. Then the person sidled up to the bar and took a position intrusively close to his left elbow. After a few seconds, Michel looked up.

"Hello, Michel," the man said, with an elaborate nod.

Michel stared at him for a moment without recognition.

"I'm sorry, but do we..." he started, then stopped himself.

He realized it was Severin Davis Marchand IV. Marchand had been Michel's and Sassy's first client when they'd opened the agency. He'd hired them to find out who'd destroyed the costume he was working on for the Bourbon Street Awards during Mardi Gras. Marchand was the last member of one of New Orlean's oldest and wealthiest families, and was a fixture on the city's gay social circuit.

While Marchand had never been attractive, he'd at least always had the look of someone who'd been pampered. Now his skin was pale and sagging, and his owlish eyes were red-rimmed and puffy. Michel guessed he'd lost at least fifty pounds.

"Severin," Michel said. "I'm sorry, I didn't recognize you for a second."

"Yes," Marchand replied dryly. "I've been on a very strict diet and working out quite a bit recently. At my age, one has to do whatever's necessary to stay beautiful."

Michel smiled, though he knew Marchand's appearance was the result of anything but diet and exercise. He was either sick or had been on an extended drug binge.

"I haven't see you in a while," Michel said.

"No, I've been spending more time at the estate," Marchand replied. "I decided I needed to take a little break."

Marchand's family estate was located on Prytania Street in the Garden District, though for years he'd lived primarily in a townhouse on Royal Street in the Quarter.

Michel nodded.

"So, are you well?" Marchand asked in his typically unctuous manner.

Again, Michel nodded.

"Yes, thank you. Everything's fine."

He studied Marchand carefully. Marchand seemed nervous and distracted, his eyes darting quickly around the room every few seconds.

Despite the fact that he found Marchand generally repugnant, Michel had actually been hoping to run into him for some time. Shortly before he died, Verle had told Michel that he'd met someone in a conservation chat room who knew Michel, and that they'd been emailing one another for several months. Based on details the person had provided and his email address—SeverinIV@yahoo.com—Michel had assumed it was Marchand, and had wanted to ask him about it.

"I thought you'd want to know that my cousin Verle passed away six months ago," he said.

"I'm so sorry," Marchand replied. "My condolences to you and your family."

It was a completely obligatory expression, lacking any genuine sympathy.

"My cousin Verle," Michel repeated, watching for a reaction. "Verle Doucette?"

Marchand just stared at him blankly.

"I don't believe I ever had the pleasure," he said.

The response seemed genuine. Michel took a sip of his drink. He suddenly felt very uneasy.

"You're sure you've never heard of him?" he asked.

Marchand looked at him impatiently.

"Quite sure."

Michel looked down at the bar and frowned.

"Because someone from New Orleans was emailing Verle," Michel explained. "Someone who knew quite a bit about me. I assumed it was you because the email address was SeverinIV@yahoo.com."

For a split second, Michel thought he saw fear in Marchand's eyes. Then it was gone, replaced by indignation.

"Are you accusing me of lying?" Marchand asked, his voice rising enough that the few other people at the bar looked up.

"I'm not accusing you of anything," Michel replied in an even tone. "I'm just trying to find out who was feeding information about me to my cousin, and since you're the only Severin I know, I figured I'd start with you."

He decided to leave out his bigger concern: that the person had been trying to get information about his past.

"I assure you, I have much better things to do than spread gossip about *you*," Marchand replied coldly.

The emphasis on "you" made it clear that while Marchand would have no qualms about spreading gossip in general, he didn't consider Michel worthy of his efforts. Michel knew from experience that in Marchand's world, a person's value was based solely on wealth, family background, or what one could provide, and for just a moment he considered mentioning that he'd inherited over $10,000,000 from Verle, just to see Marchand's reaction.

"Are there any other Severins you know?" he asked instead.

"Any other Severins?" Marchand repeated, as though the words had a bitter taste.

Michel nodded.

"Of course not," Marchand replied haughtily, "Severin is a family name."

A sudden widening of his eyes and quiver of his thin lips betrayed that Marchand realized he'd made a mistake.

"Okay, so then is that your email address?" Michel pressed.

Marchand didn't reply for a moment. Michel could see him calculating how to respond, and noticed that sweat had broken out on Marchand's upper lip.

"Possibly," Marchand replied, trying to sound casual. "My accountant set up an email for me so that he could send me documents, but I don't use it myself. Members of the staff do that for me. In fact, I don't use a computer at all."

Michel was certain that was a lie. He had no doubt that Marchand was an avid surfer of porn sites. He reached into his jacket and took out his wallet, then removed a card and handed it to Marchand.

"I'd appreciate it if you could check and let me know."

Marchand's expression went suddenly cold.

"Of course," he said.

He took an unsteady step away from the bar.

"Now if you'll excuse me," he said.

Michel nodded, then held up his right index finger.

"Just one more question," he said. "Do you belong to any conservation groups?"

Marchand snorted derisively.

"I'm sure I wouldn't know," he replied. "My accountant handles all of my charitable contributions."

Then he walked quickly to the stairs and was gone.

Freak, Michel thought.

Chapter 3

"Two, please," Michel said to the attractive young woman at the host stand.

"Do you have a reservation?" the woman asked with a pleasant smile.

Sassy looked past her to the empty tables dotting the patio, then cocked her head to the right and stared the woman down for a few seconds.

"Really?" she asked.

The woman looked momentarily unnerved, but recovered quickly. "Would you prefer inside or the patio?" she asked.

"Patio," Sassy replied immediately, without bothering to confer with Michel.

The hostess led them to a table along the back wall.

"Is this all right?" she asked, looking directly at Sassy.

"Yes, fine, thank you," Sassy replied, her tone suddenly charming and gracious.

The hostess waited until they were seated, then handed them menus.

"Alfonso will be your server this evening," she said. "He'll be right with you."

"Thank you, dear," Sassy replied.

"We're lucky she didn't seat us right outside the kitchen," Michel said, as soon as the hostess was out of earshot.

"What are you talking about?" Sassy asked.

"'*Really?*'" Michel said, imitating Sassy, but exaggerating the level of condescension in the tone.

"I did *not* sound like that," Sassy replied, slowly shaking her head. "I have never sounded like that. I'm very polite to people. That's why people like me."

Michel let out a small snorting laugh.

"Hey, whatever helps you sleep at night," he said.

Suddenly a tall, strikingly handsome man with wavy, jet black hair and light green eyes appeared at the table.

"Good evening," he said in a light Portuguese accent, "I'm Alfonso. May I get you something to drink?"

Sassy looked at Michel.

"I'm in the mood for champagne," she said. "What do you think?"

Michel shrugged.

"Sure, why not?"

"We have a very nice 2003 Jacquesson Cuvée Terres Rouge Rosé," Alfonso said.

"Perfect," Sassy replied.

"Very good," Alfonso replied.

He turned crisply and walked toward the main dining room. Sassy watched him until he was gone, then looked at Michel and sighed.

"I know what I'd get if Alfonso were on the menu," she said.

Michel laughed.

"Wow, you're certainly living up to your name tonight," he said. "What's up with that?"

"I don't know," Sassy replied. "I'm just feeling good."

Michel nodded.

"Good is good," he said.

"Oh, by the way," Sassy said, "you're paying tonight. That champagne is $180 a bottle."

Michel stared at her, his mouth open in faux shock.

"It's so nice to have rich friends," Sassy said as she picked up the napkin on her plates and dramatically shook it open.

"At this rate I won't be rich for long," Michel muttered.

"It's a small price to pay for my company," Sassy replied breezily. "Speaking of which, why are you with me tonight instead of Joel? Doesn't he leave for Orlando tomorrow?"

Michel nodded.

"Yeah, but he wanted to spend some time with Chance. Chance and Ray just broke up."

"Oh Lord," Sassy replied. "Does that mean we're going to have tears in the office on Monday?"

Michel blinked at her.

"From Chance? Yeah, right. He'll probably meet someone new tonight and be madly in love again by Monday."

"I wouldn't be so sure," Sassy replied. "I think he really liked Ray."

Michel nodded thoughtfully.

"Yeah, I think he did, too," he said.

Alfonso emerged from the dining room carrying a silver champagne stand. He gave Sassy a dazzlingly white smile as he placed it next to the table, then went back into the dining room.

"I don't know if I like him better coming or going," Sassy said. "Mmmm, mmmm, mmmm."

"I wasn't aware you'd seen him coming," Michel replied archly.

Sassy looked confused for a moment, then narrowed her eyes at him.

"Don't be taking this beautiful thing between me and Alfonso and dragging it down into the mud," she said.

Alfonso reappeared carrying a bottle and two champagne flutes. He placed the glasses on the table, then displayed the champagne first to Sassy, then to Michel. Both nodded their approval. Alfonso opened the bottle with a flourish.

"You can skip the whole tasting ritual," Sassy said. "Just fill them up."

Alfonso smiled at her, then filled their glasses while he recited the specials.

"Would you like a few minutes?" he asked when he was finished.

"Please," Sassy replied.

Again she watched Alfonso leave, then turned to Michel and leaned in conspiratorially.

"I'd like more than a few minutes, if you know what I mean," she said in a not-so-quiet whisper.

Michel sat back in his chair.

"Are you drunk?" he asked.

"What?" Sassy asked. "Of course not. I feel fine."

"Are you sure?" Michel asked. "You just seem a little...off."

While Sassy had always been capable of being humorously vulgar, in the six years he'd known her, Michel had never seen her be crass.

"It's the menopause," she said suddenly.

"Excuse me?" Michel replied.

"The menopause," Sassy said, leaning closer and looking around to make sure the hostess wasn't listening. "I've started to go through menopause."

Michel felt his cheeks flush.

"Oh," he said. "I'm sorry."

"It's nothing to be sorry about," Sassy replied. "I'll be glad to be done with all that business. But right now it's got me going through these crazy mood swings. One minute I'm about to cry, and the next I'm feeling like a giddy teenager. It's kicking my ass."

"Aren't there pills or something you can take?" Michel asked.

Sassy nodded.

"I just started taking estrogen and progestin, but it takes a while for them to kick in."

Michel wasn't sure how to respond. Instead he pretended to focus on the menu, and was relieved when he saw Alfonso coming back to the table a minute later.

"Are you ready to order?" Alfonso asked.

"I'll start with the stuffed artichokes and have the salmon," Sassy replied.

"And I'll have the duck confit and the peppered lamb," Michel said.

"Very good," Alfonso replied.

This time Sassy didn't watch him leave. Instead she stared intently at Michel.

"What?" he asked.

"That was too much information, wasn't it?" Sassy replied.

"No, of course not," Michel lied. "I'm a big boy. I can deal with lady stuff."

"Lady stuff?" Sassy replied with a chiding laugh.

"What do you want me to say?" Michel replied defensively. "That I'm okay talking about your vagina?"

"It's not my vagina," Sassy replied. "My vagina still works just fine, thank you. It's my ovaries."

"Fine," Michel replied. "I'm fine talking about your withering ovaries. Anything else? You want to tell me about your bowel movements?"

"Only if you want to tell me about yours," Sassy shot back.

Michel narrowed his eyes comically.

"We are *not* going there," he said.

Sassy broke into a warm smile.

"No, we're not," she agreed.

She lifted her glass and held it toward Michel.

"Here's to...not knowing too much about friends," she said.

Michel raised his glass and delicately tapped it against Sassy's. They each took a long sip of champagne.

"Mmm, that's good," Sassy said. "Worth every penny of your money."

Michel glowered at her for a moment, then laughed.

"So guess who I ran into on my way here?" he asked.

"I'll assume that was a rhetorical question," Sassy replied.

Michel nodded.

"Severin Marchand."

"Wow," Sassy replied without enthusiasm. "Where?"

"At the Queen's Head," Michel replied.

"Seems appropriate," Sassy replied. "So how was she?"

"Odd," Michel replied.

"There's a surprise," Sassy said.

"No, I mean really odd," Michel replied. "Way more than usual."

"How so?"

"For one thing, he's lost about fifty pounds, and he looked like hell."

"Cancer?" Sassy asked.

"I'm thinking crystal meth," Michel replied.

"That's surprising," Sassy replied. "I wouldn't have pegged him as the meth type. I would have guessed coke, maybe, and possibly Ecstasy."

"I wouldn't have either," Michel replied, "but he definitely had that jumpy junkie thing going on."

"Did you talk to him?" Sassy asked.

Michel nodded.

"For about a minute. I told him about Verle."

"And what did he say?"

"He told me to give his condolences to my family."

"He didn't mention that they were pen pals?" Sassy asked.

"No," Michel replied, "and when I asked him about it he said it wasn't him."

"You believe him?" Sassy asked.

"Yeah, but something's going on."

"What do you mean?"

"When I first mentioned the email address, he looked scared," Michel said. "Then when I asked him if it was his email, he made up some bullshit about not knowing. He said he never uses email. That the staff handles that for him."

19

"Actually that wouldn't surprise me," Sassy replied. "I'd be surprised if he even wipes his own ass."

Michel chuckled. That was the sort of blunt vulgarity he expected from Sassy.

"So what do you think's going on?" she asked.

"Well, I don't think Severin was sending the emails, but I think he knows who was," Michel replied. "And I'm pretty sure he didn't know about it until tonight."

Sassy looked down at the table with a troubled expression.

"What's the matter?" Michel asked.

"I just don't like this," Sassy replied. "I mean, I can certainly understand why someone might pose as Severin if there were an advantage to it, like if they were trying to scam other rich folks, but there was no advantage in this case. Whoever it was could have just said, 'Hey, I'm Joe Blow from New Orleans and I know your cousin Michel'."

"But they wouldn't necessarily have known that," Michel replied.

"I don't know," Sassy replied, shaking her head. "The whole thing just bothers me. Someone pretending to be Severin contacts Verle out of the blue and starts asking him questions about you, then a few months later the real Severin hires us. Seems like more than coincidence to me. I think you need to be careful."

"Okay, now you're creeping me out," Michel said.

"Good," Sassy replied.

Michel thought about it for a moment.

"Why would someone would want information on me?" he asked, as much to himself as Sassy.

Sassy shrugged.

"Not sure, but I'd watch my back until we find out."

Michel sighed and looked down at his glass.

"I think I'll swing by the Bourbon Pub later and see if any of Severin's cronies are there," he said finally. "Maybe they'll know something, or at least be able to tell me what's been going on with him."

"Seems like a good start," Sassy replied.

They were both quiet for a minute as they sipped their champagne.

"So which team do you think he plays for?" Sassy asked suddenly.

"Who?" Michel replied. "My stalker?"

"Alfonso," Sassy replied, shaking her head impatiently. "You think he plays for your team or mine?"

Michel considered it for a moment.

"Tough call," he replied. "I'm pretty sure he's Brazilian."

"What does that mean?" Sassy asked with a look of bewilderment.

"Just that all the Brazilian men I've met seem to have pretty fluid sexuality," Michel replied. "The ones who say they're gay still sleep with women, and the ones who say they're straight still sleep with guys. I think they're a lot more comfortable with sexual ambiguity."

"And I think you're a racist," Sassy replied.

"A racist?" Michel replied with a laugh. "How does that make me a racist? I didn't say all Brazilian men. I just said the ones I've met. Besides, being comfortable with sexual ambiguity is a good thing."

"Doesn't matter," Sassy said. "Having a big dick and being good in bed are also good things, but when you say all black men have big dicks and all black women are good in bed it's racist."

Michel tried to gauge how serious she was being, but her expression wasn't giving anything away.

"Well, I've never heard that about black women, anyway," he replied, unsure what else to say.

Sassy stared at him for a few moments longer, and he could feel a trickle of sweat run down the small of his back.

"Well that one happens to be true," she said finally, breaking into a teasing smile. "Even when our ovaries dry up."

Michel laughed.

"I'll try to remember that," he said.

"No need for you to remember it," Sassy replied. "You just make sure to tell Alfonso if he asks."

Chapter 4

The doors along St. Anne were open and the whistling-tea-kettle synthesizers of Britney Spears' "Toxic" could be heard half a block away. Michel walked to the corner and turned left, then entered the Pub from the Bourbon Street side. It was almost 11 PM, and the place was filling up with the later crowd. Michel hoped he wasn't too late. From what he'd observed, Marchand's clique tended to show up for happy hour early, stay for a few hours until they were on the verge of messy drunk, then head out en masse for a late dinner.

He pushed his way up to the bar and ordered a Jack on the rocks, then did a quick sweep of the room. He spotted a group along the side wall where Marchand usually held court. Most of the guys looked to be very young—the sort of eye candy that could be rented in exchange for a few free drinks—but Michel recognized the man in the center.

Michel had always thought of Scotty McClelland as the princess-in-waiting to Marchand's queen. Based on his position at the center of the group now, it was clear that he'd ascended to the throne, at least temporarily. Michel had met McClelland only once, when he'd interviewed him during the Marchand investigation. He'd found him to be only slightly less imperious and self-impressed than Marchand.

As he approached the group, several heads turned to look at Michel. Their expressions were alternately nervous or accusatory. Then McClelland saw him and broke into a wide, insincere smile.

"Detective Doucette," he trilled. "What a pleasant surprise. How are you this evening?"

"Fine, thanks, Scotty," Michel replied casually.

McClelland's faltering smile indicated that Michel's use of informal address had had its intended effect.

"I was hoping I could talk with you for a moment," Michel said. "Alone."

McClelland eyed him warily for a few seconds, then arched his eyebrows suggestively. He looked around his circle to make sure they all saw his expression, then looked back at Michel.

"Of course," he said, standing up and reflexively tugging at the bottom of his black silk shirt.

As the sheer fabric stretched unflatteringly across McClelland's doughy midsection, Michel was reminded of the expression about putting a hat on a pig. He tried to disguise his smirk by covering his mouth and coughing.

"I'll be right back," McClelland said to the group, then followed Michel to the other side of the room.

"So what can I do for you, *Michel*," McClelland asked.

"I ran into Severin earlier tonight at Good Friends," Michel replied. "Is he all right?"

"You tell me," McClelland replied, giving him a surprised look. "I haven't seen him in months."

"You haven't?" Michel asked, with equal surprise.

McClelland shook his head.

"No. But I'm sure it's because of the boy," McClelland replied.

"What boy?" Michel asked.

"Who knows?" McClelland replied. "But whenever Severin disappears like this, there's *always* a boy."

He rolled his eyes and feigned an indifferent yawn.

"So this has happened before?" Michel asked.

"Every so often," McClelland replied. "He meets some twink, falls madly in love with him, and disappears for a few

24

months. Eventually when the kid figures out he's not getting in the will, he takes off and Severin reappears. Though he is a little overdue this time."

"How long has it been since you've seen him?" Michel asked.

McClelland pursed his lips and seemed to be counting very slowly in his head.

"About a month after Mardi Gras," he replied finally.

"And you haven't talked with him either?" Michel asked.

"I tried for weeks and weeks," McClelland replied as though even the memory was exhausting. "I finally gave up because he wouldn't return my calls or emails."

Michel furrowed his brow.

"He looked terrible," he said.

"That's not surprising," McClelland replied. "Severin's always had a little problem with substance abuse. Without his friends around to keep him out of trouble, he's probably been on a binge."

Under normal circumstances, Michel would have found the idea that Marchand's friends provided a stabilizing influence laughable, but now he was genuinely concerned.

"But what about the staff?" Michel asked. "Wouldn't they look after him? Joseph?"

Michel had met Joseph at Marchand's house in the Garden District. Joseph's family had worked for the Marchands for generations, and Marchand had said that he considered Joseph to be part of his own family.

"The staff is gone," McClelland replied. "That much I know. I ran into Joseph a few weeks ago. He's living in the townhouse now. He told me that Severin let everyone else go."

"When?" Michel asked.

"I don't know," McClelland replied. "Probably when the boy moved in. For some reason, Severin always tried to keep his sexuality a secret from the staff. As if he could. But you should probably ask Joseph about it."

Michel had already made up his mind to do so.

"So is there anything else I can help you with?" McClelland asked.

His expression made it clear he'd tired of talking about the man whose position he'd usurped.

"Just one other thing," Michel said. "You mentioned you tried to email him. Did he use email very often?"

McClelland shrugged.

"As much as anyone, I suppose," he replied.

"Do you happen to know his email address?" Michel asked.

McClelland sighed as though it were a terrible imposition, but took out his cell phone and started punching buttons.

"SeverinIV@yahoo.com," he said finally.

"Thanks," Michel replied.

*****

Michel stepped out onto Bourbon Street.

"Hey there, sexy," a familiar voice called from above. "How about joining us for a threesome?"

Michel turned and looked up. Joel and Chance were standing on the balcony, a few feet from where Michel and Joel had first met. Chance had his shirt off and was leaning over the railing, while Joel held onto his left arm.

Michel took a few steps back. He wasn't afraid that Chance might fall, but from the way Chance was swaying, it was clear he might vomit at any moment.

"So what do you say?" Chance asked.

"I'm afraid I'm going to have to pass," Michel replied.

"Your loss," Chance slurred.

Michel looked at Joel, who seemed only slightly less drunk than Chance.

"Don't stay out too late," he said. "Remember you've got a flight in the morning."

"I won't," Joel replied, then began giggling.

Chance looked uncertainly from Joel to Michel, then back at Joel.

"You know that guy?" he asked. "He's kind of hot."

Michel shook his head and started toward home.

Chapter 5

"Where have you been?" Chance asked when Michel and Blue walked into the office. "Sassy's been looking for you."

"Where is she?"

"She just went to the French Market to get some coffee."

The French Market was located down by the river, on the opposite side of the Quarter from the office.

"Wow, must be really urgent if she's taking a 20-minute break to get coffee," Michel replied.

Chance looked down at an imaginary watch.

"Oh yeah, and clearly you have really important things to do, too," he replied sarcastically.

Michel mimed hearty laughter for a few seconds, as Blue walked to her customary sunny spot by the window and dropped down.

"Actually, I'm glad she's not here," he said. "I have something to talk to you about."

Chance eyed him suspiciously.

"What? You're sleeping with Ray again?"

Michel had met Ray during the Marchand investigation, and they'd dated briefly.

"No," Michel replied, "but I was sorry to hear about you guys."

"No big deal," Chance replied with a bit too much nonchalance. "I'm not going to lose any sleep over it."

From the paleness of his skin and the dark circles under his eyes, Michel could tell that he already had, but decided to let it pass without comment.

"So, I was just out at the old church on Baronne Street," Michel said.

He watched Chance for a reaction, and saw Chance's eyes narrow slightly.

"*My* church?" Chance asked. "What were you doing there?"

"Meeting with a contractor," Michel replied.

"A contractor?" Chance replied, his voice rising sharply. "Why the fuck were you meeting with a contractor at *my* church?"

"I'm sorry," Michel replied quickly. "I saw the listing on your desk on Friday and thought it would be a great place for Joel and me to live. I know, I should have asked you first."

Chance stared at him with his mouth slightly open for a moment, then shook his head.

"This is fucking unbelievable," he said. "First my boyfriend cheats on me, and now you—who I considered a friend—steal a property away from me."

Michel suddenly wished Sassy were there after all.

"I really am sorry," he said. "If you want it, it's yours. I haven't even made an offer yet. I swear."

Chance continued staring hard at him for a moment, then broke into an impish smile and chuckled.

"Oh my God, you're so gullible," he said.

"What?" Michel replied.

"I was just shitting with you," Chance said. "You should have realized that as soon as I said I considered you a friend. I can't believe you're a detective."

"You fucker," Michel exclaimed. "You already knew?"

Chance nodded.

"How?"

"Joel told me on Saturday night," Chance replied.

"He told you?" Michel asked incredulously. "Why didn't he tell me? I was dreading this all weekend."

"He probably forgot," Chance replied. "We were both kind of wasted. Or maybe he just wanted to see you sweat."

Michel shook his head. "Someone's getting a spanking when they get home," he said.

"Hey," Chance said, holding up his hands, "I don't want to know about your kinky welcome home rituals. Oh, and it's fine if you want to use Ray for the design."

"No, that's okay," Michel replied. "I'm sure I can find someone else."

"Seriously," Chance replied. "I don't mind. He may be a douche bag, but he's still a great architect."

Michel nodded, though he still felt somewhat guilty.

"So I take it you'd already decided not to buy it?" he asked.

"Are you serious?" Chance replied. "With all that termite damage?"

Michel blinked involuntarily, and Chance began laughing.

"You really are such a dumb ass sometimes," he said. "The foundation and the walls are stone."

Michel gave an embarrassed laugh.

"Oh yeah. So seriously, why did you decide against it?"

"It would have cost too much," Chance replied. "I could have put some killer condos in there, but not apartments. And there's already enough high priced real estate in that area."

Michel nodded. He felt a grudging sense of admiration. Despite the fact that he could easily have capitalized on the overheated real estate market, Chance had stuck with his original mission.

"So, what do you think about the idea of turning it into a home?" Michel asked.

"It's kind of big, but it could work," Chance replied with a shrug. "Plus you can dress Joel up like an altar boy and defile him over and over again."

Michel rolled his eyes tolerantly.

"Speaking of, have you heard from him?" he asked.

"Um, he's only been gone for a day." Chance replied, giving him a mock pitying look.

Michel ignored it.

"I tried calling him three times last night and once this morning," he said, "but I just keep getting his voicemail."

"Stalker says what?" Chance muttered under his breath.

"What?" Michel replied distractedly.

"Nothing," Chance replied, with a self-satisfied smile. "Have you tried calling the hotel?"

Michel felt himself start to blush.

"You really are the worst detective ever," Chance said, shaking his head.

He starting tapping on his keyboard, then picked up the phone and dialed.

"Joel Faulkner's room, please," he said.

There was a pause, then he looked at Michel and put his hand over the mouthpiece.

"Did he switch hotels at the last minute?" he asked.

Michel shrugged.

"Not that I know of. He's staying at the Clarion."

Chance's eyebrows knit together for a moment.

"Can you check again?" he said into the receiver.

There was another, longer pause.

"Are you sure about that?" he asked. "When?"

Michel caught the concern in Chance's voice, and walked over to his desk.

"Okay," Chance said. "Thanks."

He hung up and gave Michel a worried look.

"What?" Michel asked.

"They said he had a reservation, but cancelled it on Thursday," Chance replied.

Michel felt a chill run down his spine and pulled out his cell phone. He hit the speed dial button for Joel.

A muted ringtone came from behind Chance, and he spun around in his chair. He cocked his head toward the two file cabinets, trying to pinpoint the source.

"I think it's coming from the safe," Michel managed, though his throat had constricted and he was suddenly having trouble breathing.

Chance dropped to his knees and started quickly twirling the safe's dial. He turned to the last number and twisted the handle. As the door cracked open, the ringing became louder, then suddenly stopped.

Michel could hear Joel's voice in his ear.

"Please leave a message after the tone, and I'll get back to you."

He flipped the phone shut without thinking, and dropped it on the desk. The sound it made seemed impossibly loud.

Chance pulled open the safe door. There was a white 9 x 12 envelope lying on the top shelf. As he picked it up, the bulge in its center shifted down. He stared at it for a moment, then held it out to Michel, his hand noticeably shaking.

Michel felt as though he'd moved to some unfamiliar place in his own body—a place where his heart beat louder and his breathing echoed, a place where he had no control over his limbs. He watched as his left hand reached out and took the envelope.

From what seemed like a great distance, he could see his name printed on the front in large, neat capital letters. His left hand turned the envelope over and his right began to tear the flap open. Michel wanted to stop himself, but couldn't.

He watched as his hand reached into the envelope and pulled out Joel's cell phone, then placed it on the desk beside his own phone. He could see a piece of paper in the envelope, and his right hand sliding it out. He was dimly aware that it felt thicker and heavier than normal paper.

His hand held it up. In the same neat, capital letters it read, "$10,000,000" across the top, and "339-555-0918" below that. He heard Chance take a sharp breath and looked at him. Chance was staring at the back of the paper, his eyes wide.

Michel saw his hand flip the paper over, and a photo of a nude male sitting on a chair in a dimly lit room. The man was blindfolded, and his arms were behind the chair. In the bottom right corner of the photo was a digital time stamp: 07-17-06 5:10 AM. Earlier that morning.

Michel studied the man's nose, lips and torso. It was Joel.

With a jolt, he came back to himself. He turned the paper over and grabbed his cell phone, quickly punching in the phone number. It rang once, then there was a loud click.

"Too late," a man's voice said. "You should have gotten to work on time today."

Then the line went dead.

Michel felt a surge of panic but fought it back. He flipped the paper back over. The room in the photo was so familiar. He studied the details: the concrete floor, the vertical wood support beam, what appeared to be a bulkhead door. He knew he'd been there and closed his eyes, trying to go back to that moment.

He could remember the dampness, and a smell that was both sweet and acrid at the same time. He could remember an old rusted furnace in the corner, and the uneven surface of the floor, and the darker spots...

Blood spots, he thought suddenly.

He opened his eyes and looked at Chance.

"Call the police," he said. "Ask for Captain Carl DeRoche. Tell him about the photo, and that Joel is in the basement of Mose Lumley's old house on Poeyfarre Street. Then call Sassy and tell her to meet me there."

Mose Lumley had been a friend and coworker of Sassy's husband, Carl. During Sassy's rookie year, she'd been assigned to a case involving several missing girls. The case had culminated at Lumley's house with the deaths of Lumley and the last victim, Iris Lecher, and with Sassy being shot. Michel had gone to the house twenty-five years later while investigating a possible link between Carl and more kidnappings.

33

Chance nodded and Michel could see he was on the verge of tears. He reached out and touched Chance's shoulder.

"It's going to be okay," he said, hoping that it sounded remotely convincing.

Chapter 6

Michel turned the corner hard onto Poeyfarre Street and slammed on the brakes. His truck skidded to a stop a few inches from the back of a police car. A line of a half dozen more cars stretched up the middle of the street, their blue lights flashing in the bright morning sun. They were bracketed tightly on both sides by an array of dump trucks and flat beds carrying excavation equipment.

Michel threw the shift into PARK and jumped out so quickly that he nearly fell. He began running toward Lumley's house, awkwardly dodging the side mirrors that jutted into the narrow gap between the trucks and police cars. Behind the trucks he could see empty lots on both sides of the street, and up ahead, a bright yellow back hoe, its bucket poised in the air like a giant claw. He tasted copper as his adrenaline surged, and forced himself to run faster.

As he cleared the last truck, he stopped short and a wave of nausea welled up from his stomach. The second floor of Lumley's house was already gone, the roof and walls collapsed down into the first.

He took a ragged breath and started toward the house.

"Hey," a voice called out from somewhere close by.

Michel ignored it and walked faster. Suddenly he felt a hand close on his left arm.

"You can't go in there," the voice said.

Michel jerked his arm away and took a few more steps. Then arms closed on him from behind.

"Let me go," Michel screamed, the last word breaking as tears began welling up in his eyes.

He twisted his body hard to the right, then swung his left elbow back. It hit someone and he was free again. He stumbled forward, wiping his eyes with the back of his right hand.

There were people all around him now, though he couldn't see their faces clearly. He tried to push past them, but they blocked him. They were all talking at him in loud voices. He began throwing punches wildly.

Then suddenly he was on the ground. He clawed at the dirt, trying to drag himself forward but couldn't. A heavy weight was pressing down on his back.

"Let him up!" a familiar voice yelled. "Let him up!"

Suddenly the weight was gone, and Michel rolled to his side.

"Michel," the voice said soothingly. "It's me. Al."

Michel looked up and saw Al Ribodeau standing over him. Ribodeau was an old friend who'd been promoted to the homicide division after Michel and Sassy left.

Ribodeau knelt down and helped Michel into a sitting position.

"He's not in there," Ribodeau replied.

"What?" Michel asked, convinced he'd misheard.

Ribodeau gave him a steadying look.

"He's not in there," he repeated.

Michel took a deep, wet breath.

"Are you sure?" he replied.

His heart was racing and his tongue felt thick and slow.

Ribodeau turned to a thickset black man with short graying hair who was standing a few feet away. He waved him over.

"Michel, this is Aubrey Leveau," Ribodeau said. "He's the foreman. Mr. Leveau, this is Michel Doucette."

Leveau knelt down and nodded at Michel.

"Please tell him what you told me," Ribodeau said, looking at Leveau.

36

"We did a sweep of the house this morning," Leveau said. "There was nobody inside."

Michel felt his chest loosen slightly.

"You're sure?" he asked.

"I was in there myself," Leveau replied, nodding. "We started upstairs, then worked our way through the first floor and basement, and went out through the bulkhead. There wasn't so much as a mouse in there."

"And the house was never left unattended afterward?" Michel asked.

"No," Leveau replied. "There've been two dozen guys here since seven this morning."

Ribodeau looked at Michel.

"You're sure the photo was taken here?" he asked.

Michel took another long, wet breath, then nodded.

"Positive."

Ribodeau turned to Leveau.

"I'm afraid we're going to have to shut you down until we can get a forensics team in here," he said. "You'll have to leave everything exactly as it is, and we'll probably want to question you and your men."

Leveau sighed with resignation, but nodded.

"Is it safe for our people to go into the basement?" Ribodeau asked.

"I'm not sure," Leveau replied. "We'll need to clear some debris from the bulkhead. See if the supports are still in place."

"Fine," Ribodeau replied. "I'd like you to oversee that personally. In the meantime, you'll need to get all of your men off the property and out on the street."

"Michel!" a voice suddenly called out.

The three men turned and saw Sassy coming toward them, moving with surprising speed in the narrow lane between the police cars and construction vehicles. Ribodeau and Leveau stood and helped Michel to his feet.

"Are you all right?" Sassy asked as she reached them.

"The foreman said he's not in there," Michel replied in a small, weak voice.

"I know," Sassy replied, trying to catch her breath.

"What?" Michel asked.

"He called while I was on the phone with Chance, and left a message," Sassy replied. "He said he was at the airport in Orlando and was on his way home."

Michel looked at her with disbelief.

"You're sure it was him?" he asked.

Sassy nodded emphatically.

"No question."

"And he just called?"

"Not ten minutes ago," Sassy replied.

Michel wanted badly to believe her, but was still afraid it was some sort of mistake.

"But why didn't he call *me*?" he asked. "That doesn't make sense."

"His message said he'd been trying to call you and Chance but he couldn't get through, so he tried me," Sassy replied. "He said he'd head straight to the office when he got in."

She reached up and wiped the tears and dirt from Michel's cheeks with her thumbs. Under normal circumstances, Michel would have been bothered by the maternal gesture, but now he accepted it gratefully.

"So this was all just some sick joke?" he asked.

"Looks that way," Sassy replied.

Ribodeau frowned.

"Give us a moment, please, Mr. Leveau," he said.

Leveau nodded and walked over to join his men.

"Okay, so do we have a crime scene here or not?" Ribodeau asked, looking from Sassy to Michel with uncertainty.

"I'm thinking not," Sassy replied. "If Joel wasn't kidnapped, then he was never here."

"But whoever took the photo was," Michel replied.

"But that could have been weeks or even years ago," Sassy replied. "Obviously the photo was a fake, and that would have taken some time to do."

"But the time stamp on it was from this morning," Michel protested.

"That could have been faked, too," Sassy replied.

Ribodeau considered the arguments for a moment, then frowned.

"I don't think I can justify the manpower," he said. "Technically there's been no crime."

Michel started to protest, but then stopped himself. He realized that Ribodeau was right.

"I'm sorry, Al," he said.

"That's okay," Ribodeau replied. "You had no way of knowing."

He looked around at the dozen officers standing in the street and gave a mordant laugh.

"Our tax dollars at work," he said. "Anyway, I already sent a forensics team to your office. May as well let them see if they can pull any prints while they're there."

"I appreciate that," Michel replied.

He looked down at the ground for a moment, then winced.

"Any chance you could do me one more favor?" he asked.

"Will you buy me a donut?" Ribodeau asked.

"A dozen," Michel replied.

Ribodeau nodded.

"Can you run a trace on the phone number on the photo?" Michel asked.

"Already being done," Ribodeau replied.

"Thanks," Michel replied.

Then he looked at Sassy and smiled.

"I don't know about you," he said, "but I'm starving. Early lunch?"

Chapter 7

The hours since they'd arrived back at the office had crawled by. Michel checked his watch for the hundredth time and sighed. He'd wanted to go to the airport, but Sassy had convinced him that without knowing the airline or flight number, he'd undoubtedly miss Joel. He looked back down at the newspaper he hadn't been reading for the last hour.

When the phone rang he jumped in his chair.

"Jones and Doucette Investigations," Chance answered.

He looked up at Michel.

"Just a moment please," he said, then punched the hold button. "It's Detective Ribodeau."

Michel sat up straighter and grabbed his phone.

"Hey Al."

There was a long pause. Sassy and Chance watched Michel, trying to read his expression.

"Okay, thanks," he said finally, and hung up.

"Anything?" Sassy asked.

Michel shook his head.

"There were no prints on Joel's cell phone or the photo. They're sifting through the prints they pulled from the safe, but they're probably just ours."

"What about the phone number?" Sassy asked.

"It belonged to a bookstore on Chartres Street," Michel replied. "The cops went there, but the place has been closed for almost a year."

"And no sign anyone had been there?" Sassy asked.

"There wasn't even a phone," Michel replied.

Suddenly Blue jumped up. She cocked her head toward the door to the hall, and her tail began vibrating excitedly. Michel stood up, his heart suddenly racing.

"Who is it, girl?" he asked.

Blue looked back at him for a moment, then ran to the door and around the corner.

"There's my girl," Joel's voice carried into the room.

Michel hurried to the doorway, with Chance and Sassy close behind. Joel was squatting just inside the outer door. Blue's front paws were on his shoulders, as she enthusiastically licked his face.

"I guess you missed me, huh?" he asked.

He kissed Blue's nose, then lifted off her paws and stood up. Michel immediately closed the distance between them, and threw his arms around Joel.

"I guess you missed me, too," Joel managed through his shoulder.

"Are you all right?" Michel asked.

Suddenly Chance was beside them, wrapping his arms around them both and crying.

Joel looked at Sassy and raised his eyebrows questioningly.

"Okay, you're kind of freaking me out," he said. "I'm glad to see you guys, too, but it's only been a day."

They both hugged Joel for a moment longer, then took a step back. Now that Joel was actually there, Michel felt as though a huge knot in his chest had been loosened.

"We need to tell you something," he said.

*****

"Holy shit," Joel said when they'd finished telling him about the photo and Lumley's house. "That explains the overly enthusiastic welcome."

He sat back in his chair with a dazed look.

"I can't believe that."

"So what happened in Orlando?" Michel asked. "Why did you come back so soon?"

"It was a total cluster fuck," Joel replied. "First I went to the hotel and they told me I'd cancelled my reservation and they didn't have any more rooms, so they got me a room at some shit motel about 20 miles from the conference center. When I got there, I couldn't find my cell phone, so I tried to call you and Chance, but the phone just kept ringing."

"Did you try the office?" Chance asked.

Joel nodded.

"I left a message this morning."

Michel gave Chance a questioning look, but Chance shook his head. He'd checked the answering machine as soon as he'd gotten in that morning, and hadn't left since.

"So then what?" Michel asked, turning back to Joel.

"Then I got to the conference center this morning, and found out there was no seminar," Joel replied. "There was some big toy expo going on instead. So I went back to the motel, got my shit and went to the airport. Fortunately I was able to get a flight right away."

"There was no seminar?" Sassy asked.

Joel shook his head.

"No. Basically I got scammed out of 500 bucks, plus the money I wasted for the flights and taxis."

Sassy had a sudden sense of foreboding as she realized the level of planning that had gone into the prank kidnapping, but decided to wait to discuss it with Michel later.

"The important thing is that you're okay," she said instead. "And I think we should call it a day."

"Sounds like a plan to me," Michel replied brightly.

"But until we know exactly what's going on," Sassy added, trying not to sound overly concerned, "I think everyone should stay close to home. Just in case."

"The Rawhide is only a few blocks away," Chance said hopefully. "That's pretty close."

Sassy narrowed her eyes at him.

"I'm thinking a little closer than that," she replied. "Like inside-the-door close."

Chapter 8

Michel draped his arms around Joel's naked waist, and kissed the back of his neck. Joel looked at Michel in the bathroom mirror and smiled.

"Maybe I should get fake-kidnapped more often," he said.

"Don't even joke about that," Michel replied. "I think I've done enough crying in front of construction workers to hold me for a while, thanks."

"You cried?" Joel asked.

They'd spent the entire afternoon in bed, alternating between manic, frenzied sex and napping. It was the first time they'd talked about what had happened alone.

"Well, maybe just a few tears," Michel replied sheepishly. "And if anyone tells you any differently, they're lying."

Joel turned in Michel's arms and smiled.

"That's so sweet," he said, then leaned forward and gently kissed Michel.

"Sweet, my ass," Michel replied with an embarrassed smile. "I lost my shit in front of Al Ribodeau, a dozen other cops, and a whole bunch of burly guys in construction helmets."

"You sure you weren't at a Village People concert?" Joel joked. "Were there Indians there, too?"

"Very funny," Michel replied with a theatrical pout.

"I'm sorry," Joel said.

He put his arms around Michel's neck.

"It's just that I'm having a hard time imagining you losing control like that," he said.

"It surprised me, too," Michel said, "but when I saw Lumley's house, and thought you were trapped inside..."

He trailed off and lowered his eyes for a few moments, unsure how to explain it. Finally he looked back into Joel's eyes.

"It was just that when I thought about how scared you'd be, I wanted to protect you," he said. "I wanted to take away the fear and pain, but I realized I couldn't, and I just felt so helpless."

He paused for another moment before continuing.

"And I was scared for myself. I thought I might lose you."

He felt tears welling up, but didn't try to hide them.

Joel leaned forward and kissed Michel's right cheek, then sat back against the sink. His expression was suddenly serious.

"You realize you're not always going to be able to protect me, don't you?" he asked.

Michel nodded.

"And even if you could protect me physically," Joel continued, "you can't protect me emotionally. Bad shit is going to happen. My grandparents are going to die some day. People are going to do and say things that hurt me. You can't stop those things from happening, and you can't protect me from the pain."

"I know that," Michel replied.

"And to be honest," Joel said, "you shouldn't try. Pain is part of life. I can deal with it. I lost my parents when I was pretty young and I dealt with it, and I'm not a kid anymore."

"I'm sorry," Michel said. "I didn't mean to imply..."

"I know you didn't," Joel interrupted, "and obviously this situation was pretty extreme. I'm just saying that I hope you don't feel you have to shelter me. I'm not fragile. I won't break."

Michel wiped his eyes and gave an embarrassed smile.

"I know you won't," he said.

Joel looked at him with teasing skepticism.

"You're sure?"

"Cross my heart," Michel replied, marking an X with his right index finger.

"Good," Joel said. "So then what do you think is really going on? The truth."

Michel suddenly realized that Joel had set him up. He couldn't help but smile.

"That was very good," he said.

"Don't try to dance around the subject," Joel replied. "I want to know what's going on. Is this serious?"

Michel stared at him for a moment, then shrugged.

"I honestly don't know," he said. "I'm not sure if it was just a sick joke, or the beginning of something else."

"Any idea who would do it?" Joel asked.

Michel hesitated briefly before responding. One suspect had come to mind, though he hadn't been able to come up with a convincing motive. He was about to reply when the doorbell rang.

"Saved by the bell," he said.

Joel gave him a sour look.

"Funny. Were you expecting anyone?"

Michel shook his head.

"So should we be scared?" Joel asked, only half kidding.

"I don't know," Michel replied.

He picked up a towel from the floor and tied it around his waist, then walked to the bedroom door and opened it. Blue was standing just outside, looking at the front door. Her tail was wagging.

"So does that mean it's someone we like?" Michel asked.

He walked quietly down the hall with Blue at his side, and looked through the peephole. Sassy and Al Ribodeau were standing on the front porch. There was a third person behind them with his back to the door.

Michel looked down at his towel and thought for a second about running to the bedroom and throwing on some clothes.

"Fuck it," he said under his breath.

He opened the door and put his hands on his hips.

"Hey," he said, with exaggerated casualness.

The third person turned around. It was Stan Lecher, the former chief investigating officer for the New Orleans' Coroner's Office. Lecher had been forced to resign after participating in a rogue investigation with Michel, and had taken a teaching job at Texas State University. Iris Lecher, the girl killed at Mose Lumley's house during Sassy's rookie year, had been his daughter. Michel felt suddenly apprehensive, but pushed it away for the moment.

"Nice outfit," Lecher said. "Have you put on weight?"

"Good to see you, too, Stan," Michel replied. "Maybe if you'd called to tell me you were coming, I would have dressed more appropriately."

"Maybe if you hadn't been too busy to answer your phone, you would have known," Sassy replied.

She pushed past Michel into the hallway.

"Hey Joel!" she called. "Put on some clothes. You've got company."

Then she knelt down and began rubbing Blue's neck.

"How's my little niece?" she cooed. "Did you get locked out of the bedroom again?"

Blue wagged her tail emphatically in response.

"What are you talking about?" Joel said with a laugh, from the bedroom doorway.

He was dressed in khaki cargo shorts and a black t-shirt. Sassy looked up at him and pursed her lips disapprovingly.

"Don't play games with me," she said. "I know what goes on around here. Blue tells me everything."

She stood with a grunt and turned toward the door. Ribodeau and Lecher were still standing on the porch.

"Are you planning to come inside?" she asked.

Then she looked Michel up and down and shook her head.

"And you go put some clothes on."

Chapter 9

Michel walked into the living room wearing a pair of jeans and a white t-shirt. Ever since he'd seen Lecher at the door, his anxiety level had been climbing.

"So I take it this isn't just a social visit?" he asked.

Lecher cut a quick glance at Joel, then looked back at Michel and raised his eyebrows slightly. Joel caught the gesture and stood up.

"I guess I'll be outside with Blue," he said.

Michel nearly said "okay," then remembered the conversation they'd been having just before the doorbell rang.

"No," he said. "This obviously concerns you, too."

Joel looked mildly surprised, but sat back down in the middle of the couch next to Sassy. Michel took the end seat and looked at Lecher.

"Not that I'm not happy to see you," he said, "but what are you doing here?"

"I got the same photo," Lecher replied.

"What?" Michel replied. "Why?"

"I guess that's what we need to figure out," Lecher replied.

Michel tried to read his expression, but it was neutral.

"But obviously you're thinking something serious is going on or you wouldn't have come all the way from Houston," he said. "And Al wouldn't be here."

"Actually I was already in town," Lecher replied. "I was speaking at a symposium at LSU this morning."

"That's a pretty big coincidence," Michel replied.

Lecher stared at him blankly for a moment, then cocked his head slightly to the right and raised his eyebrows.

"You think?" he asked sarcastically.

Michel sat back. He could feel a knot forming in his stomach, and suddenly wanted a cigarette.

"I don't think we can chalk up anything that's happened to coincidence," Lecher said. "This was all planned and executed precisely. The only question is why."

"And whether this is just the beginning," Michel added.

Lecher nodded.

Michel felt a slight vibration through the cushion, and cut a quick look to his left. Joel was sitting tensely on the edge of the couch, his left leg jittering up and down. Michel reached over and squeezed his right hand reassuringly.

"So when did you get the photo?" he asked.

"It showed up in my email at nine this morning," Lecher replied, "but I didn't look at it until a few hours ago."

"Why not?" Michel asked.

"Because I knew what it was," Lecher replied. "Whenever I get a large image file from an unknown email address, I know what it's going to be."

"Excuse me?" Michel replied.

Lecher gave a slight smile.

"Believe it or not, there's a whole community of forensic groupies out there," he said. "They read our professional journals, run discussion groups, form fan clubs, etc."

"No offense, but that's kind of creepy," Sassy said.

"I agree," Lecher replied. "Or at the very least kind of pathetic. Anyway, since I left the Coroner's Office I've become sort of a superstar in the forensics world, so I get a lot of what I call 'fan letters.' Essentially staged crime scenes and doctored photos. I figured that's what it was."

"Wow, and I thought Star Trek fans were freaks," Joel murmured quietly.

Michel smiled and squeezed his hand again.

"Why do you get them?" Michel asked.

"One of my students and I developed a program that analyzes photos to determine if they've been altered," Lecher replied. "It measures light direction and intensity at multiple points to determine consistency, looks for residual artifacts from cutting and pasting. That sort of thing."

"And you did that *why*?" Michel asked.

"Studying crime scene photos is a hobby of mine," Lecher replied matter-of-factly.

"Also kind of creepy," Michel said.

Sassy shot him a chastening look.

"Does it have any practical applications for investigation?" she asked.

"That was the original intention," Lecher replied. "I mean, a lot of reconstructing crime scenes is simple physics. A bullet fired at a certain speed from a certain distance at a certain angle has a predictable trajectory. A knife wound from a particular angle should create a predictable blood spatter. It's theoretically possible that you could reconstruct exactly what happened just by analyzing photos of the final scene."

"Theoretically?" Sassy asked.

"First you'd have to remove the variables from the photography process," Lecher replied. "I don't want to get too technical, but there are a thousand minute variables that can affect a photo, and you'd have to build in compensation functions for all of them. Plus you'd have to integrate the program with a 360-degree camera on a gyroscopic base in case the crime scene isn't level."

"I take it you're not interested in that?" Sassy asked.

Lecher shook his head.

"No," he replied, "but I'm sure Aaron will run with it and probably get very rich."

"Aaron is your student?" Sassy asked.

"Was," Lecher replied. "He graduated and works for the NSA now. Anyway, the current version of the program is very good at identifying inconsistencies in photos. We published an article in *The Forensics Journal* where we applied it to several famous photos to prove they were faked. Bigfoot, a flying saucer, the Loch Ness Monster. It got a lot of attention because one of the Loch Ness photos appeared to be real. Since then, I've gotten a few 'fan letters' a week."

"So why do they send them?" Sassy asked.

"Probably to try to prove they're smarter than me. You know how us geeks are," Lecher replied with an unexpectedly self-deprecating smile.

Sassy noticed that his demeanor was more relaxed and comfortable than in the past. He'd lost some of the chilliness that had always made him seem emotionally inaccessible. His appearance, too, was more casual: well-worn jeans, rumpled white Oxford cloth shirt, blue blazer, slightly tousled hair. It gave him a look that was both professorial and kind of sexy. Sassy imagined that all of his female students, and possibly some of the males, had crushes on him.

"So what do you do with them?" she asked.

"I give them all a quick look to make sure they're not real, then just file them away," Lecher replied. "I don't respond because I don't want to encourage it."

"So when you got the photo, you thought it was just another fan letter," Michel said.

"Until I recognized Lumley's basement," Lecher replied with a nod.

"So how did you know it was fake?" Michel asked.

"I'll show you," Lecher replied.

He stood and picked up an orange envelope from the side of his chair.

"Al, why don't you move over there," he said, nodding toward the couch.

While the others shifted to make room for Ribodeau, Lecher took a stack of 8 x 10 photos out of the envelope, and placed them on the coffee table. The top photo was identical to the one Michel and Chance had found in the safe.

"Sorry for the quality," Lecher said. "I had to print them on a colleague's office printer at LSU."

He knelt beside the table and moved the top photo to the side. Joel continued to stare at it. It was the first time he'd seen it, and despite the fact that he knew it wasn't real, goose flesh rose on his arms. He picked it up as the others turned their attention to the second photo.

"As you can see, there's a very slight dark halo around the top of Joel's head and along the sides of the blindfold," Lecher said, running his index finger in a curve around a close-up of Joel's head. "That indicates that he was originally shot against a darker background."

Lecher turned to the next photo, but Joel didn't notice. He was still focused on the first photo. It seemed so real. It was obviously his actual face, but the body looked like his, too, albeit slightly thinner and less muscular than it was now. He recognized his own shoulders, his own legs, his own chest, his own penis. A distant buzzing began in his ears, and he felt slightly dizzy.

"The angle of light on his face and body is also five degrees different from the light in the background," Lecher continued.

"Wait a second," Michel interrupted. "You're saying the image of Joel is from an actual photo?"

Lecher nodded and everyone turned to look at Joel. He continued staring at the first photo for a few seconds, then looked up at Michel.

"Mr. Smith," he said quietly.

Michel stared at him without comprehension for a moment, then his eyes softened and he slowly nodded.

"Who's Mr. Smith?" Lecher asked.

Michel opened his mouth to reply, but Joel squeezed his hand to stop him.

"When I first moved to New Orleans, I was living in a boarding house in the Marigny," Joel said. "The other guys who lived there were all hustlers, and I asked to join them. Mr. Smith was my only client."

He lowered his eyes and pulled nervously at a loose thread on the right hem of his shorts.

"That was during the Clement case, right?" Ribodeau asked.

During the fall of 2004, three men had been murdered in hotel rooms in the French Quarter and Faubourg Marigny. The killer, Drew Clement, and his twin brother, Joshua, had both lived in the boarding house with Joel. At the time, they'd been going by the names Hunter and Jared.

"Ah, our transvestite serial killer," Lecher said with a knowing nod.

Joel gave Michel a questioning look.

"We all worked the case," Michel explained.

"That was almost two years ago," Sassy said.

"What did Mr. Smith look like?" Ribodeau asked.

"I don't know," Joel replied. "I had to put the blindfold on as soon as I got in the room."

"And you're sure that's when the photo was taken?" Ribodeau asked.

His tone made it clear that he wasn't making any judgment.

"It had to be," Joel replied. "The only other time I've had on a blindfold was to play pin-the-tail-on-the-donkey when I was a kid, and I'm pretty sure I wasn't naked then."

Ribodeau gave him an appreciative smile.

"Smith was staying at the Bourbon Orleans, right?" Michel asked. "Do you remember the room number?"

Joel thought about it for a moment, then shook his head.

"It was on the second floor, but I don't remember the number. Maybe if I went there I might recognize it."

Reckoning

"That would be a good start," Michel said. "We should be able to figure out the exact date by looking at the case file, and if we have the room number, the hotel can check their records to see who rented it that night."

"Seems like it's worth a try," Sassy added encouragingly.

"There's one other thing you need to see," Lecher said in a less enthusiastic tone.

He flipped through a few more photos, stopping on an enlargement of the bottom right corner of the original photo.

"The program picked up some inconsistencies in the background of the date and time stamp," he said. "I rearranged it correctly. The photo wasn't taken this morning at 5:10 AM. It was taken a year ago at 6:10 AM."

They were all silent for a few moments as they thought through the implications.

"Okay, so we have a potential suspect, and we know he's been planning this for at least a year," Michel said finally. "What else do we know?"

His calm, direct tone made it clear that he was in professional mode now.

"He knew the significance of Lumley's house, and when it was going to be demolished," Lecher replied.

"And what Joel was studying," Sassy added.

"How did you hear about the conference?" Ribodeau asked.

"I got a brochure in the mail," Joel replied. "Then I went to a website to register."

"Okay, then we know he had the resources to print a fake brochure and put up a website," Ribodeau said.

"Good," Michel said.

"He also knew where I was supposed to be staying," Joel said.

"And he must have a key to the office and know the alarm code and the combination to the safe," Sassy added. "And possibly how to block phone calls."

They were all quiet for another few seconds.

"Anything else?" Ribodeau asked.

Michel nodded.

"He knew how much I inherited from Verle," he said.

"So the amount wasn't random?" Ribodeau asked.

Michel shook his head.

"Who else would know that?" Ribodeau asked.

"Joel, Sassy, and Chance know I inherited something," Michel replied, "but I never told them exactly how much. The only person who knows that is Verle's attorney, Porter DeCew."

"You think he might have something to do with this?" Sassy asked doubtfully.

Michel shook his head.

"No, but it's conceivable this 'Smith' could have found the information in his office. He doesn't lock his files, and the building is easy enough to get into."

Michel made a mental note to call Porter to ask if there had been any strangers asking about him.

"Okay, so now let's talk about motive," he said.

"The most obvious would be money," Sassy said, "but if that were the plan, he wouldn't have hung up on you when you called. He would have tried to set something up before you figured out Joel was okay."

"And he wouldn't have chosen Lumley's house for the photo," Lecher said. "He had to have known at least one of us would recognize it. I think the goal was to taunt us."

"Us?" Michel replied.

"The photo was sent to both of us," Lecher replied.

Michel considered it for a moment, then nodded.

"Okay, so we're dealing with a taunter," he said. "But what's the point? So far all he's managed to do is scare me and humiliate me in front of Al and a bunch of hard hats."

"I hate to say it, but it feels like a warning shot," Sassy said.

"I agree," Lecher said. "But why just Michel and me?"

Sassy snorted derisively.

"What makes you so sure it's just the two of you?" she asked. "It could be all of us. Maybe the other shoe just hasn't dropped yet. You men and your egos."

"All of us?" Joel asked nervously.

"Probably not you," Michel replied with what he hoped would pass for a reassuring smile. "I think you were just the bait."

Joel gave him a doubtful look, but nodded.

"What bothers me is that we're talking about elements from two unrelated cases," Sassy said. "The Clement case and the MacDonald case."

"Or three," Lecher replied. "Lumley's house played a part in two cases."

"But Michel wasn't around for the first one," Sassy replied, shaking her head. "It's got to be something that links us all."

"But Smith wasn't really part of the Clement case," Michel countered. "He was just a john."

"So far as we know," Sassy replied quickly.

"You think he may have been involved in the killings?" Michel replied, arching his eyebrows skeptically.

"Wait a second," Ribodeau said, holding up his hands. "You're assuming that this is related to a case. Suppose it's personal, but the guy has access to police files?"

It was a possibility no one else had considered.

"Whoever it is obviously wants to play games," Ribodeau continued, "so first he's going to lead you in circles. The case connections could be meaningless. So far, all we know for sure is that he faked kidnapping Joel. That seems directed specifically at Michel, so let's not get too far ahead of ourselves."

He looked at Michel.

"Is there anyone you can think of who might want to do something like this?"

"I had an idea," Michel replied, "but now it doesn't make much sense."

Ribodeau nodded for him to continue.

"Severin Marchand," Michel said.

"Why Marchand?" Ribodeau asked.

"He and I had a run-in while we were working on his case," Michel replied. "I called him 'an ignorant, petty, frightened old queen.' At the time, he didn't really react. In fact he was pretty solicitous afterward, but I don't know. I just have a feeling he didn't forget it."

"That seems pretty thin," Lecher replied.

"On its own," Michel said, "but when I was in Bayou Proche visiting Verle six months ago, he told me he'd been emailing with someone in New Orleans who knew me. The guy's email address was SeverinIV@yahoo.com. I ran into Marchand on Saturday night and asked him about it. He said it wasn't him, but he seemed sort of unnerved."

"He'd certainly have the resources to pull something like this off, and probably has a connection in the department to get the files," Sassy said.

"And I don't think it's beyond the realm of possibility that he was Mr. Smith," Michel said. "He has a taste for young guys, and I wouldn't be surprised if he's got a sadistic streak when he's anonymous."

"Okay, so then why don't you think he make sense as a suspect now?" Ribodeau asked.

"The timing," Michel replied. "He was emailing Verle six months before I even met him. And the photos of Lumley's house and Joel were taken long before then. He wouldn't have had any reason to go after me at that point."

"Plus he has no connection to me," Lecher added.

"Again, that we know of," Sassy said.

They were all quiet again for a few moments, then Sassy made a low murmur of realization. Everyone looked at her.

"Are you sure you never had any contact with Marchand before he hired us?" she asked, looking at Michel.

"Not that I remember. Why?"

"I was thinking about what Al said. That maybe this isn't related to any case. Suppose Marchand is obsessed with you, and has been for a few years?"

"Excuse me?" Michel replied with a look of revulsion.

"Hear me out," Sassy said. "It makes some sense. These kinds of things are generally progressive. It starts with watching from afar, then turns into stalking, and the next thing you know, the President's getting shot."

"So you mean an actual clinical obsession?" Lecher asked.

Sassy nodded.

"So first he was just watching you in the bars," she said. "Then he started collecting information on your cases. When that wasn't enough, he found Verle and started checking into your past. Finally he took the big step of contacting you personally when he hired us, but you essentially rejected him. That's what pushed him over the edge."

Michel considered it.

"Okay, I can see that," he said, "but what about the photos of Joel and Lumley's place? Why would he have taken them in the first place unless he was already planning to use them? The photos don't make sense *until* he had a motive."

"For all we know, he's taken photos of every crime scene you've ever visited," Sassy replied. "That could be part of his obsession. As far as Joel goes, maybe he was planning to use the photo to drive you two apart."

"I'm not following," Michel replied.

"Maybe he saw you together and got jealous," Sassy replied. "He found out Joel was living at Zelda's and assumed he was an escort, so he called her to set things up. Then he took the photo with the idea of sending it to you so you'd see what Joel was doing and dump him."

Miss Zelda had owned the boarding house where Joel had lived, and had been the figurehead of the escort service.

"No," Joel said. "That doesn't make sense. Smith didn't request me. Zelda told me he usually hired one of the other boys, but Peter was busy that night. I think it was Hunter's idea to send me instead. It was his big test to see how far I'd be willing to go to be part of the group."

"And if he was planning to use the photo to break us up, why did he hold onto it for two years?" Michel added.

Sassy studied the coffee table thoughtfully for a few seconds.

"Okay, maybe he didn't request Joel," she said finally, "but it certainly wouldn't surprise me if Marchand was a regular customer, and maybe taking photos was part of his kink. Then later when he saw you together, he realized he could use the photo he'd taken of Joel."

Michel gave her a dubious look.

"Okay, so it's not a perfect theory," she admitted. "You have anything better?"

Michel looked down and shrugged.

"Not at the moment."

"I'm not saying it doesn't make some sense," Lecher said, "but I still can't help feeling that this involves all of us. If it's Marchand, it doesn't explain why he sent the picture to me."

"You said it yourself, Stan," Sassy replied. "You're a superstar now. If Marchand had access to police files, he'd know that you worked with Michel. Maybe he saw the article you published and decided it would be fun to get you involved, too. Or maybe it's part of throwing us off the track by making us think it involves a case."

Lecher looked like he was going protest for a moment, then nodded instead.

"I think we're getting ahead of ourselves again," Ribodeau said. "We don't have to fit all the pieces together right now. We've got some solid leads to work, so let's just work them and see where we get."

"We?" Sassy said. "So you're here as more than just a friend?"

Her tone was both hopeful and mildly surprised.

"Yeah, why?" Ribodeau replied.

"Well, because there really hasn't been a crime," Sassy replied, "and certainly not a homicide."

"Consider it a professional courtesy," Ribodeau said. "Besides, you know how slow it gets during the summer. The Captain would rather keep me busy."

"Well, if it's an official investigation, does that mean you're going to deputize us?" Michel asked, trying to disguise his excitement at the idea.

"No," Ribodeau replied flatly. "Besides, you're already licensed to investigate and carry a gun. What more do you need?"

Michel gave him a deflated frown.

"But I will get you a copy of the Clement file so you can try to narrow down the date Joel was with Smith," Ribodeau continued.

"That won't be hard," Michel replied. "It was the night before Clement was killed."

Ribodeau nodded.

"Okay. In the meantime, I'll arrange to have Marchand brought in for questioning."

"Can I be there for that?" Michel asked, his enthusiasm quickly returning.

"I'll see what I can do," Ribodeau agreed.

"We should also find out who owns the URL for the conference website," Sassy said.

"We can handle that," Ribodeau replied. "Anything else?"

Lecher looked at Michel and Sassy.

"If it's all right with you, I'd like to bring Aaron to your office tomorrow morning. I think he might be able to shed some light on how Marchand or whoever has been getting information. He's a little arrogant, but he's solid."

"One of your students? Arrogant?" Michel replied. "I wonder where he learned that?"

Lecher just stared at him in reply.

"He's in the area?" Sassy asked.

"Yeah, he's an analyst at the local field office," Lecher replied. "I already spoke to him. He's on vacation this week, so the timing is perfect. He was actually excited to help out."

"He's on vacation, and he's excited to help us out?" Sassy replied, wrinkling her nose. "That's just wrong. Shouldn't he be sitting on a beach somewhere sipping pina coladas?"

"I'm pretty sure Aaron's not the beach or the pina colada type," Lecher replied, smiling.

"Anything that might help," Ribodeau said. "Just don't get the Feds pissed at us for using their boy."

Lecher nodded.

"Then I think that's it for now," Ribodeau said.

He looked around the group for agreement, but Joel was looking down at the floor with a worried expression.

"What?" Michel prodded.

"This may be a really dumb question," Joel replied hesitantly, "but what about Jared? I mean, Joshua."

Michel sat back and let out a loud sigh.

"Wow," he said. "Four experienced investigators in the room, and look who notices the elephant in the corner."

Despite the fact that the situation was now potentially far more serious than he'd originally thought, Michel felt suddenly energized, almost giddy. It was the familiar rush he'd experienced so often during his years on the force.

"We all worked the case," he said, "and if anyone would have a reason for revenge, it would be him."

"And he could have known Smith and gotten the photo of me from him," Joel added.

"Shit," Sassy said with a mock scowl. "And just when I was thinking I was in the clear."

"If it is Joshua, you're screwed," Michel teased, opening his eyes wide. "You were the one who blew his brother's head off."

"While saving your life," Sassy replied.

Michel held up his hands defensively.

"Hey, I'm just saying," he said. "If I were Joshua..."

Sassy narrowed her eyes at him.

"Well then I hope it's Marchand, and that he kidnaps your bony ass and makes you his love slave," she said.

Michel let out a comic shudder.

"Wow, that's low even for you," he said.

He gave Sassy a wide smile, and she smiled back. It felt like old times. Michel could tell that she was sharing his excitement.

"Are you done?" Lecher asked.

Michel and Sassy looked at him. He and Ribodeau were staring at them impatiently.

"Um, yeah, I guess so," Michel replied with a sheepish grin.

"Sorry," Sassy said, then exchanged another furtive smile with Michel, like two incorrigible children in the back of a station wagon.

Ribodeau rolled his eyes but couldn't hold back a slight smile, too.

"Okay, so now we have two suspects," he said. "I'll run a check on the brother to see if he's surfaced anywhere."

"You might want to check with the Louisville police first," Michel said. "Both brothers were suspects in the murders of their parents and a local priest. If he showed up somewhere, he might have been brought back there to stand trial."

Ribodeau nodded.

"Okay," he said. "I'll call you as soon as I know when Marchand is coming in. In the meantime, I suggest everyone watch their backs."

Chapter 10

Chance was sitting at his desk, his face close to the computer screen, when Sassy walked into the office a few minutes before 9 AM. He immediately hit a button on his keyboard and sat up straight.

"Hey," he said quickly. "I was just doing some invoicing. What are you doing here so early?"

"Just a busy day," Sassy replied distractedly.

She walked stiffly to her desk and sat down. As she took a sip of coffee from a paper cup, Chance could see her eyes darting furtively around the room.

He heard hushed voices from the hallway and turned to see Michel and two other men just outside the door. Michel nodded at Chance's desk, then started slowly toward his own.

"Good morning," he said breezily as he passed Chance.

Chance looked back at the doorway. The two men had taken a step into the room and were looking around curiously.

The one on the right looked to be in his mid-fifties. He was medium height and compactly built, with short graying hair, and was dressed in jeans, a wrinkled blue pinstripe shirt with rolled up sleeves, and scuffed brown loafers.

The one on the left was taller and much younger, really more of a boy. He was thin and pale, with a mass of untamed, soft brown curls, and the beginnings of a light, patchy beard on his cheeks and chin. His large attentive eyes surveyed the room through stylishly thick rectangular-framed glasses. As his gaze settled on Chance, he smiled in a disarmingly friendly way.

"Don't mind me," he whispered. "In fact, just pretend I'm not here and keep doing what you were doing."

Chance looked doubtfully from the young man to Sassy and Michel, who both nodded. Chance looked back at his computer and began typing. After a few seconds, it had turned to gibberish. The presence of the strangers had him too unnerved to concentrate.

The young man looked around the room for a moment longer, then walked to the back of Chance's desk. Chance fought the urge to look up at him and continued typing. The young man grabbed the power cord on the back of Chance's computer and yanked it out.

"What the fuck?" Chance shouted, as his screen went blank.

"Sorry," the young man said.

He leaned forward and extended his hand.

"I'm Aaron," he said, smiling.

"Like I give a shit," Chance replied angrily, ignoring the hand. "Why the fuck did you unplug my computer?"

Aaron's smile faltered, and he looked suddenly unsure what to do or say.

"Relax, Chance," Michel said firmly as he got up.

"But he just wiped out all my invoices," Chance whined.

"Don't worry about it," Michel replied.

"Are we safe?" Sassy asked.

"Should be," Aaron replied. "I don't see any other cameras in the room."

"What about our computers?" Michel asked.

Aaron looked at the outdated behemoths on the other two desks that Michel had rescued from the curb in front of a neighbor's house.

"You mean the Sperry Univacs?" Aaron asked with a laugh. "I don't think so. They don't even have cameras or microphones."

"Cameras or microphones?" Chance said. "What the fuck are you talking about, and who are you?"

"Aaron works for the NSA," Michel said. "And that's Stan Lecher. He used to work for the Coroner's Office."

Lecher nodded at Chance, whose expression suddenly grew worried.

"Does this have to do with the photo of Joel?" he asked.

Sassy pushed back her chair and stood up.

"Yes," she said, "but we'll explain that later. Aaron's here to figure out how someone's been getting information from here."

Chance gave her a wary look, as though she'd accused him.

"It wasn't me," he said forcefully.

"It probably was," Aaron replied, "but not on purpose. I think your computer's bugged."

"Seriously?" Chance asked, looking down at his computer as though it had suddenly sprung legs and antennae.

Aaron nodded, and Chance jumped up.

"It's okay," Aaron said. "That's why I unplugged it."

"Why didn't you warn me first so I could save my files?" Chance asked.

"We wanted to make it look like a power failure in case you were being watched," Michel replied.

"Watched?" Chance repeated.

"I'm afraid so," Aaron replied. "At least I think so."

"Okay, so what do we do?" Michel asked eagerly.

Aaron looked at him as though he'd just belched loudly.

"I'd suggest you just take a seat," he said. "Unless, of course, you have some computer expertise I'm unaware of."

There was an unmistakable note of condescension in his tone that set Michel's teeth on edge, but he decided to let it go for the moment. He walked over to the low file cabinet next to Chance's desk and sat down.

"It's okay," Aaron said more gently to Chance. "You can sit back down. I won't need your chair for a few minutes."

He took the red messenger bag from his shoulder and set it on the floor, then tipped the iMac facedown onto the desk.

"If it were me," he said, "the first thing I'd do is set up a feed from Chance's computer."

He opened his bag and took out a ratchet screwdriver.

"What does that mean?" Sassy asked.

"The computer already has a built-in camera and microphone," Aaron replied as he began unscrewing the back panel. "If someone accessed it, they could hear everything that was happening in the room and see anything that went on behind the desk."

"Like opening the safe?" Chance asked.

Aaron looked up at him and smiled.

"Exactly," he said.

"So how would someone do that?" Chance asked.

"Well, the simplest thing to do would be to disable the camera light so you wouldn't know it was on, sign you into a video chat, then hide the window."

He lifted the back off the computer and placed it to the side, then leaned in close and began examining the computer's components.

"Do you ever do any video chatting?" he asked.

"Um, sometimes," Chance replied, then quickly looked down at the floor.

"Have you noticed if the light's been on?" Aaron asked.

"I'm not sure," Chance replied.

"I'll check when I put it back together," Aaron said.

He continued studying the inside of the computer for another few seconds, then straightened up.

"So what are you looking for?" Sassy asked.

"Well, there are a couple of ways that someone could link into a computer," Aaron replied, looking over his right shoulder at her. "One would be to enable remote access by another computer through the internet, another would be to install spyware, and the third would be to install some kind of transmitter. That's what I was looking for. I also wanted to make sure there wasn't an additional microphone or any keylogging hardware."

"Then it's clean?" Michel asked.

"The guts are," Aaron replied. "I have to check the keyboard."

Aaron placed the backplate on the computer and screwed it on, then inserted the plug and disconnected the internet cable.

"All right, now I'm going to need your chair," he said as he stood the iMac back on its base.

Chance got up and moved behind his chair. Aaron walked around the desk and slid into it. He picked up the keyboard and began examining it.

"Looks fine," he said after a few seconds.

"So now what?" Michel asked.

"So now we turn this bitch on," Aaron replied.

"But won't that enable the camera and microphone?" Michel asked.

"Yes, but since I disconnected the internet cable, it probably won't matter," Aaron replied.

He gave Michel a patronizing smile, and Michel could feel his ears burning.

"But just to be safe," Aaron continued, "do you have any Post Its?"

"Middle drawer," Chance replied.

Aaron opened the drawer and pulled a Post-It off the yellow pad. He stuck it over the camera lens near the top of the computer.

"Gee, you NSA guys sure are high tech," Michel said dryly.

Aaron blinked at him through his glasses, but didn't reply.

"You can all come back here and watch if you want," he said instead. "Just stay quiet until I've checked to make sure there's no wireless connection set up."

Michel was struck by the similarity between Aaron's tone, gestures, and mannerisms to those of Lecher. Unlike Lecher, however, Aaron didn't seem content to simply be the smartest person in the room; he seemed compelled to demonstrate it.

Aaron waited until Lecher and Sassy had joined Chance behind the chair, then turned on the computer. The familiar start-up tone filled the room. The screen was blank for a few seconds, then the Apple logo appeared, followed a few seconds later by the desktop.

Aaron immediately opened the Preferences Pane and clicked the Network icon. Chance leaned in close to his shoulder to watch what he was doing. He noticed that Aaron's hair smelled like strawberries.

"We're not connected to anything," Aaron said, pointing at the row of red lights in the pop-up window.

"You're sure?" Michel asked.

"Yeah, I'm sure," Aaron replied with a hint of annoyance.

He went back to the Preferences Pane, and clicked on the File Sharing icon.

"And no remote access has been set up."

He closed the Preference window and clicked on the iChat icon at the bottom of the screen, then went to the File dropdown menu at the top.

"And you weren't signed into any chats when I unplugged the computer," he said, "so that rules out those options."

He exited iChat and double-clicked the hard drive icon in the upper right corner of the screen, then began quickly opening and closing folders.

"Now what are you looking for?" Chance asked.

"Just anything unusual," Aaron replied.

He closed the window and looked up at Michel.

"There's a CD case in my bag," he said. "Could you get it for me, please?"

Although it was a reasonable request given that he could reach the bag most readily, Michel couldn't help but feel that Aaron had purposefully left the bag on the floor near him so that he'd have to retrieve it. It seemed like a calculated power play to establish a hierarchy between them.

He reached down, grabbed the bag, and handed it to Aaron. Aaron stared at it for a few seconds, then took it.

"Thanks," he said, though he looked slightly peeved.

He reached into the bag and took out the CD case.

"What's that?" Sassy asked.

"It's a scanning program I designed," Aaron replied as he opened the case and popped out the CD. "It searches for viruses, worms, spyware. That sort of thing. It's a little more sophisticated than the off-the-shelf stuff you can buy."

He slipped the CD into the slot on the right side of the computer and waited until the disk icon appeared on the screen. He double-clicked it, then selected the icon for the hard drive and hit the START button.

"This should just take a few minutes," he said. "Do you have any coffee?"

"Sure," Chance replied immediately. "How do you like it?"

Michel and Sassy exchanged incredulous looks. In all the time he'd been working with them, Chance had never once offered to get either of them coffee.

"Black with two sugars, please," Aaron replied.

"Mr. Lecher?" Chance asked.

"No, thanks," Lecher replied.

Chance moved out from behind the desk, and Lecher took his place directly behind Aaron.

"So if you find something, will you be able to trace where the information is being sent?" Michel asked.

"Doubtful," Aaron replied.

"Why not?" Michel asked.

"Because computers aren't directly connected to each other like tin-can telephones," Aaron replied dismissively. "Each one is connected to an internet service provider, along with a few million other customers."

He pulled the Post-It from the computer and drew a circle with ten spokes coming off of it.

"This is your internet service provider," he said, writing ISP in the center of the circle, "and this is you."

He drew an X at the end of one spoke.

"Every time you visit a website or send an email, the information is routed through your ISP's server..."

He drew a line from the X to the circle.

"...or more likely, a series of servers."

He continued the line to the end of another spoke, then drew another circle and added ten spokes around the outside.

"So the final destination could be any one of these other computers," he said, tapping the spokes with his pen, "or it might be going to another server first, and then to the final destination. And each time it goes through a server, the number of possible end points grows exponentially. If this guy has any clue what he's doing, he's going to bounce the information through at least a couple of relay points."

"But even if he bounced it ten times, wouldn't we be able to trace it from computer X to Y to Z to wherever?" Michel asked. "I mean, isn't that how you guys track down terrorists and pedophiles?"

Aaron gave a grudging nod.

"Yeah. It could be done, but you'd have to subpoena the records from every ISP in the chain, and it would take weeks to review them."

"Why so much time?" Michel asked. "I thought computers had traceable IP addresses."

He was mildly proud of himself for remembering the term from an article he'd read in his dentist's waiting room.

Aaron sighed deeply.

"IP addresses aren't static," he replied, shaking his head. "At least not for most personal computers. There's a limited number of them, so each ISP gets a block of them, and they assign them to their customers as they're needed. So each time you log onto the internet, you get assigned a different number from their block. It's called Dynamic Host Configuration Protocol, aka DHCP. "

Michel looked both deflated and slightly confused.

"You're also assuming that the information's only being bounced to one computer at each point," Aaron continued. "It could be going to multiple computers, or even to every computer connected to a server."

"Someone can do that?" Sassy asked.

"If they know what they're doing," Aaron replied. "It's possible the information on Chance's computer is being sent to every customer who uses the same service provider."

"So everyone in the city could be watching me?" Chance asked nervously, as he walked over carrying two coffee mugs.

"The information's probably being encrypted," Aaron replied with a reassuring smile, "so they could only see it if they had the decoding program. Otherwise, they wouldn't even know it was on their computer."

He took a mug from Chance just as the iMac emitted a dinging tone.

"Let's see what it found," he said.

He took a sip of coffee, then put the mug on the desk and began scrolling through a list of code that had appeared on the screen. The others moved closer to watch.

"What is all that?" Michel asked.

"Basically it's the structure of the computer's operating system," Aaron replied. "The program traces it so I can see if there's anything unusual going on."

He stopped scrolling and pointed at the screen.

"Like this."

"What is it?" Sassy asked.

"The keystrokes are being rerouted," Aaron replied.

"To where?" Sassy asked.

Aaron double-clicked the hard drive icon and opened a series of folders.

"To here," he said. "Those are data logs. Everything that's typed on the keyboard is being recorded and stored here."

"What would be the purpose?" Michel asked.

"To monitor everything that gets typed into the computer, like emails, what websites have been visited, passwords..."

"Passwords?" Sassy interrupted.

Aaron nodded. Sassy looked at Chance and Michel.

"I guess that explains how that $10,000 was mysteriously transferred from the checking to the reserve account," she said.

"Which means they've been monitoring Chance's computer for at least six months," Michel replied.

"Since January 28th, to be exact," Aaron replied, pointing to a file.

He placed the cursor on another file and double-clicked. A window popped open. It was filled with a solid block of keyboard characters.

"This is the file from this morning," he said.

"That just looks like gibberish," Michel said.

"That's because it's encrypted," Aaron replied, as though he were explaining to a toddler.

He reached into his bag and pulled out another CD case, placing it on the desk.

"Okay, let's save this to text...," he said to himself, as he began selecting windows on the desktop and hitting keys, "exit this... drag this to here..."

The CD in the computer popped out of the slot on the side, and Aaron pulled it out. He replaced it in its case, opened the other case, and put the new CD into the slot. When the disk's icon appeared on the screen, he double-clicked it, then clicked the icon inside the opened folder.

"So what were you typing just before I pulled the plug, Chance?" he asked.

"What?" Chance stammered.

"What were you typing?" Aaron repeated, turning to look at Chance, who was beginning to turn red.

Chance hesitated for a moment, then looked down at the floor.

"'Who's the hot nerd, and why is he standing behind my desk?'" he replied in a small voice.

Aaron let out a laugh.

"Seriously?" he asked.

"I thought you were working on invoices," Michel said.

"I was," Chance replied in plaintive voice, "but it was kind of hard to concentrate."

He looked at Aaron.

"Sorry about the nerd thing."

"That's okay," Aaron replied with a smile. "At least you said I was hot."

"Do you two want us to leave you alone?" Michel asked sarcastically.

Aaron ignored him and turned back to the computer.

"Okay, so we know four equals w," he said as he began entering the information in a window in the upper left corner of the screen, "question mark equals h, i equals o..."

He continued on for almost a minute.

"All right, let's try this," he said finally, as he hit the ENTER button.

The text in the data log window began changing into recognizable words.

"So what did you do?" Sassy asked.

"I used a decryption program," Aaron replied. "Encryption is done using algorithms to translate letters or words to alternate characters. If you know what letters some of the characters equate to, the program can extrapolate the rest."

He studied the screen for a moment.

"It would take days to go through all of these logs to figure out what information they could have gotten, but to be safe, you should reset all your passwords."

He put a finger against the screen and looked up at Chance.

"You like that site, too?" he asked.

"What site?" Michel asked, quickly leaning closer.

Aaron immediately closed the window. Michel looked up at Chance and gave him a chastening look.

"You better not be looking at porn on this computer."

"So now the question is how they're accessing the logs," Aaron said.

He opened another window to display the operating system code again, and began slowly scrolling down. After a minute, he stopped and leaned closer to the screen.

"What is it?" Sassy asked.

"It looks like a parallel system," Aaron replied in a tone that sounded more like he was thinking aloud than answering the question.

He double-clicked the hard drive icon again, and started opening more folders.

"That's pretty clever," he said after a few seconds.

He double-clicked an icon and a window opened. It was identical to the Preference Pane he'd opened earlier. He clicked on the File Sharing icon.

"That's not good," he said.

"What?" Michel asked.

"You see all these numbers here?" Aaron replied, pointing at a list in the lower right corner of the window. "Those are all IP addresses. He's granted access to those thirty computers."

"I thought you said IP addresses weren't static," Michel replied. "How's that possible?"

"I said IP addresses for most *personal* computer aren't static," Aaron replied. "Businesses that have their own servers need fixed IP addresses, so they buy them."

"So the information's being sent to a business?" Sassy asked.

Aaron nodded.

"Probably three of them since there are three main numbers, and based on the number sequences, each one has ten computers sharing the same internet connection."

"So then we just have to find out who bought those addresses," Michel said. "That makes things easier, right?"

"Not if the owner is an internet cafe or library or someplace else with public access," Aaron replied.

He looked up to make sure the others were comprehending the full implication of what he was saying. From their expressions, it was clear they were.

"Okay," Michel said with a sigh, "so whoever we're dealing with is pretty computer-savvy."

"Well, it's not like they're a genius," Aaron replied with what seemed a hint of grudging admiration, "but yeah, they know their way around a computer and how to cover their tracks."

"But you can turn off the keylogger thingie and make it so they can't access Chance's computer anymore, right?" Sassy asked.

"Yeah, but are you sure you want to do that?" Aaron asked.

"Why wouldn't we?" Michel asked.

"Because right now, whoever it is doesn't know we know how they're getting information," Aaron replied. "You might be able to use that to your advantage. That's one of the reasons I wanted to make it look like you had a power failure, so they wouldn't realize we were checking the computer."

"How would we use it to our advantage?" Sassy asked.

"Set a trap," Aaron replied. "For example, you could pretend to open a new bank account, but we'd set it up so that if someone enters the fake account ID and password on the bank site, it would activate a trace back to the user's computer."

"You can do that?" Michel asked.

"The NSA can," Aaron replied.

"But what would be the point if he's using a public computer?" Sassy asked.

"The public computers are probably just being used to re-route the information," Aaron replied. "I don't imagine he's sitting in a cafe watching and listening. Other patrons might tend to notice something like that. Plus he needs a computer with the encryption key on it to read the data logs. I guarantee you he's linked into the chain somewhere along the line."

Sassy and Michel exchanged questioning looks.

"It's your choice," Aaron said with a shrug, "but once I disable the connection, he's going to know you're on to him."

"What do you think?" Sassy asked.

"If it were just the keylogging, I'd be okay with it," Michel replied, "but the idea that we're being watched and listened to, that kind of creeps me out."

"Me, too," Chance added quickly. "Especially since it's mostly me being watched."

Michel almost made a comment about Chance keeping his pants zipped in the office, but decided against it.

"I think we should disable it," he said instead. "Maybe if he knows we're onto him, he'll back off."

Sassy hesitated for a moment, then nodded.

"Done," Aaron said.

He punched a key on the keyboard, then spun around in the chair to face the others.

"So what else do you need from me?" he asked indulgently.

Sassy saw Michel's jaw tighten, and fought back a laugh.

"The phones," she said quickly. "Joel said he tried to call Michel and Chance on their cell phones, but they just kept ringing. He also said he left a message on the office phone, but there was no message."

"Where was he calling from?" Aaron asked.

"A motel room outside Orlando," Sassy replied.

"So on a land line?" Aaron asked.

Sassy nodded.

"Do you have your phones?" Aaron asked.

Michel and Chance pulled out them out and handed them to him. He flipped open Michel's phone and started hitting buttons.

"When was the last time you received a call?" he asked.

Michel thought about it for a few seconds.

"Friday, I think," he replied.

Aaron put the phone in his lap and opened Chance's.

"What about you?" he asked.

"Saturday," Chance replied. "I talked to Joel a few times because we were going out that night."

Aaron didn't say anything for a few seconds as he focused on Chance's phone, then he picked up Michel's phone, too, and held them both out with the screens facing the others.

"They were both set to Call Forwarding," he said. "To the same number."

Michel took his phone and looked at the screen.

"That's the same number that was on the picture in the safe," he said.

"So we know that's going to be a dead end," Sassy said. "What about the office phone?"

"I can take it apart to see if I can find anything, but if he had access to the office, he might have just come in and erased the message," Aaron replied.

"Well, at least we can get our phones dusted for prints," Michel said.

"Wait a second," Chance said uneasily. "So he actually had our phones at some point?"

Aaron nodded.

"But I never leave mine anywhere," Chance replied. "It's always in my pocket. Do you think he broke into my place while I was sleeping or something?"

"It's a possibility," Michel replied. "On the other hand, you were pretty drunk on Saturday night. Someone could easily have taken it out of your pocket for a minute."

Chance gave him a confused look.

"How do you know how drunk I was?"

"Because I saw you," Michel replied. "Remember? You and Joel on the balcony at Parade? You asked me if I wanted to have a threesome?"

Chance looked down at the floor for a moment, then an expression of comic horror came over his face.

"Oh my God, that was you?" he asked.

Michel nodded with a smirk.

"Wow, I *must* have been drunk," Chance replied. "I thought it was somebody hot."

"Whatever helps you sleep," Michel replied.

"And what about *your* phone?" Sassy interrupted.

"It's usually in my jacket," Michel replied, "but when I'm out, I usually just throw that over the back of my chair. It would be easy to grab my phone if I were in the bathroom."

"What about your keys?" Aaron asked.

Michel stared at him for a moment, then his eyes widened.

"Shit," he said.

"Nice, Michel," Sassy said with an exasperated sigh. "So now we know how he copied the office key, and Lord knows what other keys."

"Sorry, I didn't realize I was being stalked," Michel replied.

"Even so," Sassy said, "do you really think it's a good idea to leave your keys and cell phone unattended in a bar?"

"Well, I always figured they'd just take my wallet instead," Michel replied, with a defensive shrug.

"You leave your wallet in your jacket, too?" Sassy asked incredulously. "You know what? You deserve to be stalked. And robbed. And have your identity stolen. And everything else that happens to stupid people."

"I'm telling mom you called me stupid," Michel replied, attempting a sad puppy dog face.

"You're not even a little cute right now," Sassy warned.

She looked back at Aaron.

"What about the alarm? Any idea how he got past that?"

"How many numbers in the code?" Aaron asked.

"Four," Sassy replied.

"That would be easy," Aaron replied. "You'd just have to dust the keypad to see which numbers were being pressed. With four, there are only 24 possible combinations."

"What would you suggest?" Sassy asked.

"Six numbers with two of the digits repeating should do it," Aaron replied. "You should also set it so that if the wrong code is punched in more than a few times, it sets off the alarm."

"Okay, so we need to change the lock and alarm code, and reset the password for the bank account," Sassy said. "Chance, can you take care of that?"

Chance nodded.

"Okay, anything else we should be doing?" Sassy asked, looking back at Aaron.

"I think that's it for now," he replied, "but if it's okay, I'll stick around for a while to check out the phone, and I may as well scan the other computers while I'm here, just to be safe."

"That's fine," Sassy replied.

She turned to Michel and Lecher.

"You hungry?"

"Sure," Lecher replied.

Michel nodded.

"We'll be back in an hour, Chance," Sassy said.

Chance gave her a hurt look.

"What about us?" he asked.

"You have work to do," Sassy replied.

"Yeah, but I'm hungry, too," Chance protested.

Sassy fixed him with an indifferent look.

"Well then maybe next time you'll eat breakfast instead of spending your morning looking at porn on the office computer," she said.

Chapter 11

"You were unusually quiet this morning," Michel said, as soon as the waitress left the table.

Lecher smiled.

"Well, I figured I'd let Aaron take the lead," he said. "Give him his moment in the sun."

"Oh yeah, because clearly he suffers from self-esteem issues," Michel replied sarcastically. "Seems to me he thinks he *is* the sun."

"I did warn you he's a little arrogant," Lecher replied.

"I didn't think he was arrogant," Sassy said. "I just think he was anxious to prove himself."

"Oh sure, because he was nice to you," Michel replied.

"Yeah, I did notice a little tension between the two of you," Lecher said. "What was that about?"

"It's a gay thing," Michel replied.

Sassy let out a laugh.

"A gay thing? What kind of a gay thing?"

"Sometimes when a gay man is attracted to another gay man, he masks it by being a bitch," Michel replied authoritatively. "It's a form of self-protection, especially if he senses that the attraction isn't mutual."

Sassy gave him a deadpan look.

"So you're saying that Aaron was attracted to you?"

Michel nodded.

"Seems to me he was a lot more attracted to Chance," Sassy replied, "and I didn't see him being a bitch to him. I've already told you what your problem is. You need to be nicer to people. I'm nice. That's why people like me."

Lecher laughed.

"I'm glad to see some things haven't changed," he said.

"I'm glad someone is," Michel replied dryly.

Sassy wrinkled her nose at him.

"So what about you, Stan?" she asked. "How've you been?"

"Great," Lecher replied brightly. "Leaving the Coroner's Office was probably the best thing that ever happened to me. I didn't realize how little life I had outside the job until I left."

"You ever miss it?" Sassy asked.

"Not really," Lecher replied. "It certainly gave me a sense of purpose, but teaching is very rewarding. I'm training a whole new generation of investigators, and there's something really satisfying about that."

Sassy studied him for a few seconds, trying to gauge the sincerity of his enthusiasm.

"But you miss the excitement a little," she said finally.

"Okay, maybe just a little," Lecher replied, laughing softly.

"That's what I thought," Sassy said with a knowing smile. "So what about outside of work? How's that going?"

"Believe it or not, I actually have a social life now," Lecher replied. "I've got some colleagues I get together with regularly for dinner and cocktail parties and barbecues. It's nice."

"Hey, we had lunch together that one time," Michel said.

"Yeah, because you were trying to pump me for information," Lecher replied, then looked back at Sassy. "No, overall it's a good life. My hours are regular. I have time to spend on my hobbies. I get the summers off. I can't complain."

Sassy nodded. "You do seem a lot more relaxed."

"So I know I don't need to ask him," Lecher said, nodding at Michel, "but what about you? Do you miss the job?"

"Hey wait a second," Michel cut in. "Why don't you need to ask me?"

"Because I saw the look in your eyes last night," Lecher replied. "Just being close to a police investigation had your panties all wet."

"Ewww," Michel replied, making a face. "Did you really need to say that? And was it really that obvious?"

"Yeah, it was really that obvious," Sassy replied.

"Well, you were excited, too," Michel shot back.

"No, I wasn't," Sassy protested.

"Don't lie to me," Michel replied. "I've known you for too long. You were getting off on it as much as I was. You miss the rush of real police work."

"Okay, maybe a little," Sassy replied, mimicking the tone of Lecher's earlier admission, "but that doesn't mean I want to go back to it full time. I'm getting old, Michel. I'm tired."

"That's just because your hormones are all whacked," Michel replied.

"That's true," Sassy replied with a nod. "That wasn't actually excitement you saw last night. That was just delirium from the drugs."

"What are you talking about?" Lecher asked.

"I've started taking estrogen and progestin," Sassy replied, "but they're doing a number on me. I'm supposed to take them in the morning, but if I do, I can't function during the day. About an hour after I take them, I start nodding off like a drug addict, and the next thing I know it's morning."

"They shouldn't affect you like that," Lecher replied with a concerned look.

"You're sure?" Sassy asked.

"I did go to med school," Lecher replied, nodding. "You need to call your doctor."

Sassy shrugged. "Okay. I'll call her this afternoon."

She took a sip of coffee.

"So you feeling any better about things this morning?" she asked, looking at Lecher.

He looked down at his cup for a moment, then frowned.

"Not really," he replied. "I'm glad Aaron figured out how the information was being accessed, but I'm still not buying Marchand as the suspect."

"Why not?" Michel asked.

"Maybe I just have a tremendous ego," Lecher replied, "but I don't think I would have gotten the photo unless this involved me, too. And that would also rule out Mr. Smith and Joshua Clement since my involvement in that case was only peripheral. I'm thinking this has something to do with MacDonald."

Maxwell "Mac" MacDonald had been the sheriff of New Orleans. He'd also been responsible for the kidnapping and murder of at least three young girls, including Iris Lecher.

"But MacDonald's dead," Michel replied, "so who'd be coming after us?"

"Maybe he wasn't working alone," Lecher replied.

"Maybe," Michel replied doubtfully, "but if you'd helped kill three little girls and you'd gotten away with it for decades, would you want to draw attention to yourself?"

"No, I suppose not," Lecher agreed, "but that's the case that ties us together most closely, and it involved Lumley's house."

"I keep going back to what Al said about the case allusions being used to throw us off track," Sassy said. "Given that there's no connection between the Clement and MacDonald cases besides us, that sounds feasible to me."

"You think it involves another case entirely?" Michel asked.

"Not sure," Sassy replied. "But this is feeling a little like our greatest hits collection. Clement and MacDonald were two of the biggest cases we ever worked on. If Deacon Lee suddenly pops up, I'm going to know someone's playing with us."

"So does this mean you've changed your mind about Marchand?" Michel asked.

"No," Sassy replied. "Maybe he's not responsible for everything, but I can't help but feel he's involved on some level."

"Speaking of Marchand, have you heard from Al yet?" Lecher asked, looking at Michel.

"Not yet," Michel replied. "I figured I'd give him until noon, and then call him if I still haven't."

"So what until then?" Sassy asked. "Back to the office to watch the boy genius at work?"

Michel shook his head.

"Joel and I are going to go by the Bourbon Orleans to see if he can remember which room Smith was in," he replied.

"Where is he now?" Sassy asked.

"At home," Michel replied.

"You think that's safe?" Sassy asked.

"Yeah," Michel replied. "I told him not to answer the door unless it's someone he knows well, and he's got Blue with him. She can be pretty fierce when she perceives a threat."

Sassy nodded.

"Well, hopefully it'll just turn out to be Marchand so we can stop worrying altogether," she said.

Chapter 12

Chance kept his head down, pretending to be concentrating on invoicing, and stole another look across the room. While he didn't normally go for the "hot nerd" type, there was something about Aaron that he found intriguing.

"So what do you do for the NSA?" he asked abruptly.

Aaron looked up from Michel's computer and smiled.

"I'm an analyst," he replied. "Basically I spend all day decoding and sorting through data, looking for signs of terrorist activity."

"Sounds interesting," Chance lied, wanting to keep the conversation going.

Aaron gave a small laugh.

"Not very, but it pays pretty well."

He looked back at the computer and Chance frowned. Another minute of silence passed, then Aaron stood up.

"Both clean," he said.

"That's good," Chance replied automatically.

He watched as Aaron stretched elaborately, his green t-shirt lifting to reveal a few inches of very pale, flat stomach.

"So what's up with your boss?" Aaron asked as he lowered his arms.

"Which one?" Chance replied.

"Michel."

"What about him?"

"He seems like kind of a dick," Aaron replied.

Chance laughed.

"No, he's all right," he said. "He just has a stick up his ass sometimes. But he's a good guy when you get to know him."

"I'll take your word for it," Aaron replied.

He walked across the room and settled onto the file cabinet next to Chance's desk, pulling his legs up and wrapping his arms around them.

"No, seriously," Chance replied. "I mean, I didn't like him at first either, but once I got to know him I realized he's actually pretty cool. In an uptight sort of way."

"So why didn't you like him?" Aaron asked.

"Probably because I was afraid he was going to change things between Joel and me," Chance replied.

"Have things changed?" Aaron asked.

Chance felt suddenly uncomfortable. The question seemed inappropriately personal from someone he'd just met.

"Sorry, I didn't mean to pry," Aaron said quickly, apparently reading his discomfort. "I have a bad habit of asking a lot of questions. When I was a kid, my mother used to call me 'The Inquisition'."

Chance laughed and relaxed a little.

"That's okay," he said. "I don't mind."

He considered the question for a moment.

"Yeah," he said finally. "Things have changed, but not because of Michel. At least not in a bad way."

"I'm not going to ask a follow-up, in case you were wondering," Aaron said with mock seriousness, "but feel free to expound if you want."

Chance laughed again.

"I was in kind of a bad place when Joel moved here," he said. "Actually I was working as a hustler."

"Seriously?" Aaron asked.

Rather than the surprise Chance had expected, Aaron was studying him closely, seemingly trying to decide if Chance was teasing before reacting. Chance nodded.

"Wow, I'll bet you were pretty successful," Aaron said.

"Why's that?" Chance replied, with exaggerated offense. "Because I'm a big whore?"

"No, because you're really cute," Aaron replied quickly. "I always think of hustlers as being like skanky crack addicts, but I'd definitely pay you for sex."

He stopped and looked suddenly stricken as he realized what he'd said. He began to blush

"I mean...if I were to pay for...not that I think you would..." he stammered.

Chance found Aaron's sudden awkwardness charming, and despite the fact that he enjoyed seeing him flustered, he decided to throw him a lifeline.

"I know what you meant," he said gently.

"Whew!" Aaron said, pretending to wipe sweat from his brow, though he was obviously still flustered.

He took a few theatrically deep breaths.

"So what happened?" he asked.

"I got stabbed," Chance replied.

"By who?" Aaron asked, this time showing surprise.

"A guy by the name of Hunter," Chance replied, "though his real name was Drew something."

"Clement?" Aaron asked.

Now Chance looked surprised.

"Yeah, how did you know that?" he asked.

"Professor Lecher told me a little about it," he said. "He said the police were checking on Clement's brother because they thought he might have something to do with the photo of Joel."

"Fuck," Chance said, sitting back hard.

"Are you all right?" Aaron asked.

Chance stared down at the desk for a few seconds.

"Yeah," he said, nodding slowly. "I just didn't see that one coming. I figured the photo was just some kind of joke, but if Jared's involved, it could be a lot more serious."

"So Jared is the twin?" Aaron asked.

Chance nodded.

"When I knew them, they were Hunter and Jared," he said. "We all lived in a boarding house owned by a transvestite named Miss Zelda, and we all worked for her. Or at least I thought we did. It turned out Hunter was running the whole operation. Oh, and he was a serial killer."

He let out a small giggle.

"What?" Aaron asked, looking slightly alarmed.

"It's just that when I say it out loud, it all sounds pretty absurd," Chance replied, holding back another laugh. "And I haven't even gotten to the best part yet."

"The best part?" Aaron asked, with a look that suggested he wasn't really sure he wanted hear what Chance considered "the best part."

Chance nodded, and Aaron could see his lips twitching as he tried to keep a straight face.

"The best part," Chance said, pausing for dramatic effect, "is that he did it dressed as a woman!"

Then he dissolved into hysterical laughter. For a moment Aaron looked confused and slightly horrified, then he began laughing, too.

"Okay, yeah, that does sound pretty absurd when you say it," he said, causing Chance to laugh even harder.

They both continued laughing hard for a full minute, then slowly it began to subside. Chance sighed and wiped his eyes.

"Anyway," he said, "after a while two of the other boys and I went out on our own. When Joel got here, he moved in with me, but when he found out I was hustling, he moved into Zelda's house. Long story short, eventually Hunter got Joel to turn a trick, then basically kidnapped him. I tried to rescue him and I got stabbed. I went back to Mississippi to recuperate, and while I was there I inherited some money and started a real estate development company."

"So I'm confused," Aaron said. "You own a development company, but you work here?"

"I do affordable housing projects," Chance explained. "Rentals. And I put most of the profits back into the company."

Aaron nodded.

"Plus the business doesn't take up very much time," Chance continued. "I figured working here would keep me out of trouble. I'm starting school in the fall, so at that point I'll probably only work a few hours a week."

"What are you planning to study?" Aaron asked.

"Business," Chance replied.

He suddenly noticed that Aaron's right leg was lightly touching his own right knee, and wondered when Aaron had unfurled his legs from the top of the file cabinet.

"That's pretty impressive," Aaron said.

"You think?" Chance replied with surprise.

"Yeah," Aaron replied. "You basically reinvented your whole life. I think that's impressive."

Chance smiled and pressed his knee against Aaron's leg a little harder.

"If you say so," he said. "Anyway, to get back to your original question, back when we were growing up in Natchez, Joel and I were best friends, but we really didn't talk about much. Except being gay, of course. I mean we talked all the time, but not about what we were feeling or anything. We were just kids, you know?"

Aaron nodded.

"Then when he'd come to visit me here, it was mostly just about having fun and partying," Chance continued. "So when he moved here, I figured that's what it was always going to be. Two small town gay boys on an endless party in the big city."

"But it's not," Aaron said.

"No," Chance replied. "We still have a lot of fun when we go out, but we don't go out as often. I hate to say it, but I guess we've matured. It's like we spend less time together now, but I think we're actually closer, if that makes sense."

"It's about the quality of the time rather than the quantity," Aaron replied.

Chance considered it.

"Yeah, that's a good way of putting it," he said.

He suddenly felt mildly embarrassed that he'd shared so much about himself with a stranger.

"So what about you?" he asked quickly. "What's your hard luck story?"

Aaron smiled broadly, and Chance noticed for the first time that he had dimples.

"No hard luck story here," he replied. "I had things pretty easy. Great parents, close with my brother and sister, stable home life, nice town."

"Where'd you grow up?" Chance asked.

"Connecticut," Aaron replied. "A town called Greenwich."

"What was it like?" Chance asked.

"Rich," Aaron replied with a laugh.

"So your parents are rich?" Chance asked.

"Yeah," Aaron replied, "but they're sort of like old hippies. My dad worked on Wall Street years before I came along, then he retired and they moved to Greenwich to live 'a simpler life.' But they're the kind of hippies who like nice things. I think my dad was the first guy in town to buy a hybrid car, mom shops at the organic market even though everything costs three times as much, and they collect a lot of art. They're definitely not the types who'd live in a commune or anything like that. They're like high-end hippies."

"And you're still close with them?" Chance asked.

"As much as I can be from 1500 miles away," Aaron replied. "They weren't exactly thrilled when I told them I wanted to go into intelligence work, but they got over it, and they've been pretty supportive since I joined the NSA."

"Why weren't they thrilled?" Chance asked. "Seems like a pretty important job."

"I think they've got this fear of government left over from the Nixon years," Aaron replied with a laugh.

"Nixon?" Chance replied. "Wasn't that in like the early 70s? How old are they?"

"My mom's 68 and my dad just turned 70 last month," Aaron replied.

"So they had you pretty late," Chance replied.

"Actually they adopted me," Aaron replied. "I think it was 'empty nest' syndrome because my brother and sister were already in high school and mom got scared when she realized she wouldn't have anyone to nurture once they were gone."

"It sounds kind of selfish when you put it that way," Chance replied with a serious look.

"I didn't mean to make it sound that way," Aaron replied. "They're both awesome parents, and I'm really thankful they adopted me."

They were both quiet for a few moments, and Chance worried that he'd killed the moment with his last comment. He noticed that Aaron's leg was no longer touching his own, and tried to think of a way to get things back on track.

"So where do you live now?" he asked.

"Metairie," Aaron replied.

"Why?" Chance asked, wrinkling his nose.

"It's close to work and it's cheap," Aaron replied, shrugging. "Plus I'd never been here before I moved, so I didn't really know the area."

He smiled, and Chance relaxed a little.

"So do you ever go out to the bars or clubs?" Chance asked.

"Not yet," Aaron replied. "I was hoping I could make some friends first so I wouldn't have to go out alone."

"But how are you going to make friends if you don't go out where you can meet people?" Chance asked.

"Good point," Aaron replied, laughing. "I've tried to meet some people online, but all they want to do is hook up."

Chance nodded as he wondered what Aaron's online profile pictures looked like.

"Well, if you want, we could go out together some night," he ventured, trying to sound casual.

He felt Aaron's leg press against his knee again.

"Great. How about tonight?" Aaron replied enthusiastically.

Chance almost said 'sure,' then remembered Sassy's admonishment to stay close to home until they knew what was going on.

"I can't," he said instead.

He could read the disappointment in Aaron's eyes.

"Okay. Another night, I guess," Aaron replied dejectedly.

Chance looked down at their legs for a moment, then looked up and smiled suggestively.

"Or you could just come over to my place and hang out," he said.

Chapter 13

Michel and Joel walked along Royal toward the Marigny. Michel realized that Joel hadn't spoken since they'd left the Bourbon Orleans five minutes earlier.

"You okay?" he asked.

"Is it too early for a drink?" Joel replied, only half kidding.

Michel looked at his watch. It was just before noon.

"It is for me," he replied, "but we can stop for lunch somewhere and you can get one, if you want."

Joel shook his head.

"No, I'm not really hungry."

They reached the corner of Esplanade Avenue, and waited for a truck to pass.

"So, did it bring back bad memories?" Michel asked.

Joel stared across the street for a moment, then gave a sad smile.

"Kind of," he said.

"You want to talk about it?" Michel asked.

"Not really," Joel replied.

They crossed to the median strip.

"It felt more like I was remembering a movie than something that actually happened to me," Joel said, apparently changing his mind.

"You were a different person then," Michel replied sympathetically.

"Not to mention that I was pretty fucked up that night," Joel replied, with a bitter laugh.

They crossed to the far side of the street and started up the block toward Frenchman Street.

"I'm really sorry," Joel said.

Michel stopped and put his left hand on Joel's shoulder.

"For what?" he asked.

Joel stopped and turned to face him.

"For what happened back then," Joel replied.

Michel sensed he meant more than the night with Smith.

"You don't have to apologize for anything that happened back then," he said. "You got caught up in bad situation and made some mistakes, that's all."

"I know," Joel replied, "but if I hadn't, things might have been different with us. We might not have wasted a year and a half doing whatever it was we were doing."

"You blame yourself for that?" Michel asked.

Joel hesitated, then nodded.

"I think you're forgetting an awful lot," Michel replied. "I wasn't exactly in a great emotional space for a relationship at that point either, and I was the one who pushed you away during the MacDonald investigation. If anyone's to blame, it's me. You made it pretty clear you were ready long before I did."

Joel studied Michel's face for a moment, then smiled.

"Yeah, you were kind of a pain in the ass for a while there," he said.

"Thanks a lot," Michel replied sarcastically.

"Playing all hard to get," Joel teased, "and as old as you were, too. That wasn't right. You should have jumped at the chance to get a fine young piece of ass like this."

Michel took a step forward, and draped his arms over Joel's shoulders.

"Well, I've got him now," he said, "and I'm not going to let him go."

He leaned forward and kissed Joel.

"Promise?" Joel asked.

"Promise," Michel replied. "We've got the rest of our lives to make up for that year and a half."

They kissed again, and Joel smiled.

"Good," he said. "So what do you say we go home and lock Blue out of the bedroom?"

Suddenly Michel's phone began to ring.

"So much for that idea," Joel said.

Michel gave an apologetic look as he pulled out his phone.

"Hey Al," he answered.

"Marchand is on his way in," Ribodeau replied.

"Great. When?"

"He should be here in an hour," Ribodeau replied.

"I'll be there," Michel replied. "Oh, and Joel and I were just at the Bourbon Orleans. He's pretty sure Smith was in room two-seventeen."

"Great," Ribodeau replied. "I'll get our guys working on it."

"Okay, see you in a while," Michel said, then hung up.

"I know," Joel said resignedly. "Duty calls."

Michel sighed and nodded contritely. Then he arched his eyebrows and smiled.

"But not for an hour."

Chapter 14

"Is he here yet?" Michel asked as he hurried into the squad room five minutes late.

Ribodeau nodded.

"In the interrogation room. Along with his lawyer."

"His lawyer?"

"I think he was expecting us," Ribodeau replied.

"I'm not sure if that's good or bad," Michel replied.

"Me neither," Ribodeau replied, "but I'm guessing it means he's guilty of something."

He grabbed a note pad from his desk, then gave Michel a questioning look.

"Are you okay? You look kind of flushed?"

"I'm fine," Michel replied, a bit too casually. "I just ran part of the way."

Ribodeau moved closer and made a show of sniffing the air.

"Ran, huh?" he asked, narrowing his eyes.

"Oh stop it," Michel replied, slapping him lightly on the shoulder. "You're getting as bad as Sassy. Let's go."

*****

The Severin Marchand seated on the other side of the glass looked like a different person from the one Michel had seen just three days earlier. While he was still much thinner than he'd been in the past, he appeared clear-eyed and healthy, and was immaculately groomed and turned out in a seersucker suit.

"Is he wearing makeup?" Michel asked.

"Looks like a bronzer to me," Ribodeau replied.

Marchand sat straight in his chair, his hands folded in his lap, staring directly into the two-way mirror. His expression was serene, almost beatific.

"Who's the lawyer?" Michel asked, looking at the younger, intense-looking man to Marchand's right.

"Lewis Stanhope," Ribodeau replied. "He's a partner at Goldman & Marshall."

Michel knew the name. They were one of the largest criminal defense firms in the southeast, based out of Atlanta.

"They don't have a local office, do they?" he asked.

"Nope," Ribodeau replied. "He's from the main office."

Michel gave him a questioning look.

"Like I said," Ribodeau replied, "I think he was expecting us. So anything special you want me to ask him?"

Michel smiled.

"Yeah, ask him where he got that suit."

Ribodeau left the observation room. A few seconds later, the door to the interrogation room opened and he walked in. He closed the door and took a seat on the opposite side of the table from Marchand, with his back facing the window.

"Thank you for coming in so quickly, Mr. Marchand," he began immediately.

"Of course," Marchand replied with a benevolent smile.

"I have a few questions to ask you about Michel Doucette," Ribodeau said.

"Michel," Marchand repeated warmly, then looked directly into the mirror as though he could see Michel on the other side. "What about him?"

"You know him?" Ribodeau asked.

"Yes, I hired him and his partner, Miss Jones, to help me with a private matter several months ago," Marchand replied, looking back at Ribodeau.

"And you didn't know him prior to that?" Ribodeau asked.

"I didn't *know* him," Marchand replied, "but I certainly knew *of* him."

"How's that?" Ribodeau asked.

"I saw him on occasion in some of the establishments I frequent, and was told he was a police detective," Marchand replied. "Later, I heard he'd left the department and started a private investigation agency."

"What about Joel Faulkner?" Ribodeau asked. "Did you know of him, too?"

Marchand looked up at the ceiling and pursed his lips for a moment, then shook his head.

"That name doesn't sound familiar," he said.

"What's this all about, Detective?" Stanhope cut in. "Why is my client here?"

"Joel Faulkner is Mr. Doucette's boyfriend," Ribodeau replied without hesitation, as though he'd been expecting the question. "Yesterday morning, Mr. Doucette received a photograph suggesting Mr. Faulkner had been kidnapped, along with a ransom note for $10,000,000."

"Oh dear," Marchand said with exaggerated concern. "I hope the boy's okay."

"He's fine," Ribodeau replied. "It was a hoax."

"So what does that have to do with Mr. Marchand?" Stanhope asked.

"I'm not sure," Ribodeau replied, "but whoever was behind it obviously had access to some personal information about Mr. Doucette."

He looked back at Marchand.

"Is your email address SeverinIV@yahoo.com?"

Marchand looked at Stanhope, who nodded.

"Yes it is," Marchand replied.

"Mr. Doucette told us that his cousin, Verle Doucette, was communicating with someone with that email address last year," Ribodeau said. "He also told us that he asked you about it on Saturday night, but you said it wasn't you. Is that correct?"

Marchand hesitated for a moment, then gave what seemed intended as an embarrassed smile.

"I'm afraid that was a lie," he said.

"So then you were in touch with Verle Doucette?" Ribodeau asked.

"Yes," Marchand replied.

"For what purpose?" Ribodeau asked.

Marchand looked at the mirror again for a few seconds, then back at Ribodeau.

"I was intrigued by Michel," he said, "and wanted to learn more about him."

"Intrigued?" Ribodeau replied.

"Yes. As I said, I'd seen him around for a while, and thought he was...interesting," Marchand replied, emphasizing the last word in a way that suggested his interest had been sexual.

"What did you and his cousin discuss?" Ribodeau asked.

"Mostly environmental issues," Marchand replied, "but I did ask him some questions about Michel's childhood and his family. That sort of thing."

"And why would you want to know about those?" Ribodeau asked.

"Just curiosity," Marchand replied smoothly. "Wouldn't you want to know as much as possible about someone in whom you had an interest, Detective?"

"Yes, but I would ask them personally," Ribodeau replied.

"Unfortunately, that option wasn't open to me at the time," Marchand replied.

"At the time?" Ribodeau repeated.

"Yes, it seemed that the opportunity to meet Michel never came up," Marchand replied, "but when he and Miss Jones opened their agency, I hired them so that I could get to know him better. Unfortunately, we didn't hit it off."

"And why's that?" Ribodeau asked.

"He was quite rude," Marchand replied, making a sour face.

"And how did you feel about that?" Ribodeau asked.

"Well, I certainly didn't appreciate it," Marchand replied with a long-suffering sigh, "but if you're asking whether it bothered me enough that I'd want to seek some sort of retribution, the answer is no. I have far more important things to worry about."

"Such as?" Ribodeau asked.

Marchand smiled thinly.

"Just an expression," he replied.

Ribodeau looked down at his note pad for a moment.

"Are we done?" Stanhope asked impatiently.

"Just one more thing," Ribodeau replied, looking back up at Marchand. "Would you be willing to give us access to your computer files?"

Marchand leaned close to Stanhope for a moment, and they exchanged whispers. Then he sat up straight again and smiled with self-satisfaction.

"I'd be willing to let you do anything that I'm legally obligated to do," he said.

*****

"Wow, he's a piece of work," Ribodeau said, as he walked back into the observation room. "If police brutality didn't already exist, it would be invented for guys like that."

Michel smiled appreciately.

"He was lying about not knowing who Joel was," he said.

"Yeah, I noticed that," Ribodeau replied. "He called him a 'boy,' even though I never said anything about his age."

"That's not going to be enough to get a warrant for his computer, though," Michel said.

"No," Ribodeau agreed. "So what did you think about his explanation?"

"It's bullshit," Michel replied. "First of all, who shows up for an informal interview with a high-priced criminal attorney? Second of all, it's not like I walk around with armed bodyguards to keep people away, and he's not exactly the shy type. If he wanted to meet me, he would have done it. Plus, I don't buy for a second that he'd be interested in me in the first place because I actually have to shave."

Ribodeau nodded.

"What really bothers me, though, is that his reason was so close to what Sassy said last night," Michel finished.

"You think your place might be bugged?" Ribodeau asked.

"It's not beyond the realm of possibility," Michel replied. "Stan's former student came by the office this morning. Chance's computer was set up so it could be accessed by 30 other computers."

"Was he able to trace them?" Ribodeau asked.

"No," Michel replied. "He got the IP addresses, but didn't think they'd be much help because they appear to belong to businesses with multiple computers."

"Send them to me, anyway, and I'll get our guys working on it," Ribodeau said. "Did he find anything else?"

"Everything that was typed on the keyboard was being recorded and stored," Michel replied.

"What about your phones?" Ribodeau asked.

"Our cells were set on call forwarding to the old bookstore," Michel replied. "He was checking the office line when I left."

"Sounds like maybe you ought to have him check your house, too," Ribodeau said.

"Yeah, unfortunately," Michel replied.

"What does that mean?" Ribodeau asked, looking at him curiously.

"Just that he's kind of an arrogant prick and I'd rather not have him in my house," Michel replied, with a small laugh, "but I think you're right. So anything on your end?"

Ribodeau nodded.

"We tracked down the owner of the domain name for the phony conference website," he said. "A Dr. Michael Gunn. Ring any bells?"

"Nope."

"I didn't think so," Ribodeau replied. "He was a professor at Johns Hopkins."

"Was?"

"He retired last year," Ribodeau replied. "Parkinson's Disease. The symptoms got too severe to continue teaching. Turns out the conference was real, except he stopped running it two years ago."

"Did you talk with him?" Michel asked.

"His wife," Ribodeau replied. "Apparently his speech is pretty badly impaired. She said he still owns the domain name, but was planning to let it lapse when it came up for renewal next year. She's trying to track down information on who built her husband's old site."

"Why would that be relevant?" Michel asked. "You think our guy would have hired the same person?"

"No, but whoever put up the fake site would need the administrative password," Ribodeau replied.

Michel nodded slowly, not entirely sure what that meant.

"What about Joshua Clement?" he asked. "Anything there?"

"Oh yeah," Ribodeau replied emphatically. "Not pretty. He was arrested in Tucson for solicitation about a year ago. It was meant to be a catch-and-release to scare some of the hustlers out of the area, but when he couldn't produce any ID, the judge ordered him held. After a week, he told them who he was, and of course when they checked for priors, they found out he was wanted for killing his parents and the priest."

"Did they send him back to Louisville?" Michel asked.

Ribodeau nodded. "But the Commonwealth's Attorney couldn't convince the grand jury he should stand trial, so they had to let him go. A month later, he was found beaten to death in a motel room back in Tucson. Police think he was killed by a trick."

Michel let out a sigh.

"I know this is an awful thing to say," he said, "but I have to admit I'm relieved. He was the wild card who made me the most nervous."

"Understandably," Ribodeau replied.

"So I guess that's it for now," Michel said.

"Not quite," Ribodeau replied. "I spoke with the manager at the Bourbon Orleans just before you got here. He said they had some kind of computer virus about a month ago."

"Let me guess. It wiped out their records?" Michel replied.

"Not entirely," Ribodeau replied. "They still have records of all their previous guests, including credit card information. They just don't know when they stayed at the hotel, or which rooms they were in."

"A targeted virus," Michel replied. "Isn't that convenient? So that pretty much narrows things down to Smith."

"Or someone who knows that Smith can identify them," Ribodeau said.

"Either way we're screwed," Michel replied.

"Not necessarily," Ribodeau replied. "Joel said that Smith usually hired one of the other boys, which means he was a regular customer. If he was a regular, then maybe Zelda knows who he is."

Michel gave him an impressed look.

"Gee, you're actually pretty good at this cop stuff, Al."

"That's why they pay me the big bucks," Ribodeau replied, with a dry chuckle.

Chapter 15

"When was the last time you saw her?" Michel asked.

"A while ago," Joel replied, looking down guiltily at the kitchen counter.

A few months after the Clement case, Miss Zelda had been diagnosed with early-stage Alzheimers, and had moved into a nursing home. For the first few months, Joel had visited her regularly, but as her symptoms had progressed he'd found it more and more painful to spend time with her, and had eventually stopped going altogether. It had been four months since his last visit.

"Was she still coherent?" Michel asked.

"Off and on," Joel replied in a small voice. "She was in pretty bad shape."

"Well, it couldn't hurt to visit her and find out what she remembers," Michel replied.

"Maybe Chance should go with us," Joel said.

"Chance?" Michel replied. "I thought he and Zelda hated one another."

"They did," Joel replied, "but he started visiting her when he came back to town. He goes every Sunday. She'd probably be more comfortable with him there."

"Okay," Michel said with a shrug. "It's fine with me."

"Do you think we should bring Blue, too?" Joel asked.

"Blue?"

"Yeah. I was reading about how people bring dogs to nursing homes. It's supposed to be therapeutic for the patients."

"I'm not sure that's such a good idea," Michel replied.

"Why not?"

"Because you know how she reacts to people who walk funny," Michel replied, "and a nursing home's going to be filled with people who walk funny. She'll be knocking people down, ripping out IVs, overturning wheelchairs."

"No, she won't," Joel replied. "I've taken her to Washington Park in the morning when all the old guys are sitting on the benches, and she's really gentle with them. I think she'd like it."

Michel looked at Blue, lying in the living room a few feet away. She looked back at him and raised her eyebrows questioningly.

"Okay," he said, "but if you eat any old people, you're not getting your allowance this week."

*****

"The smell is a little overwhelming at first," Chance said as they walked up the path to the door of the nursing home, "but you get used to it after a few minutes."

"The smell?" Michel replied, grimacing.

"Yeah, you know how old ladies' clothes usually smell like stale perfume?" Chance replied. "Well multiply that by ten, then add in piss and shit."

"That's disgusting," Joel said.

"You better get used to it," Chance replied, smirking, "because you'll be visiting him here before you know it."

He cocked his head toward Michel.

"Funny," Michel replied, without amusement. "I may be the first one in here, but I have a feeling you'll be the first one in diapers."

Chance gave Michel a withering look, but didn't reply.

"Hey Chance," the woman behind the reception desk said warmly, as soon as they walked through the door. "What are you doing here? It's not Sunday."

"Hey, Myra," Chance replied. "I brought some friends for a visit. Is it okay if we bring the dog with us?"

The woman looked at Blue, and a shadow of doubt crossed her face.

"She looks kind of wild," she said.

"I know, but she's really sweet," Chance replied.

Michel looked down at Blue. As if on cue, she cocked her head and smiled. The woman's expression softened, and she smiled back.

"Okay," she said, "but you be sure to clean up after her if she has an accident."

Chance nodded.

"This way," he said.

He lead Michel and Joel through a pair of doors to the left of the reception desk.

"I thought Zelda's room was the other way," Joel said.

"It was," Chance replied. "I had her moved to a private room."

"*You* had her moved?" Michel asked.

"Yeah, I'm her legal guardian," Chance replied casually.

"Since when?" Joel asked.

"Since a few months ago," Chance replied. "We were going over her finances, and she told me she wanted to sell Chanel's house. Her doctor said she wasn't mentally competent to sign the paperwork, so I petitioned the court to have myself declared her legal guardian and get power-of-attorney. Instead of selling the house, I took out a reverse mortgage and used the money to move her to a private room."

"Why didn't you sell it?" Joel asked.

"Because I was afraid her tenants were going to get kicked out," Chance replied.

"And what about the boarding house?" Joel asked. "Does she still own that?"

"She sold it right after she moved out," Chance replied, shaking his head, "and she got almost nothing for it."

"So how come no one's living there?" Joel asked.

Chance shrugged.

"They're probably still trying to get a permit to convert it to condos."

Michel stopped. Joel and Chance continued for another few steps, then realized he wasn't following and turned back.

"Given your history with Zelda, why would you do that?" Michel asked with genuine curiosity. "And why didn't you mention it?"

Chance's expression turned serious.

"Someone had to do it," he said simply, "and I didn't think anyone else would care."

He turned and started back down the hallway. Michel and Joel exchanged surprised looks, then followed after him, Blue padding along closely beside them.

They reached the end of the hall, then walked up a flight of stairs to another hall. Rather than the sterile tile floors and plain yellow walls below, this one was carpeted, and bracketed on both sides by dark crown moldings and wainscoting.

They paused for a moment to let an old man in a green flannel bathrobe pet Blue, then continued down the hall.

"It doesn't smell in here," Michel whispered.

Chance smiled slyly in response.

"Here we are," he said, stopping in front of an open door on the left side of the hall.

He knocked on the frame and peeked his head inside.

"Zelda?"

"Chance!" Zelda's voice came back. "Come in, darling."

Chance walked into the room. Michel looked at Joel and mouthed the word "darling," with an expression of disbelief. Joel suppressed a laugh, and motioned for Michel to go in.

Chance was leaning over the bed, hugging Zelda. He stood up and pointed toward the door.

"Look who came to see you," he said.

Zelda stared at Michel and Joel blankly for a moment, then looked down at Blue and broke into a wide smile.

"Aren't you a beautiful girl?" she said, patting the bed lightly beside her.

Michel gave Joel a questioning look. Joel shrugged. Michel unhooked Blue's leash, and she immediately trotted to the bed and jumped up next to Zelda. As Zelda began stroking her side, she settled down and let out one of her bovine groans.

"Yes, you're a sweet thing, aren't you?" Zelda murmured, leaning down to look into Blue's eyes. "What's your name?"

"Blue," Chance said.

"That's a nice name," Zelda cooed to Blue. "I'm Miss Zelda, but you can call me Auntie Zelda, if you want."

Joel noticed that Zelda looked much better than she had the last time he'd seen her. She was almost back to her normal weight, and wasn't wearing the matted brown wig she'd been favoring at the time. Her natural hair was short and neatly brushed, and she was dressed in a colorful floral housecoat.

Joel looked around the room. It looked more like an actual bedroom than a hospital room. The walls were painted a warm burnt orange, and there were curtains on the windows. A large oriental rug covered most of the floor. Joel recognized the rug, the bed, the divan in the corner, and the painting above the mantle from Chanel's house.

"So who are your friends, Chance?" Zelda asked after a moment of focusing on Blue.

"You remember Michel Doucette, don't you?" Chance asked hopefully.

"Of course I do," Zelda replied. "Detective Doucette."

"Nice to see you again, Miss Zelda," Michel said.

Zelda looked at him suspiciously for a few seconds, then turned back to Chance.

"Is he coming?" she asked.

"Is who coming?" Chance replied.

"Detective Doucette," Zelda replied.

Chance gestured toward Michel.

"That's him."

"No, I mean the other one," Zelda said. "The nice one. I never liked this one. He was always so full of himself."

Chance looked up at Michel and smirked.

"I guess she really does remember you," he said.

"Please don't talk about me like I'm not here," Zelda said, with a hint of testiness. "It's not polite."

"Sorry," Chance replied.

Joel noticed that Chance didn't talk down to Zelda. His tone was no different with her than with anyone else.

"What about Joel?" Chance asked. "Do you remember him?"

"He used to live at my house," Zelda replied.

"That's right," Chance replied.

Zelda studied Joel for a moment.

"Will he be coming with Detective Doucette?" she asked, looking back at Chance.

"I think so," Chance replied, then looked back at Michel and Joel and gave an apologetic shrug.

"So who are your friends?" Zelda asked again.

"That's Steve and Bill," Chance replied. "I think I've told you about them."

"Of course," Zelda replied, smiling at Michel and Joel. "It's a pleasure to meet you both. Why don't you come in and sit down for a while? This is my dog, Blue."

*****

"I'm really proud of you for helping Zelda," Joel said, as they watched Michel and Blue walk the perimeter of the field next to the parking lot.

"Don't be a douche," Chance replied dismissively.

"What?" Joel replied. "You don't want anyone to know you actually have a heart?"

"It's not like I'm being totally selfless," Chance replied. "She made me her sole beneficiary."

"But that's not the reason you did it," Joel replied, looking at him expectantly.

Chance rolled his eyes.

"Okay, fine. I care about her."

"See," Joel said. "That wasn't so hard now, was it?"

They were both quiet for a few moments.

"I care, too," Joel said finally, his tone more serious.

"I know you do," Chance replied.

"But earlier you said you didn't tell anyone what you were doing because you didn't think anyone else cared," Joel replied.

"I said I didn't think anyone else *would* care," Chance replied. "I meant I didn't think anyone would be bothered by it."

"You sure about that?" Joel asked, studying him closely.

Chance gave him a questioning look, then broke into a teasing smile.

"I'm just her legal guardian, you know," he said. "I'm not empowered to give absolution on her behalf."

"What? I wasn't asking you to," Joel replied too quickly.

"You sure about that?" Chance mimicked.

Joel blinked at him with his mouth slightly open for a few seconds, then began to laugh.

"Okay, maybe just a little," he admitted. "And fuck you."

"I get it," Chance replied. "I probably wouldn't be doing what I'm doing if I didn't feel guilty, too."

"But why do you feel guilty?" Joel asked. "You're actually helping her."

"*Now*," Chance replied. "But not when she really needed it."

"I'm not following," Joel replied.

Chance looked down at the ground for a moment, seemingly collecting his thoughts.

"Maybe if I hadn't been such a dick to Zelda, things would have turned out differently," he said finally.

"I'm still not following," Joel said.

Chance groaned.

"Do I really have to get into this?" he asked.

"Too late now," Joel replied, smiling sympathetically. "You already opened the can. Time to set the worms free."

Chance smiled back, then took a deep breath.

"Okay," he said, shaking his arms and shoulders like he was about to step into a boxing ring. "Why did I have a problem with Zelda?"

"Is that rhetorical?" Joel asked.

"No," Chance replied.

Joel gave him a wary look.

"Well, I guess because you've always had a slight problem with authority figures, and she was your pimp," he ventured.

"Exactly," Chance replied. "It was my usual defensive bullshit."

"Okay. Still not sure where you're going with this," Joel said.

"It didn't have to be that way," Chance replied. "Yeah, she could be a bitch sometimes, but it wasn't like she treated me badly. She didn't deserve to be treated the way I treated her."

"I'm with you so far," Joel replied.

"And if I hadn't treated her like that, maybe we could have been friends," Chance continued. "Or at least not enemies."

Joel nodded encouragement.

"Then when Hunter, or whatever the fuck his name was, started blackmailing her, maybe she would have told me and I could have stopped it," Chance finished.

Joel let out a small sigh of understanding.

"But Chanel was her *best* friend, and she didn't tell her what was happening," he replied.

"Because she was trying to protect Chanel. But maybe if she'd had someone else she could trust..." Chance trailed off.

They were quiet for a moment, then Joel wrapped his left arm around Chance's shoulders.

"I think you're putting an awful lot on yourself," he said. "Hunter was a killer. I'm not sure there's anything you could have done to stop him."

"Maybe not," Chance replied, "but at least Zelda wouldn't have had to go through it alone."

Joel felt a lump in his throat, and swallowed hard. He fought the urge to tell Chance again how proud he was of him.

"So you're doing this as penance?" he asked instead.

"That's how it started," Chance replied, nodding, "but now I actually like the crazy old bitch. Go figure."

Joel took his arm off Chance's shoulder and they both straightened up as they saw Michel and Blue approaching

"Did Sassy say where she was going to be?" Michel asked. "I just called her and got voicemail."

"She said she was going home," Chance replied. "She wanted to take a nap."

Michel frowned.

"I guess I'll try her later," he said.

Chapter 16

"Hey, it's me," Sassy said.

"Hey," Michel replied. "I tried calling you last night. You sound terrible. You okay?"

"Just exhausted," Sassy replied.

"Couldn't sleep?" Michel asked.

"Oh no, I slept like a dead woman," Sassy replied. "For 14 hours. But I'm still exhausted. I must have slept right through your call."

"Did you call your doctor yet?" Michel asked.

"Not yet," Sassy replied.

"Sas, come on," Michel chastised. "You need to call her this morning. As soon as we hang up."

"Fine, I will," Sassy replied. "But I'm not so sure it's the hormones anymore. I think I'm just fighting something off."

"Maybe," Michel replied, "but you need to call her and find out for sure."

"Yes, mom," Sassy replied. "Anyway, I was thinking about staying home today. You need me for anything?"

"No, I think we've got it covered," Michel replied.

"Anything important I should know about?" Sassy asked.

"Well..." Michel began.

"Hang on," Sassy interrupted. "I'm going to need to get some more coffee or I might not make it through this."

"Are you implying that I'm boring?" Michel replied with mock offense.

"No, I'm not *implying* anything," Sassy replied. "I'm *saying*

I'm tired. And as far your boring-ass stories go, I learned to deal with those a long time ago."

There was a loud clunk in Michel's ear, and he made an annoyed face at the phone. He could hear Sassy pouring her coffee, and the refrigerator opening and closing, then a spoon clinking against the sides of a cup.

"Okay, I'm ready now," Sassy said finally.

*****

"I can't say that I'm sorry about him being dead," Sassy said after Michel finished filling her in on Marchand's interview, the hotel's database, and Joshua Clement's murder. "I mean, of course it's sad that he died, but I'm kind of relieved we don't have to worry about him."

"I know what you mean," Michel replied. "I felt the same way. It really is kind of tragic, though, how much violence touched both brothers' lives."

"It didn't have to be that way," Sassy replied firmly. "A lot of kids go through terrible experiences, and they don't all end up as prostitutes and killers."

"I know," Michel replied, "but it's still sad."

"So what do you make of Marchand's explanation?" Sassy asked.

"It was a little too close to your explanation, for my taste," Michel replied.

"You think your place is bugged?" Sassy asked.

"It's a definite possibility," Michel replied. "Stan and Condescending Boy are on their way over now to check."

"You must be looking forward to that," Sassy replied, with a half-hearted laugh.

"Oh yeah," Michel replied. "Highlight of my day."

"Look at the bright side," Sassy replied. "Once you know there are no cameras, you can stop worrying about you and Joel showing up on the internet doing the nasty."

There was a long pause.

"Gee, thanks," Michel replied finally. "I hadn't been worrying about that before, but now..."

"I'm just saying," Sassy replied. "I could have sworn I saw your bedroom on there last night. Does Joel have a little French maid's costume?"

"Goodbye," Michel replied in a singsong. "I'm hanging up now."

"I was just trying to be helpful," Sassy replied.

"Yeah, I could tell," Michel replied. "Anyway, get some rest. And call your damn doctor."

"I will," Sassy promised. "And you call me if Aaron finds anything."

"Will do," Michel replied.

*****

"So what is that thing?" Joel asked.

"It's an RF sweeper," Aaron replied, holding the walkie-talkie-like device out in front of him. "It detects radio frequencies emitted by audio bugs."

"What about video?" Joel asked.

Aaron reached into his back pocket, and took out what looked like small camera.

"This is for video," he said, handing it to Joel. "The red light on the front is a laser. It can pick up lens reflection on even tiny cameras."

"Can I try it?" Joel asked.

"Sure," Aaron replied. "Just press that button on the front, then look through the lens. If you see a red dot, it means there's a camera. Or something else with a reflective surface."

Joel hit the button and lifted the device up to his eye.

"Cool," he said, as he began to turn in a slow circle.

Aaron walked to the couch and moved the sweeper's wand back and forth a foot above the seat cushions. He adjusted the frequency dial and repeated the process, then turned toward the coffee table.

"Looks like this is going to take a while," Michel said from his perch on the kitchen counter.

"Looks like," Lecher agreed. "So what should we do while the boys play with their toys?"

Michel cocked an eyebrow at him.

"You do realize how dirty that sounded, right?" he asked.

Lecher laughed.

"Not until I heard myself say it, unfortunately."

He looked at the digital display on the microwave.

"Too late for breakfast and too early for lunch, and brunch is just wrong on a weekday."

Michel nodded agreement.

"So what do you want to do?"

"I don't know. What do you want to do?" Lecher replied.

"I asked you first."

"No, I asked you first," Lecher replied. "Besides, it's your house and your town."

Michel made a face and looked down at the floor. Then his expression brightened.

"You want to go to the station and see what Al's up to?"

Lecher nodded.

"Sounds good. Should we see if Sassy wants to go?"

"No. I talked to her just before you got here," Michel replied. "She's going to stay in today and sleep. She thinks she may be coming down with something."

"Did she call her doctor about the hormones?" Lecher asked, frowning slightly.

"She hadn't when I talked to her," Michel replied, "but I gave her shit about it, and she promised she would."

Lecher nodded.

"Good. So you think they'll be all right alone?" he asked.

Michel looked into the living room. Aaron was running the

sweeper wand along the back wall, while Joel studied the ceiling through the scanner. Blue lay by the patio door, watching them.

"Yeah, I think so," Michel replied. "So long as Aaron doesn't start getting bossy."

Lecher looked into the living room, too.

"I think he'll be okay," he said. "He seems pretty comfortable letting Joel handle his equipment."

"Again with the dirty," Michel replied with a smirk.

Lecher smirked back.

"That time I meant it to be."

*****

Joel lowered the scanner.

"I don't see anything in here," he said.

"It can be tricky," Aaron replied. "It takes a little while to know what you're looking at."

He ran the sweeper under the cabinets over the coffee maker, then turned to Joel.

"I'm done in here. Where to next?"

"The bedroom, I guess," Joel replied.

He headed into the hallway, with Aaron behind him.

"So you and Chance have been friends for a long time," Aaron said.

"Since kindergarten," Joel replied.

"That must be nice," Aaron replied. "I haven't had any friends for that long."

They walked into the bedroom and Aaron looked around.

"This is nice," he said.

"Thanks," Joel replied, "but I can't really take any credit. It was like this when I moved in."

Aaron nodded.

"So how long have you guys been together?" he asked.

"Off and on for about two years," Joel replied, "but on for the last six months."

"Why off and on for so long?" Aaron asked.

Joel thought about how to respond.

"I guess neither of us was in the right place for a relationship when we met," he said finally. "You know what I mean?"

"Not really," Aaron replied with a self-deprecating laugh. "I've never been in a relationship."

"Really?" Joel replied. "Why not?"

"I've never really had the opportunity," Aaron replied. "The town I grew up in was pretty conservative. I mean it was liberal politically, but it wasn't like there were any openly gay people."

"Tell me about it," Joel said.

"But at least you had Chance," Aaron replied.

"That's true," Joel replied. "He was the one who told me we were gay. I didn't even know there was a name for it, or that we were different until then. I figured that eventually we'd find girlfriends, get married, and have kids just like everyone else in town. But Chance always had dreams of something else."

"Were you guys boyfriends?" Aaron asked.

"No," Joel replied. "We were more like brothers. Though we did fool around together for a couple of years."

"I wish I'd had a friend like that," Aaron said emphatically.

"It didn't suck," Joel replied, with a laugh. "So to speak."

"Chance is really hot," Aaron said.

"I guess," Joel replied. "I don't think of him that way now."

"I do," Aaron replied with a shy smile.

Joel studied his face for a few seconds.

"Is there something going on between you two?" he asked.

Aaron chewed his lower lip for a moment, then broke into a wide smile.

"I spent the night at his place," he said.

"Wow, that didn't take long," Joel replied, thinking about Ray Nassir.

Aaron's smile faltered.

"What does that mean?" he asked in a wounded tone.

"Nothing," Joel replied quickly. "I just meant that you only met yesterday."

He realized he was digging himself a deeper hole.

"Not that there's anything wrong with that," he said. "I mean, Michel and I spent the night together the first night we met, and that obviously turned out fine."

Aaron seemed to be trying to gauge Joel's sincerity. Finally he nodded and gave a diffident smile.

"So, do you think this could be going somewhere?" Joel asked, trying to sound enthusiastic.

"I don't know," Aaron replied.

He looked down at the bed for a moment, then looked up at Joel and his smile grew wider.

"But it sure was fun," he said.

"I'll bet," Joel replied, not wanting to hear the details.

He looked around the room.

"Shall we get started?"

"Why don't you start in here, and I'll start in the bathroom," Aaron replied, "then we can switch. I don't think there's enough room for both of us in there at the same time."

"Oh, you'd be surprised," Joel replied, raising his eyebrows suggestively, then gave an easy laugh.

Aaron looked at him curiously for a second, then smiled.

*****

Joel saw a small red dot on the wall above the bed, and lowered the scanner.

"I think I may have found something," he said.

"What?" Aaron replied from the bathroom.

"I said I think I may have found something," Joel replied.

He stepped up on the bed and lifted the scanner again. He relocated the dot and walked toward it. When he reached the wall, he lowered the scanner and leaned in close. A tiny silver dot shimmered just above the headboard. Joel licked his index finger, then touched it. He lifted his finger and looked at the tip.

"Fucking glitter," he mumbled.

He jumped down from the bed.

"I've got something in here," Aaron said excitedly.

Joel walked toward the bathroom door.

"What is it?"

As he reached the door, Aaron suddenly stepped in front of him and kissed him. Joel froze for second, then quickly jumped back as he felt something poke him just below his belt. He looked down. Aaron was naked and aroused.

"What the fuck?" Joel exclaimed, taking another step back. "What are you doing?"

"I thought this was what you wanted," Aaron replied with a mixture of hurt and confusion.

"Why would you think that?" Joel asked incredulously.

"Because of what you said," Aaron replied defensively. "That I'd be surprised about how we could both fit in the bathroom at the same time."

Joel stared at him for a moment, then shook his head.

"I didn't mean us," he said. "I meant Michel and me. That we'd fooled around in there."

He looked down at Aaron's naked body again for a second.

"Fuck," he said, with an exasperated sigh.

"I'm sorry," Aaron replied, taking a half step toward him.

Joel took another full step back, and held his hands out in front of him.

"Just stay there," he said. "You already touched me with your dick once."

He reflexively looked down again, and despite his discomfort, felt a small twinge of excitement. He closed his eyes and took a deep breath.

"And what about you and Chance?" he asked.

"Well, it's not like we're dating yet," Aaron replied.

"But he's my best friend," Joel replied.

"And you guys used to fool around," Aaron said. "I thought maybe..."

"You thought wrong," Joel cut him off. "Chance and I don't have sex anymore, and we don't share fuck buddies. Michel and I have a monogamous relationship."

"I didn't know," Aaron replied. "I'm new to this gay stuff."

He looked like he was on the verge of tears.

"It's okay," Joel said brusquely, not wanting to give in to the sympathy he was feeling. "But you need to leave, and we're going to forget this ever happened."

Aaron took a deep breath and nodded.

"Thanks," he said, "and I really am sorry."

He turned to get his clothes, and Joel stole a quick look at his ass.

"Under different circumstances..." he thought, shaking his head.

Chapter 17

"So why are you here exactly?" Ribodeau asked.

"To help you?" Michel tried unconvincingly.

Ribodeau gave him a skeptical look.

"Okay, fine," Michel said. "Aaron and Joel are looking for surveillance bugs at the house and we got bored."

"So you figured you'd come bother me?" Ribodeau asked.

"It was too early for lunch," Lecher replied.

"And where's the third musketeer?" Ribodeau asked.

"At home," Michel replied. "She's feeling a little under the weather."

Ribodeau regarded them for a few seconds, then sighed with resignation.

"Okay, sit down."

He began sifting through the neat stack of folders on the corner of his desk.

"Here you go," he said, pulling one from near the bottom and handing it to Michel.

Michel opened it and held it to his left so Lecher could see the contents as well. It was a list of the IP addresses Aaron had found on Chance's computer. Next to each was the location of the corresponding computer. Ten were located at an address in Carrollton, eight on Carondelet Street in the Central Business District, and twelve on Toulouse Street in the Quarter.

"So what's at these addresses?" Michel asked.

"Internet cafes," Ribodeau replied.

"Aaron called that one," Lecher said.

"I don't suppose they keep records of who uses their computers?" Michel asked.

Ribodeau shook his head.

"The manager at the one on Toulouse said they average 120 users a day. Most just stop in for a few minutes to check email."

"So much for that avenue," Michel said, closing the folder.

He tossed it onto Ribodeau's desk. Ribodeau stared at it for a few seconds, then gave Michel an expectant look.

"Oh, sorry," Michel said. "Old habits."

He picked up the folder and handed it to Ribodeau.

"Thanks," Ribodeau said, as he placed it back in the same order in the stack.

"Any luck with the hotel's guest list?" Lecher asked.

"I can tell you that Marchand isn't on it," Ribodeau replied. "And there are about two dozen Smiths who are. Not that I think any of them are our guy."

"So another dead end?" Michel asked.

"Afraid so," Ribodeau replied. "Without transaction records, we can't really do anything. And we can't get those from the credit card companies without a court order. And since there's no evidence of an actual crime..."

Michel and Lecher both nodded.

"And I take it you didn't have any luck with Zelda?" Ribodeau asked.

"No," Michel replied. "She didn't even recognize Joel and me. She knew our names when Chance said them, but couldn't connect that we were the same people."

"I told you I thought you'd put on weight," Lecher said.

Michel gave him a blank look.

"Don't you have a body to examine or something?" he asked. "Oh, that's right. You don't work here anymore."

"At least I'm not sitting on the wrong side of my own desk," Lecher shot back.

"Now, now, children," Ribodeau said. "Play nice."

"So is that it?" Lecher asked.

"What about the conference website?" Michel asked.

"I was just getting to that," Ribodeau replied.

He pulled another folder from the stack and opened it.

"The site was built and maintained by a company in Baltimore," he said. "Big Awesome Web Design."

"Subtle," Lecher said.

"I spoke to the project manager this morning. A guy by the name of Luke Marshall," Ribodeau continued. "He checked his records and told me 15 people worked on the various incarnations of the site, dating back six years."

"Anyone who might be a lead?" Michel asked.

Ribodeau nodded.

"He sent me their W-2s and we ran a check. One kid was using a fake social security number. The number tracked back to a woman in Florida who's been dead for ten years."

"Was she murdered?" Lecher asked.

"No. She was 94," Ribodeau replied.

"What was the kid's name?" Michel asked.

"Jason Brown," Ribodeau replied.

"It's certainly nondescript enough for an alias," Michel said.

"According to his application, he was a student at the University of Maryland," Ribodeau continued. "He worked for the company for a few months in early 2005."

"Did you check with the school?"

"They won't give out that information without a court order," Ribodeau replied, "but the address he gave is a chicken and waffle house."

"Did Marshall give you a description?" Michel asked.

"He was either a short redhead, a tall brunette, a medium blond, or a chubby black guy," Ribodeau replied.

Michel and Lecher both smiled as though he were kidding.

"No, I'm serious," Ribodeau replied. "They hire a lot of college kids, and most of them work offsite and only come into the office for occasional meetings. Marshall said he's had 50-plus kids work for him over the last two years. That's the best he could narrow it down to."

"So in other words, another dead end," Michel said.

"For the moment," Ribodeau replied. "I left a message for a friend of mine who went to Maryland. I'm hoping there's an alumnae directory he can access for us."

"Good idea," Lecher replied.

"You know," Michel said. "A tall brunette. That could be your boy Aaron."

"Just because someone doesn't fawn all over you and kiss your ass doesn't make him a suspect," Lecher replied.

"What's that supposed to mean?" Michel replied.

"Nothing," Lecher replied with exaggerated innocence.

"Oh, come on," Michel replied. "My ego is *not* that fragile. The fact that he was an arrogant prick to me has nothing to do with it. He just happens to be a tall brunette arrogant prick with mad computer skills."

"Did you really just say 'mad computer skills'?" Lecher asked with a look of distaste.

"Yeah. Why?" Michel replied.

"Because that's the sort of thing my students say," Lecher replied. "They're at least a dozen years younger than you. You shouldn't say it anymore."

Michel curled his upper lip in response.

"Besides, Aaron was at Texas State then," Lecher said, "not in Baltimore. And I met his family at graduation, so I know his identity checks out. Not to mention the fact that he works for the NSA. I'm pretty sure they vet their employees carefully."

Michel gave a dissatisfied frown, and Lecher sighed.

"What do you want to do?" he asked sarcastically. "Send a photo of him to this Marshall guy to see if he recognizes him?"

"Do you have one?" Michel asked quickly.

"Are you serious?" Lecher asked.

Michel shrugged.

"It couldn't hurt. I mean we have to be sure that everyone on the team is actually working *for* the team, right?"

"He's got a point," Ribodeau said.

Lecher looked from Ribodeau to Michel and back.

"Fine," he said. "I've got some photos from graduation on my computer. I'll email you one."

Ribodeau nodded.

"Thanks," Michel said.

A squealing noise caught his attention and he looked to his right. A janitor was pushing a large wheeled trash barrel down the center of the room. He stopped and began emptying the trash cans from the desks on both sides into the larger barrel.

Michel started to look away, but then turned back. There was something familiar about the man. He tried to place his face, wondering if he'd seen him in a bar.

Suddenly the janitor looked up and saw Michel watching him. He nodded sullenly, then his eyes seemed to register recognition. He put down the trash can he was holding, then turned and began pushing the barrel in the opposite direction.

"Who is that guy?" Michel asked quickly, nodding toward the man.

Ribodeau looked across the room and squinted.

"His name's Speck," he replied. "Why? You think you know him from somewhere?"

Michel didn't reply immediately. He began searching his memory for a last name.

"Speck Boucher?" he asked finally.

"I'm not sure," Ribodeau replied, "but I can check the personnel files."

He started typing into his computer.

"Close," he said after a few seconds. "Bouchard."

"Why's that so familiar?" Michel asked, as much to himself as the others.

Ribodeau started typing again, then suddenly stopped and gave Michel a worried look.

"Because you interrogated him," he said. "He was the clerk at the Creole House the night Clement killed his first victim."

They all looked back at Bouchard. He was nearing the door.

"Speck!" Ribodeau called. "Hold on a second. You missed my trash."

Bouchard didn't respond. Instead he quickened his pace.

"Dumb shit," Ribodeau said, shaking his head as Bouchard left the room and turned left.

Ribodeau picked up his phone and punched in a few numbers.

"Hey, Curtis. It's Al. Is the janitor headed your way?"

There was a brief pause.

"Yeah, the one with the dark hair. Speck. Can you do me a favor and grab him?"

Another pause.

"Yeah, cuffs if necessary," he said. "Thanks."

*****

Michel watched Speck Bouchard through the window of the observation room. Although he looked much healthier than he had two years earlier, he still had the same nervous, darting eyes and defensive posture.

"Any chance you'd let me have a crack at him?" Michel asked, his eyes widening optimistically.

Ribodeau knelt down and put his palm on the floor for a few seconds.

"Sorry," he said, shaking his head. "Still not frozen over."

"Was that really necessary?" Michel asked as Ribodeau slowly stood. "A simple 'no' wouldn't have sufficed?"

"Actually I enjoyed that," Lecher chimed in.

Michel fixed him with a dull stare.

"Sorry," Ribodeau replied, "but I couldn't resist. Anyway,

I'm afraid you're going to have to watch this one from the sidelines. Anything special you want me to ask him?"

Michel thought about it for a few seconds.

"No," he said. "I'm sure you can handle it."

*****

Ribodeau walked into the interrogation room and closed the door. Speck Bouchard sat up straighter and folded his hands in his lap. Though he was making an obvious effort to appear relaxed, the wariness in his eyes was unmistakable as he watched Ribodeau take the chair on the opposite side of the table.

"What are you doing here, Speck?" Ribodeau asked immediately.

Speck looked at him with cautious confusion.

"I don't know," he replied. "You're the one who put me here. Why don't you tell me?"

Ribodeau smiled indulgently.

"I don't mean right here," he clarified. "I mean what are you doing working at the station? We have a policy against hiring convicted criminals. How'd you manage to get around that?"

Speck's expression remained fixed.

"I don't know," he replied with a shrug. "I just applied for the job and I got hired. I didn't know there was any policy or anything. I guess somebody just didn't notice."

"You're sure you want to stick with that story?" Ribodeau asked calmly.

"If you think I lied about my record, you're wrong," Speck replied adamantly. "I put it on my application."

"I don't think you lied," Ribodeau replied. "I just think you had a little help getting the job."

Speck didn't respond, but reached into his shirt pocket and took out a pack of cigarettes.

"Uh uh," Ribodeau said, slowly shaking his head. "No smoking in the building. You should know that."

Speck reluctantly slid the pack back into his pocket, then laid his hands palms-down on the table. He stared at them for a moment, as though unsure what to do with them.

"So you like working here?" Ribodeau asked.

Speck looked up at him.

"It's okay, I guess," he said.

"You like it better than being in jail?" Ribodeau asked, the threat in his voice unmistakable.

Speck's body tensed and his eyes narrowed.

"What are you talking about?" he replied. "I didn't do anything wrong."

"Have you ever heard of obstruction of justice?" Ribodeau replied. "We're conducting an investigation. I asked you a question and you're not telling me the truth. Parole boards have a tendency to frown on obstruction."

He watched for a response, hoping that Speck wouldn't realize it had just been a carefully constructed bluff. He could see Speck assessing his options.

"What do I get?" Speck asked finally.

"Get?" Ribodeau replied. "This isn't a negotiation, Speck. You don't *get* anything."

"What about my job?" Speck asked quickly. "Can I keep my job?"

There seemed to be a touch of desperation.

"Assuming you haven't broken any other laws," Ribodeau replied, though he wasn't sure he could back it up.

Speck looked back down at his hands for a long moment, then nodded to himself.

"Severin Marchand," he said.

Ribodeau sat back in his chair and tried to keep the surprise from his face.

"How do you know Severin Marchand?" he asked.

"He used to be a customer," Speck replied.

"A customer?"

"When I was hustling," Speck replied, meeting Ribodeau's gaze evenly. "And then again when I was dealing."

"And he got you the job?" Ribodeau asked.

Speck nodded.

"Okay, from the top," Ribodeau said. "Tell me exactly what happened."

He saw Speck anxiously look down at the cigarettes in his pocket, and nodded.

"Go ahead."

Speck pulled out the pack and quickly lit a cigarette. He took a long drag, then eased back in his chair, blowing a large cloud of smoke up toward the ceiling.

"He came to see me about a week after I got out of jail," he said finally.

"So you'd stayed in touch?" Ribodeau asked.

Speck shook his head.

"I hadn't seen or heard from him since I got arrested. I don't even know how he knew where I was living."

"What did he want?" Ribodeau asked.

"Crystal meth," Speck replied. "But I told him I wasn't dealing anymore."

Ribodeau nodded for him to continue. Speck took another drag from his cigarette first.

"He stayed for a few minutes and we just talked," he said. "He asked me what I was planning to do, and I told him I was looking for a job. Then he left. Two days later he called and told me he had a friend in the police department who could get me a job here."

"Do you know who the friend was?" Ribodeau asked.

Speck looked at him like he'd just said something unbelievably stupid.

"Like I asked?" he replied with a derisive grin.

Ribodeau sat forward and gave Speck a hard look. Speck reflexively pulled back and lost the smile.

"So why do you suppose Marchand got you a job?" Ribodeau asked. "I've met him. He doesn't strike me as the charitable type."

Speck took another long drag, squinting against the smoke, and shook his head.

"No. He wanted a favor.".

"What kind of favor?" Ribodeau asked.

"He called me about a week after I started and said that he wanted me to get him some files," Speck replied. "Cases that Detective Jones and Detective Doucette worked on."

"Did he tell you why he wanted them?" Ribodeau asked.

Speck gave him the same look again.

"So did you get them for him?" Ribodeau asked.

"Hell no," Speck replied emphatically. "Even if I'd wanted to, I couldn't. The file room is always locked, and I don't have a password for the computers."

"Then you tried," Ribodeau said.

"Only so I could tell him why I couldn't get them," Speck replied. "I swear I wouldn't really have given them to him."

Again his voice carried a tone of desperation. Ribodeau studied him for few moments.

"Why not?' he asked.

Speck looked genuinely surprised by the question, and cocked his head to the right. He seemed to be considering the answer for the first time himself.

"I guess because I'm tired of being used," he replied quietly after a moment.

Ribodeau gave him a questioning look.

"I'm not stupid," Speck replied. "I know that Marchand doesn't give a shit about me. I've known him since I was 15, and the only times he ever wanted anything to do with me were when he was looking for ass or dope. Otherwise I didn't exist."

Ribodeau nodded, imagining that was probably true.

"I figured this was a one-time thing," Speck continued.

"That once I gave him the files, he wouldn't need me here anymore and I'd get fired."

"So you strung him along for a while, telling him you were still working on it?" Ribodeau asked.

Speck nodded.

"It may not be much," he said, "but I get a paycheck and I know I earned it. And working here helps me stay clean."

"But you had to figure he'd catch on eventually, or lose his patience," Ribodeau replied.

"I was hoping that by then maybe they'd want to keep me around anyway," Speck replied. "If I did a good enough job."

Ribodeau nodded again. He'd seen Speck around enough to know that he was a hard worker.

"Okay, I think we're done for now," he said.

The surprise returned to Speck's eyes.

"Then I can go back to work?" he asked.

Ribodeau nodded.

"And I'm not in trouble?" Speck asked.

"Not so long as you were telling the truth," Ribodeau replied.

Speck stood up slowly, as though expecting Ribodeau to change his mind at any moment.

"Oh," Ribodeau said, and Speck froze. "I'm going to need an official statement from you when you finish your shift, and I wouldn't plan any vacations without checking with me first. You'll probably be called as a witness if we charge Marchand with anything."

"Okay," Speck replied.

He stood awkwardly at the table for another few seconds, trying to decide whether Ribodeau was actually done with him this time. Then he nodded and quickly walked to the door.

*****

"You think he's telling the truth?" Ribodeau asked.

Michel nodded.

"I'm hesitant to say it because I know it doesn't happen too often, but I think he's actually trying to turn his life around."

He rapped his knuckles three times against the wood window frame.

"I agree he's telling the truth about wanting to keep his job," Ribodeau replied, "but if he didn't steal files, then how's Marchand been getting his information on your cases?"

"Probably from whoever got Speck his job," Michel replied. "In fact, my guess is that Marchand never really expected Speck to steal anything in the first place. He just told him he did."

"I'm not following," Lecher replied.

"I think Speck was just insurance," Michel replied. "Get him a job. Ask him to snoop around. Plant some case files under his mattress if things go wrong. I think he was set up as the potential fall guy to protect Marchand's real contact."

"And you're basing that on what?" Lecher asked. "Intuition?"

"Would you put all your eggs in a basket being carried by Speck?" Michel replied. "The guy's been a junkie most of his life. Odds were he was going to relapse. Not exactly the most dependable accomplice you could choose. Plus Marchand's contact has to be pretty high up if he could get Speck a job. I'm sure he knew Speck couldn't get access to the files."

Lecher considered it for a few seconds, then nodded.

"Well, in any case," Ribodeau said, "I think Speck just gave us enough to bring Marchand back in, and get a warrant to search his house and computer."

He looked down at his watch.

"I don't know about you guys," he said, "but I'm ready for some lunch."

"Sounds good," Michel replied. "I just want to call Sassy first and let her know what's going on."

He pulled out his phone and hit the speed dial. The phone rang four times, then Sassy's voicemail picked up.

"Hey, it's me," Michel said. "Just wanted to let you know we caught a break. Marchand is going to be picked up, and we're getting a search warrant. Call me as soon as you get this."

He hung up and looked at the others.

"All right," he said. "Let's eat."

Chapter 18

The buzzing of her cell phone stopped, but the doorbell rang again. Sassy finally opened her eyes. She willed herself to sit up, and swung her legs to the side, planting her feet firmly on the floor. The doorbell rang again.

"I'm coming!" she tried yelling, though the words were barely audible.

She put both hands on the arm of the couch and pushed herself up with a loud groan. The doorbell rang again.

"Fucking asshole," she mumbled.

She took a few lumbering steps to the hall, then stumbled as her right foot caught the edge of the runner that ran to the front door. She threw her left arm out and managed to catch the corner of the wall, though she was distantly aware of pain in her middle finger. She stood there for a few seconds, blankly staring at the blood seeping out from under her torn fingernail while she waited to regain her equilibrium.

"I said I'm coming!" she yelled more clearly as the doorbell rang again, then started down the hall, keeping her left hand on the wall for balance.

As she reached the door, the bell rang again.

"Motherfucker," she hissed sharply.

She put her left hand on the door jamb and peered through the peephole. A young blond woman in sunglasses stood on the porch, facing the door. She was wearing a red skirt and jacket, and had her hair pulled up, with just a few chin-length strands framing her face prettily.

"Who the fuck?" Sassy muttered.

She took an unsteady step back and turned the deadbolt, then pulled the door open.

"What?" she slurred.

The woman smiled, then took a step forward.

"Remember me?" she said in a male voice.

Chapter 19

Al Ribodeau swallowed the last bite of his sandwich and looked at his watch again.

"I thought we'd hear something by now," he said.

"The judge probably couldn't be bothered to come in off the golf course to sign the warrant," Michel replied dryly.

He signaled the waiter for another iced tea.

"So I've been meaning to ask you something, Al," he said. "How come you don't have a partner?"

"Uh, because I'm not gay?" Ribodeau replied in a mock questioning tone.

"No, I mean at work," Michel replied, rolling his eyes.

"Oh," Ribodeau replied. "I did have one, but she's on maternity leave right now."

"I take it you don't approve?" Lecher asked with a laugh, noting that "maternity leave" had sounded like a dirty word.

"It's not that I don't approve," Ribodeau replied. "I get the desire to have kids and all, and I think that cops should be able to have normal lives like other people, but I don't get the timing. She just got her shield six months ago. She should have waited until she'd logged some time and had a few cases under her belt. That's what I would have done."

"But that's a slippery slope," Michel replied. "You wait a year, and then the timing's still not right so you wait another year, and before you know it it's too late."

Ribodeau and Lecher both gave him curious looks.

"So you wanted to have kids?" Lecher asked.

"Hell no," Michel replied with a revolted look. "But it's the same with everything when you're a cop. You put off having kids because you're worried the timing's not right and it could hurt your career. Or you put off buying a house because you know there are going to be budget cuts and you're not sure if you're going to have a job in six months. Or you put off getting into a relationship because you don't know if you have enough room in your life for both the job and another person. But if you always put the job first, what do you have left when that's gone?"

"Usually a bottle and a 45-caliber pacifier," Lecher replied.

"Exactly," Michel replied.

Ribodeau stared at them both for a moment, then narrowed his eyes.

"So in other words, I'm going to end up a suicidal spinster?" he asked.

"Not you, Al," Michel replied lightly as he made a show of looking from Ribodeau's plain, jowly face to his soft, protruding belly. "You've still got that second career as a male model to look forward to."

Ribodeau opened his mouth to reply, but stopped when his phone began to ring. He picked it up from the table and frowned at the display.

"It's the Captain," he said.

He hit the answer button and put the phone to his ear.

"What's going on, Captain?" he asked.

There was a long pause, then Ribodeau looked at Michel. Michel felt his pulse suddenly speed up.

"We'll be there in five minutes," Ribodeau said. "What about Sassy, Joel, and Chance?"

Another, briefer pause.

"Okay," Ribodeau said, then hung up.

"What's wrong?" Michel asked immediately.

"Marchand is dead," Ribodeau replied.

"How?" Michel asked.

"Beaten to death," Ribodeau replied. "We're taking everyone into protective custody. Squad cars are on the way to pick them up."

Michel had his phone out before Ribodeau finished speaking, and hit the speed dial for home. He closed his eyes and listened to it ring, willing Joel to be there. When he heard a click after the third ring, he felt a wave of relief wash over him.

"Hey," Joel said.

"Hey. Where are you right now?" Michel asked, keeping his tone calm.

"On the patio," Joel replied.

"Is Aaron still there with you?" Michel asked.

"No," Joel replied. "He left about an hour ago."

There was something odd in his tone, but Michel decided to let it pass.

"Okay," he said. "There's a police car on its way to pick you up and take you to the station. I want you to wait inside."

"Why? What's wrong?" Joel asked.

"Severin Marchand was murdered," Michel replied.

For a moment Joel didn't respond.

"You still there?" Michel asked.

"Yeah," Joel replied finally in a tight voice. "What about Chance?"

"He's being picked up, too," Michel replied. "Can you call and let him know? I've got to call Sassy."

"Okay," Joel replied.

There was another pause.

"It's going to be okay," Michel said, sensing Joel's anxiety. "You can bring Blue with you and I'll meet you there."

"Promise?" Joel asked.

"Promise," Michel replied. "We're on our way now."

"Okay," Joel replied, sounding only slightly comforted.

"I love you," Michel said.

"I love you, too," Joel replied.

Michel hung up and looked at Lecher.

"Aaron's not there," he said. "I doubt he's in any danger, but you should probably call and have him meet us at the station anyway."

Lecher nodded and Michel immediately hit speed dial again.

"Come on, Sas. Pick up," he thought as he heard each successive ring.

After the fourth ring, Sassy's voicemail picked up. Michel hung up and waited ten seconds, then hit REDIAL, hoping the ringing might annoy Sassy into waking up. When he heard her voicemail pick up again, he sighed.

"Fuck," he muttered as he waited impatiently for her outgoing message to finish.

"Sassy, it's me," he said finally. "Marchand's been killed and the police are on their way to pick you up to take you into protective custody. Please call me as soon as you get this."

He hung up and looked at Ribodeau and Lecher.

"The car will probably get there before she even hears the message," he said.

"You want to swing by and get her?" Ribodeau asked.

"If you wouldn't mind," Michel replied with obvious relief.

"Not a problem," Ribodeau replied.

Chapter 20

"Looks like she's home," Ribodeau said, as he guided the car to the curb, directly behind Sassy's car.

Michel searched the windows of the house for a moment, then reached for the door handle. Suddenly the lock popped down, with a mechanical *thunk*.

"What the hell?" Michel exclaimed.

He turned to face Ribodeau.

"I think the front door is open," Ribodeau said, his face tight with concern.

Michel felt a jolt of adrenaline and quickly turned back toward the house. He could see a thin shadow along the right side of the door. He reflexively grabbed the door handle and yanked on it three times.

"Let me out of the fucking car, Al," he said angrily.

"Hold on," Ribodeau replied, keeping his own voice even.

"I'm not waiting for backup," Michel said.

"I'm not either," Ribodeau replied. "But we go in together, and we do it by the book. Okay?"

Michel was taken by surprise, and stared at Ribodeau distrustfully for a moment. Then he nodded slowly. The door lock popped up.

"You have your weapon?' Ribodeau asked.

Michel nodded.

"What about me?" Lecher asked from the back seat.

"Stay here and call it in," Ribodeau replied.

He and Michel stepped out of the car and pulled their guns.

They checked the magazines, then moved quickly to the front porch steps.

"Remember, you're just backing me up," Ribodeau said. "I go first."

"Okay," Michel replied.

Ribodeau walked quietly up the steps and positioned himself to the left of the door. Michel followed, taking the position to the right. Ribodeau looked at him to make sure he was ready, then pushed the door open with his left hand. He waited a few seconds, then stepped into the doorway, his pistol in the high-ready position.

"Sassy!" he called.

He cocked his head to the left and listened for a response or any movement.

"Okay," he said quietly, then began moving down the hall as Michel came in behind him.

*****

Ribodeau slipped his pistol back in his holster and frowned as he looked around the living room. He could hear the distant wail of sirens.

"What do you think?" he asked.

"I don't see any sign of forced entry or a struggle, or anything unusual," Michel replied. "It's like she just walked out and forgot to close the door behind her."

"What about the blood on the wall here?" Lecher asked.

Ribodeau and Michel both started a little, then turned to face him. He was standing at the near end of the hallway.

"I thought I told you to wait in the car," Ribodeau said.

"I got bored," Lecher replied, shrugging.

"What blood?" Michel asked anxiously.

"Right here," Lecher said, as the others moved closer.

He pointed to a barely visible horizontal streak on the cocoa brown wall.

"There are eight of these leading toward the door," he said, "and a spot about the size of a nickel on the left side of the doorframe."

"Any guesses?" Ribodeau asked.

"From the height and the amount of blood, I'd say that Sassy—or someone—was bleeding from a finger, and using the wall for balance as she walked to the door."

"How can you be sure the blood was coming from the finger?" Michel asked. "She could have had blood on her hand from covering a bullet or stab wound."

Lecher shook his head.

"In that case, the blood would have been on more than one finger, and we'd have a lot up at this end of the hall and very little by the door. These marks are pretty consistent. The finger that was touching the wall was actively bleeding."

"You're sure?" Ribodeau asked.

Lecher nodded.

"And since there's no blood on the floor or the door handle, it doesn't look like she had any other wounds. At least not serious ones."

"So then maybe she really did just walk out of here," Ribodeau said.

Michel walked back into the living room. Everything was in its usual place except for the sofa pillows. They were both leaning against the far arm of the sofa.

"Maybe she sleepwalked," he said, only half-kidding. "It looks like she was taking a nap."

He pulled out his phone and dialed Sassy's number. A muted ringing came from the direction of the hall.

"It's in here," Lecher said from the kitchen doorway.

Michel snapped his phone shut. He suddenly had an unsettling sense of deja vu, flashing back to the night Sassy was kidnapped by Mac MacDonald.

Lecher walked into the living room with Sassy's handbag.

"Okay if I look inside?" he asked, over the sound of the approaching sirens.

"Sorry," Ribodeau replied, holding out his hand.

Lecher looked momentarily annoyed, but handed him the black leather bag.

"Okay, but tell the lab to check her medications," he said.

Chapter 21

Sassy had been awake for almost five minutes, just listening and trying to get her bearings. She knew she was lying on her back, and that her right arm was extended above her head. Aside from a headache and a dull throbbing in the middle finger of her left hand, she seemed to be okay.

Slowly she opened her eyes, wincing at the harsh light of the bare bulb directly above her. She blinked a few times, then turned her head to the left. A young man with blond hair was sitting in a worn, green leather chair a few feet away, intently watching her. Though she'd seen Drew Clement only once, and he'd been wearing a wig at the time, the resemblance was unmistakable.

"You're supposed to be dead, Joshua," she said, in a dry rasp.

The young man smiled slightly. "Joshua *is* dead."

Sassy gave him a uneasy look.

"What does that mean?" she asked, wondering if there'd been a third brother she and Michel hadn't known about.

"Joshua and Drew have been dead since my brother killed our parents and Father Cleary," the young man replied.

"So then you're Jared?" Sassy asked uncertainly.

"For now," Jared replied with a nod.

Sassy tried to read his expression, but it was neutral. She didn't sense that she was in any immediate danger.

"Can I get some water?" she asked.

Jared nodded to his right, and Sassy looked up. There was a plastic cup on the battered nightstand next to the bed.

"Sit up slowly," Jared said. "I hit you pretty hard."

Sassy tried to bring her right arm down, but it wouldn't move. She looked up at her wrist. It was encircled by a thick leather strap that had been chained to an eyebolt in the heavy wood bedpost.

"I don't suppose you'd consider taking that off, would you?" she asked, looking back at Jared..

"Not at the moment," Jared replied, with an amused smirk.

Sassy pulled her knees up and braced her feet on the mattress, then propped her left elbow next to her hip and began to push herself upward, rocking from side to side until her back was resting against the headboard. She took a deep breath, trying to will away the pain that had exploded in her head from her efforts, then looked around the room. She was in the attic bedroom of Zelda's old house.

"I figured you'd recognize it," Jared said. "After all, it's where you killed my brother."

"I prefer to think of it as the place where your brother tried to gut me like a fish and kill my partner and Joel," Sassy replied, keeping her tone even.

She reached for the cup and noticed with surprise that her middle finger had been bandaged. She picked up the water and took a small sip as she looked around. The mannequins that had once crowded half the room were now all stripped and piled against the far left wall.

"I like what you've done with the place," she said, then took another sip.

She looked back at Jared.

"You hit me, huh?" she asked.

Jared nodded.

"With what?" Sassy asked.

"My fist," Jared replied.

Sassy nodded.

"Then you must hit like a girl," she said.

She watched Jared carefully for any sign of anger, but he just smiled benignly.

"A girl who knocked you out," he replied.

Sassy took another sip of water. Clearly Jared wasn't going to be baited that easily. She decided to try a different approach.

"You said Drew and Joshua have been dead since your brother killed your parents and the priest," she said. "So you didn't have anything to do with the murders?"

Jared stared at her for a moment, then shook his head.

"No, but I was glad they were dead," he said, then paused two seconds before adding, "Just like you and your partner were when you thought I was dead."

The surprise registered on Sassy's face before she could stop it, and she silently cursed herself. Jared's response had obviously been calculated to elicit a reaction, and she'd given him one. She realized she was going to have to be more careful with him.

"Yeah, I know pretty much everything you've said or done for the last six months," Jared said in an oddly casual way.

"But why?" Sassy asked.

"Because you killed my brother," Jared replied.

"But why the games? Why the long preparation?" Sassy asked. "You could have just waited outside my house and shot me one night."

"Because I haven't made up my mind about killing you yet," Jared replied.

He stood up before Sassy could reply.

"We'll have plenty of time to talk later," he said. "You should get some more sleep. Let the drugs work their way out of your system."

"What drugs?" Sassy asked.

"Zolpidem and Promethazine," Jared replied. "I substituted them for your estrogen and progestin. That's why you've been sleeping so much."

Sassy looked at him with disbelief.

"Are you telling me that on top of everything else, you anticipated my menopause?" she asked.

Jared laughed.

"No offense," he replied, "but I would have figured you'd have gone through that a long time ago. That was just a lucky coincidence."

Then he turned and walked to the stairs.

"Yeah, lucky," Sassy said to herself as he descended from sight.

A moment later, the light went out and she was left in near-total darkness.

Chapter 22

Michel, Ribodeau, and Lecher arrived at the station two hours later. Though it wasn't even 3 PM yet, Michel felt like he'd been awake for days, and he wanted a cigarette badly.

"The others are in Conference Room B," Ribodeau said, as they stopped outside the homicide squad room. "Why don't you go join them while I find the Captain."

Michel nodded, and he and Lecher continued down the busy corridor. He could see Joel, Chance, and Aaron through the large windows of the room at the end. Joel was sitting on the left side of a rectangular table, with Blue at his feet. Chance and Aaron were sitting on the opposite side, their chairs almost touching. The way that Chance leaned toward Aaron suggested a level of intimacy.

"That didn't take long," Michel thought.

When Blue saw him coming, she jumped up and her tail began wagging vigorously. Joel looked up and Michel could see the worry in his eyes. He attempted a reassuring smile, but from Joel's reaction, he knew he'd failed.

Joel got up and opened the door. Blue darted out and cantered excitedly down the hall. Michel got down on one knee, and Blue buried her face against his stomach while he rubbed both sides of her neck.

"Did you miss me?" Michel asked in a low, soothing tone.

Blue lifted her head and nipped the end of his nose.

"I missed you, too," Michel replied with a tired smile, then kissed the top of her head.

He stood up as Joel and Chance reached them. He wanted to say something to comfort them, but his mind went blank. Then Joel wrapped his arms around him and hugged him hard. Michel closed his eyes and sighed, just enjoying the feeling for a moment.

"Do you think Sassy is okay?" Joel asked finally.

Michel reluctantly took a step back.

"I don't know," he replied. "There was some blood on the wall in her hallway, but it wasn't much."

"So now what?" Chance asked.

"The police are canvassing her neighbors to see if anyone saw anything," Michel replied, "and checking with cab companies and hospitals in case she left on her own. So far nothing."

He looked over Joel's left shoulder and saw Aaron standing a few feet back.

"Did you find anything at our house?" he asked.

"No," Joel said before Aaron could respond. "Aaron's scanner broke, so he has to come back."

Michel looked at Aaron and he nodded confirmation, though Michel noticed that he seemed unsettled.

"It won't matter," a familiar voice said from behind Michel. "You won't be going back there until this is all over."

Michel turned and saw Captain Carl DeRoche standing in the middle of the hall. Michel smiled reflexively at his old boss, then realized what DeRoche had said.

"Wait a second, you're not putting me into protective custody," he protested.

"Why not?" DeRoche asked.

"Because I don't need it," Michel replied.

DeRoche just stared at him unyieldingly.

"It hasn't been that long since we worked together," he said. "Do you really think you're going to change my mind?"

Michel looked back at him with an equal amount of determination, then his expression softened slightly.

"I'll make a deal with you," he said. "Let me help out during the day, and you can lock me down at night. And I promise I won't leave Al's side."

"I don't have to make any deals," DeRoche replied, though his tone suggested he was considering the proposition. "Besides, what makes you think I want to put Al in danger like that?"

Michel looked at Ribodeau for support. He just shrugged.

"It's up to the Captain," he said, "but it's all right with me."

Michel looked back at DeRoche hopefully. DeRoche studied him for a few seconds, then gave a slight nod.

"Okay, but if you even step close to the line, never mind over it, I'm locking you up. And I don't mean in some nice hotel room."

"Thank you," Michel replied with genuine gratitude.

"So what's going on?" Joel asked. "Where are we going?"

"We've booked a wing on the top floor of the Chateau LeMoyne on Dauphine," Ribodeau replied. "The whole floor is closed down for renovation, so it'll be easy to secure."

"What about Blue?" Joel asked. "Can she come with us?"

"I'm afraid not," Ribodeau replied.

"She can board with our K-9 unit," DeRoche offered.

Joel gave Michel an uneasy look.

"She'll be fine," Michel assured him. "The dogs are very well cared for, and she'll get plenty of exercise. Plus it's all shepherds, and you know how much she likes shepherds. She probably won't want to come home."

"Will we be able to visit her?" Joel asked.

"I'll see what we can do," DeRoche replied. "Hopefully you won't be separated for long, anyway."

Joel nodded grudging acceptance.

"All right then," DeRoche said, looking at Michel and Lecher. "Let's go to my office."

"Should I come, too?" Aaron asked.

DeRoche looked at him curiously.

"That depends," he replied. "Who are you?"

Aaron blinked twice, as though surprised that DeRoche didn't know everything about him.

"Aaron Brooks," Lecher replied. "He's a former student of mine. He's an analyst for the NSA now, and he's been helping us out."

"Then I guess you should come with us," DeRoche said.

He turned crisply and started down the hall. Lecher, Ribodeau, and Aaron fell in behind him, but Michel hung back. He knelt down and cradled Blue's head in the crook of his left arm. Blue let out a snorting sigh and leaned against him.

"You be a good girl and play well with the other dogs, okay?" he said. "And we'll all be home together soon."

He kissed the top of Blue's head, and she suddenly backed away and shook her whole body.

"Okay, I know," Michel said with a resigned smile. "Too much love."

"Not for me," Joel said.

Michel stood and put his arms around Joel's neck.

"It's going to be okay," he said.

"I know," Joel replied. "Just be careful, okay?"

"I will," Michel replied.

He was suddenly aware of people watching them, and smiled to himself, knowing that he would never have been so openly affectionate while he was still on the force.

"I love you," he said.

"I love you, too," Joel replied.

Then they kissed, almost desperately, as though neither of them wanted it to end. Finally Michel pulled back.

"I'll see you in a few hours," he said. "Keep the bed warm."

"I will," Joel replied with a sexy smile.

Michel turned and followed the others down the hall.

*****

"Okay, so where do we stand?" DeRoche asked as soon as everyone was settled.

"The forensics team is almost done at the house," Ribodeau replied, "and we've interviewed all but two neighbors within a one-block radius. So far nothing."

"What about cab companies and hospitals?" DeRoche asked.

"No pick ups for anyone matching Sassy's description anywhere near the area, and nothing at the hospitals," Ribodeau replied.

DeRoche nodded.

"What about this Jason Brown at the web design place?" DeRoche asked. "Find out anything more on him?"

Ribodeau didn't respond for a moment, and DeRoche gave him a questioning look.

"Al?"

"Nothing yet," Ribodeau replied tersely, then looked down at his hands.

DeRoche raised his right eyebrow.

"Do you care to elaborate on that?" he prompted.

Ribodeau seemed to be struggling with what to say, then suddenly turned to Aaron.

"Would you mind giving us a minute?" he asked.

"Uh, sure," Aaron replied, clearly taken aback.

He stood slowly, seemingly unsure what to do.

"Should I just wait outside?" he asked awkwardly.

"Yeah, that'll be fine," Ribodeau replied. "This won't take long. Thanks."

Aaron gave Lecher a confused look, then walked to the door and let himself out.

"What's going on, Al?" DeRoche asked, as soon as the door was closed.

"I just don't think we should be talking about Jason Brown in front of him," Ribodeau replied.

"Why not?" DeRoche asked.

"Yeah, why?" Michel echoed.

Ribodeau looked at him incredulously.

"If I'm not mistaken, you're the one who was worried he might *be* Jason Brown," he replied.

Michel looked suddenly stricken.

"Oh yeah," he replied sheepishly.

"What's this about?" DeRoche asked.

"I wanted to send Aaron's picture to the project manager at the web design company where Brown worked, just to make sure he's not Brown," Michel replied.

"You really think he might be?" DeRoche asked skeptically.

"Probably not," Michel replied, "but he does have the skills to do everything that's happened so far."

DeRoche considered it for a moment, then nodded.

"Okay, let's do it," he said, "We may as well rule him out."

"And what do we do with him in the meantime?" Ribodeau asked.

"What exactly has he been doing?" DeRoche asked.

"He figured out how information was being accessed through one of the computers in our office," Michel replied. "And this morning, he was checking the house for surveillance equipment, though his scanner broke."

"That's nothing our guys can't handle," DeRoche replied.

"So what are you saying?" Michel replied. "You just want to send him home?"

DeRoche shrugged and Michel felt a flash of anger.

"Sassy's missing and we've got an NSA whiz kid willing to help us out, and you want to just cut him loose?" he asked, barely concealing the edge in his voice.

"Unless you can figure out some way to keep him around but away from the investigation until we've cleared him," DeRoche replied.

Michel looked at Lecher.

"Where's your computer?" he asked.

"In my hotel room," Lecher replied.

"And you're sure you have a picture of him on it?" Michel asked.

Lecher nodded, and Michel looked at DeRoche.

"Can you send someone to pick it up?"

"Sure," DeRoche replied.

"Okay, so let's do that quickly," Michel replied. "Then hopefully we'll just have to keep him busy for a few hours until we get confirmation he's not Brown."

"How?" Ribodeau asked.

Michel considered it for a moment.

"We could ask him to set up surveillance cameras at the hotel," he replied.

"For what?" DeRoche replied. "We're going to be locking down the elevators and the stairwells for that floor."

"But he doesn't know that," Michel replied.

DeRoche looked at him doubtfully.

"Seems kind of thin," he said. "Besides, how are you going to explain Al asking him to leave the office?"

"I'll think of something," Michel replied.

He looked around at the others for confirmation.

"Okay," DeRoche replied finally. "It's worth a try."

"Good," Michel said. "I'll go talk to him."

*****

Aaron looked up expectantly when the office door opened, then frowned slightly when Michel stepped out and closed it behind himself.

"Hey," Michel said.

"Hey," Aaron replied.

"Sorry about that," Michel said. "Detective Ribodeau was just being a little paranoid."

"About what?" Aaron asked.

Michel gave a faux sigh of exasperation.

"About mentioning Jason Brown in front of you," he replied.

"Why? Who is he?" Aaron asked.

"We don't know yet," Michel replied. "Maybe no one. It's just a name that came up."

"Then why wouldn't Detective Ribodeau want me to know about him?" Aaron replied with a hurt look.

Michel smiled reassuringly.

"Don't take it personally," he said. "It's just a cop thing. They have a tendency not to play well with other law enforcement agencies."

Aaron studied him for a few seconds, then smiled grudgingly in response.

"So we need your help with something else if you're still game," Michel said immediately, hoping to steer the conversation away from Jason Brown.

"Sure," Aaron replied. "What do you need?"

Unlike before, Michel didn't detect any sense of superiority in the question.

"We'd like you to set up some surveillance cameras at the hotel," Michel replied.

"What kind of surveillance?" Aaron asked.

"In the stairwells," Michel replied.

"Aren't the doors going to be locked?" Aaron asked.

Michel nodded.

"But there are four of them on every floor, and the locks aren't exactly high tech," he said. "If the officer-on-duty could monitor them all simultaneously, it would be really helpful."

Aaron gave him a skeptical look.

"Why don't the police just set it up?" he asked. "It's not rocket science."

"No," Michel agreed, "but right now the only members of the department who know where we'll be staying are the Captain and Detective Ribodeau. I'd like to keep it that way."

"Because you think there's a security leak?" Aaron asked.

Michel shrugged noncommittally, but put on an expression that seemed to confirm it. Aaron nodded slowly in response.

"Yeah, I can do that," he replied. "Where do I get the equipment?"

"Just put together a list of what you need, and we'll get it for you," Michel replied.

"I'll need to scope out the place first," Aaron replied.

"That's fine," Michel replied. "You can probably catch a ride with Joel and Chance if they haven't left yet."

"Okay," Aaron replied. "Then I better get going."

"Thanks," Michel said, trying to sound as sincere as possible. "I really appreciate it."

*****

"So how'd it go?" DeRoche asked, as Michel walked back into the office.

"I think he bought it," Michel replied.

"How'd you explain me asking him step outside?" Ribodeau asked.

"I told him you were a paranoid old man who doesn't play well with others," Michel replied.

"Thanks a lot," Ribodeau deadpanned.

"Hey, I had to improvise and it was the first plausible thing that came to mind," Michel replied.

Ribodeau gave him a sour smile.

"Did he ask about Brown?" DeRoche asked.

Michel nodded.

"I was vague. I told him it was a name that came up, but that we didn't know anything about him yet."

"I guess that's the best you could do in the circumstances," DeRoche replied, then looked at Ribodeau. "So what *is* going on with Brown?"

"There are 16 Jason Browns living in the New Orleans area," Ribodeau replied. "So far, we can't find a connection between any of them to Michel, Sassy, or Stan, and I'm still waiting to hear back from my friend who went to Maryland."

"Call him again," DeRoche replied. "Let him know we've got a probable kidnapping and it's urgent."

"Will do," Ribodeau replied.

DeRoche sat back in his chair and laced his hands behind his head. He looked from Ribodeau to Lecher to Michel.

"Any theories on who else Brown might be?" he asked.

"If he weren't already dead, I'd say Joshua Clement," Michel replied.

"Because of motive?" DeRoche asked.

"Motive, plus he was about the same age as Brown, and he fit one of the descriptions that the project manager gave us," Michel replied. "He was also definitely Marchand's type."

"Meaning?" DeRoche asked.

"Young, blond, and a hustler," Michel replied.

"You know for certain that Marchand was involved with hustlers?" DeRoche asked with mild surprise.

"Speck Bouchard told us that Marchand used to be a client when he was hustling," Michel replied.

"Speck? The janitor?" DeRoche replied with more pronounced surprise.

Ribodeau nodded.

"We talked to him just before lunch," he said. "I didn't have a chance to fill you in yet. Sorry."

"Why did you talk to Speck?" DeRoche asked.

"I recognized him," Michel replied. "He was the clerk on duty at the Creole House when the priest was killed there. I interrogated him at the time."

"He told us that Marchand used a connection to get him his job here," Ribodeau added, "then a few days later, asked him to get copies of Michel's and Sassy's case files."

"Wait a second," DeRoche said. "You're saying Speck was Marchand's mole?"

"That was Marchand's plan," Ribodeau replied, "but Speck says he didn't give him anything."

"And you believe him?" DeRoche asked.

"I do," Ribodeau replied with certainty.

"But he may know something about Marchand's boy," Michel said.

"What boy?" DeRoche asked.

"I ran into Marchand's friend Scotty McClelland the other night," Michel replied. "He said he thought that Marchand was holed up with a boy."

"Jason Brown?" DeRoche replied.

"Maybe," Michel replied. "McClelland never saw the kid. He was just speculating that he existed based on Marchand's previous history."

"And you think Speck may have seen this kid?" DeRoche asked.

"Not sure, but I think it's worth asking him," Michel replied. "I also think we should talk to Marchand's former house manager, Joseph."

"*Former* house manager?" DeRoche asked. "Any idea where he is now?"

"He's living in Marchand's townhouse on Royal," Michel replied.

"Okay, let's bring him in," DeRoche replied.

He stared down at his desk for a few moments, and his expression grew troubled.

"Are we sure that Joshua Clement is really dead?" he asked finally. "Michel is right. He would seem like the most likely suspect, and the fact that Speck had a connection to the first murder Drew Clement committed makes that even stronger. Everything seems to point to him."

"Everything except me," Lecher replied. "I worked the case, but my role was minimal. It doesn't explain why the picture of Joel was sent to me."

"That's true," DeRoche replied, "but so far, this all seems to be more targeted at Michel and Sassy."

"So far," Lecher repeated.

DeRoche looked at Ribodeau.

"Did you get a picture of Clement from either the Tucson or Louisville police?"

Ribodeau shook his head.

"Let's do that," DeRoche replied. "Have Joel and Chance take a look at it to make sure it was really him. And find Speck."

Chapter 23

After Jared had gone downstairs, Sassy had lain quietly for what felt like hours, listening to him moving around the house. Finally she heard what sounded like a distant door closing, then the house was silent. She waited a few more minutes, then slowly pushed herself up to a sitting position.

The only light in the room was coming through a narrow gap in the wall to her right, but it was enough that she was able to make out basic shapes. Other than the nightstand to her left, there didn't seem to be anything close by. She scooted to her right and swung her legs over the edge of the bed. As her feet came down, her right heel struck something, and there was a loud metallic clatter.

Sassy froze, and time seemed to stop as she listened for movement downstairs. Finally, after what felt like an hour, she let out a slow breath, and reached down with her left hand. Her fingers closed on the edge of something cool and curved. She tapped it lightly with a fingernail and heard a dull clink. She gripped the edge and slowly pulled it out from under the bed.

"Charming," she muttered to herself, looking down at an aluminum pail.

She ran her fingers around the top, and felt a chain on the right side, passing through a hole just below the rim. She pulled on the chain and felt it catch after a foot.

"So much for hitting him in the head," she said sitting up.

She looked down at her right hand and made a fist, then jerked her arm hard. It didn't give at all. She twisted her wrist and could make out a heavy padlock on the back of the cuff.

"Fucker," she muttered.

She was suddenly aware of a dull throbbing in her bladder, and looked back down at the bucket.

"Okay, how am I going to manage this?" she sighed with resignation.

She stood slowly and tested her legs. They felt surprisingly steady. She stepped closer to the bed post so the chain on her wrist was slack, then unbuttoned and unzipped her pants. She pushed them to her knees along with her panties, then shook her legs until they both dropped to her ankles.

"Dignity is so important," she thought, as she grabbed the bed post with her right hand and squatted down.

*****

"Speck's gone," Ribodeau said as he came back into DeRoche's office.

"What do you mean, 'gone'?" DeRoche asked.

"I mean we can't find him," Ribodeau replied. "He didn't punch out, but his locker's empty."

"Shit," DeRoche said. "Maybe he was feeding Marchand information after all."

"I don't think so," Michel said. "It sounded like he was telling Al the truth. My guess is he just got scared. Speck doesn't strike me as the type who deals well with pressure."

"I hope you're right," DeRoche replied, shaking his head. "You put out an APB on him?"

Ribodeau nodded.

"And we've got an unmarked parked down the block from his place."

"Okay," DeRoche replied. "What about Marchand's house manager? Any luck?"

"A neighbor was at the townhouse feeding his cat," Ribodeau replied. "She said he was in Sarasota visiting his sister.

162

He's supposed to be home tomorrow. I got a number for him, and left a message."

"Seems like we're hitting walls in every direction," DeRoche replied with a hint of annoyance.

"Not entirely," Ribodeau replied. "I heard back from Luke Marshall, the project manager at Big Awesome Web. He said Aaron definitely wasn't Jason Brown."

"That's a relief," Michel said. "Especially since he's setting up surveillance for us."

"And I got this," Ribodeau said, handing Michel a folder.

Michel opened it and saw a mug shot of a cute young blond. Even without a lopsided blond wig or murderous rage in his eyes, he looked eerily familiar.

"Joshua Clement," he said.

"Let's hope Joel and Chance agree," Ribodeau replied.

"What about your friend from University of Maryland?" DeRoche asked.

"Still nothing," Ribodeau replied.

"If you don't hear from him by morning, let's try to get a subpoena for the school's records," DeRoche replied.

Ribodeau nodded.

"So it looks like we're at a standstill for the moment," DeRoche said, turning to Michel. "You may as well head to the hotel and get some rest. I don't think there's anything more you can do here tonight."

Michel nodded reluctantly.

"I'll just wait for Stan."

"Where is he?" Ribodeau asked.

"Down in the lab making sure they don't fuck up the tests on the blood and Sassy's medication," Michel replied.

"I'm sure they're loving that," Ribodeau replied, smirking.

"Actually they seemed pretty excited to see him," Michel replied. "It was like he was a returning king."

"King of the socially retarded lab rats," Ribodeau muttered.

"I heard that," Lecher's voice said sharply behind him, causing Ribodeau to jump.

"Sorry," he said with a theatrically guilty look.

"That's okay," Lecher replied. "At least you said I was king."

"So?" Michel asked.

"The blood belonged to an African-American woman, and it matches Sassy's blood type," Lecher replied.

"And the drugs?" DeRoche asked.

"Zolpidem and Promethazine," Lecher replied.

"I take it those aren't usually prescribed for menopause?" Michel asked.

Lecher shook his head.

"Zolpidem is a sleeping pill. Promethazine is an antihistamine antiemetic, but it's also a strong sedative."

"So she's been doped up for days," Michel said.

"Yeah," Lecher relied. "We tested the blood and found significant concentrations of both in it."

"That would explain why there were no signs of a struggle," Ribodeau said. "She was probably so out of it she didn't even know what was happening."

"It also suggests that Brown or whoever is planning to keep her alive for a while," Michel added. "Otherwise why bother to sedate her, right? He must have wanted to take her someplace without a fight."

He looked at the others hopefully for agreement. After a moment, they all nodded.

"So now we just have to figure out who he is and where he took her," Ribodeau replied with a dark grimace.

Chapter 24

"You're sure it's him?" Michel asked.

"Definitely," Joel replied.

"No question," Chance added, looking up from the photo. Michel frowned.

"So we're still at square one, with no suspects," he said.

"There's got to be somebody else you guys pissed off when you were cops," Chance replied.

"I'm sure there are plenty," Michel replied, "but this is different. It's so...personal."

"Which is why I think it has to be somebody connected to all three of us," Lecher said. "I just can't believe I was sent Joel's photo on a whim."

"I know," Michel replied, sighing wearily, "but most of our cases together were pretty cut-and-dried. We did our work, you did your work. It's not like we all rushed in together at the end to make the arrests."

"Could it be someone who was wrongly convicted?" Joel offered.

Michel shrugged.

"Maybe, but innocent people have a tendency to keep appealing their conviction. So far as I know, that's never happened with one of our cases."

"We should probably check with the DA's office, just in case," Lecher said. "See if anyone managed to get a conviction overturned. It's an angle we haven't considered."

He gave Joel an appreciative smile.

"Good idea," Michel said. "I'll call Al and ask him to check into it. In the meantime, I'm starved. Room service?"

"Not like we have any other choices," Lecher replied.

"I'm going to wait to see if Aaron comes back," Chance said.

"Where is he?" Lecher asked.

"I don't know," Chance replied, shaking his head. "He finished setting up the cameras and said he was going to take a walk. He seemed kind of bummed out."

Lecher gave Michel a concerned look.

"He's pretty perceptive," he said. "I wonder if he realized he'd been put on the bench."

"What are you talking about?" Chance asked.

"Setting up surveillance was just a way to keep him busy while we checked him out," Michel replied without thinking.

For a moment, Chance didn't react. Then his cheeks flushed and his expression darkened. Michel wished he could go back five seconds as he braced himself for the coming storm.

"And why would you want to check him out?" Chance asked, his voice much sharper.

"Because I was worried he might be involved," Michel replied.

Chance shook his head slowly, then unleashed a harsh, scornful bark of laughter.

"And why the fuck would you think that?" he asked, his tone ripe with disdain. "Because he thinks you have a stick up your ass? Then I guess you'd better check out everyone who's ever met you."

Michel took a steadying breath.

"No. I wanted to check him out because he has the technological skills to pull off everything that's happened," he replied. "That's all. I just wanted to be sure."

"And are you *sure* now?" Chance asked in a mocking voice.

"Yes," Michel replied simply, refusing to be baited.

"Good," Chance replied dismissively. "I could have told you he was okay."

"Because your instincts are so flawless?" Joel cut in.

Chance blinked at him in disbelief for a moment, but Joel just stared him down.

"Fuck you," Chance said.

"Hey, I'm just saying," Joel replied. "Just because you're fucking someone, doesn't exactly mean they can be trusted. Why was it things didn't work out with Ray, again?"

Chance's pale blue eyes flashed both anger and hurt.

"Enough," Michel said emphatically. "We're all just tense because we're worried about Sassy. Let's not start ripping each other apart."

Chance glared at Joel for a few more seconds, then abruptly stood up.

"I'm going back to my room," he said.

Chapter 25

A sudden bright light startled Sassy awake, and she shielded her eyes with her left hand. She wondered how long she'd been asleep. She could hear soft footsteps on the stairs, and squinted at the doorway. Jared appeared, holding a tray. He was dressed in pale blue boxer shorts and a white ribbed tank top.

"Is that for me," Sassy asked, "or did you just want some company while you eat?"

"It's for you," Jared replied, without emotion.

As he came toward the bed, Sassy could smell coffee, chicory, and the unmistakable odor of something fried. She was suddenly ravenous.

She worked her way up to sitting, and Jared placed the tray on the bed beside her. Next to a cup of black coffee was a paper plate with three powdered beignets. Sassy knew immediately that they'd come from Café du Monde.

"What time is it?" she asked, trying to sound casual.

"Does it matter?" Jared replied.

His mood seemed darker than it had earlier, and Sassy wondered if something had happened to cause it.

"I suppose not," she said, then took a sip of coffee.

Jared stood next to the bed watching her for a moment, then suddenly turned toward the stairs.

"I'll be back," he said.

"I'll be here," Sassy replied.

She began devouring the first beignet before Jared had even reached the door. She thought she'd never tasted anything so delicious in her life, and savored each sweet, greasy bite before swallowing it.

"Well, at least the food's good," she thought, as she watched Jared disappear down the stairs.

*****

A few minutes later as she was wiping her mouth, she heard footsteps on the stairs again. She took a long sip of coffee and watched Jared over the rim of the cup as he came toward her. Though his body was taut, he wasn't very muscular, and Sassy guessed that he weighed no more than a hundred-and-sixty pounds. She couldn't imagine him being able to carry her all the way to the attic by himself.

"So did Severin help you get me up here?" she asked suddenly, hoping to take him off guard.

Jared didn't react. He just stared at her dully for a few seconds, then picked up the tray and moved it to the floor.

"What do you think?" he asked, as he sat in the green leather chair. "Does Severin seem like the manual labor type to you?"

"Not really," Sassy replied. "I think he'd be worried about breaking a nail."

The idea that Jared might be working with another unknown partner filled her with unease.

"So then how'd I get up here?" she asked.

"The dumbwaiter," Jared replied. "It runs from the kitchen to the third floor, so I only had to drag your fat ass up one flight of stairs."

Sassy chuckled.

"How's about you unlock my right hand and we see if my fat ass can whip your boney ass?" she replied.

Jared just stared at her humorlessly in reply.

"Are you always this grouchy in the morning?" Sassy asked.

"What makes you so sure it's morning?" Jared replied. "Café du Monde is open 24 hours a day."

Sassy smiled benignly, though she wished badly she could kick Jared in the head.

"So are you satisfied?" Jared asked.

"You mean with the accommodations or the service?" Sassy asked.

Jared nodded at her right wrist.

"I mean that you're not going anywhere."

"Yes," Sassy replied.

"I was a little surprised you didn't try dragging the bed anywhere," Jared said.

Sassy kept her eyes fixed on him, fighting the urge to look around for a camera.

"Well, I wouldn't want to do everything on the first day," she said. "Otherwise I might get bored later on."

For the first time, Jared showed a hint of a smile. He studied Sassy for a moment, then leaned forward, resting his elbows on his knees.

"So why did you become a cop?" he asked with what seemed to be genuine curiosity.

"Why did you become a hustler?" Sassy replied.

"When you're 16 and on the run for killing your parents, you don't have a lot of options," Jared replied matter-of-factly. "It's kind of hard to get a real job when you don't have any ID."

The response seemed sincere, and Sassy nodded. She took a sip of coffee, then set the cup in her lap.

"Because I wanted to help people," she said finally.

"But there are lots of jobs where you could have helped people," Jared replied. "You're smart. You could have been a doctor or a lawyer or a teacher or a shrink. Why a cop, and why a homicide cop?"

His use of the word "shrink" seemed intended both to make it clear that he knew about Sassy's background and to convey his contempt for the profession.

"In those jobs you don't get to shoot people," Sassy replied.

Jared sat back in his chair and gave her a hard look.

"Why would you even say that?" he asked. "Don't you think that's kind of stupid given the situation?"

"Whether you kill me today or tomorrow or the next day, I'm still going to end up dead in the end," Sassy replied.

"I already told you that I haven't made up my mind about killing you yet," Jared replied with a hint of frustration.

"And how are you going to make that decision?" Sassy asked.

Jared stared down at the floor for a moment.

"I need to know that it was...right," he replied finally, looking back up at Sassy.

"Me killing your brother?" Sassy replied, giving him a confused look.

Jared nodded slowly.

"I understand," he said. "In that situation, you didn't have any other choice. But why were you in that situation in the first place? That's what I need to understand."

"Why? What difference would it make?" Sassy asked. "If it hadn't been me, it would have been someone else eventually. Your brother was killing people. He was going to get caught, and chances are he was going to get killed."

"Maybe," Jared replied. "But the fact is *you're* the one who was there, and *you're* the one who killed him. I need to understand how you ended up there."

Sassy stared at him for a long moment.

"Jesus, Jared, that's a big question," she replied, sighing. "That's like asking someone to go back through his entire life to figure out how he ended up getting into a car accident in a specific place on a specific date."

"So you're saying that you being there was just an accident?" Jared replied.

Sassy considered it.

"In some ways, yes," she replied. "It was just chance that

171

Michel and I were assigned that case. It was just chance that Lady Chanel woke up when she did and told us it was your brother. That whole day could have played out a thousand different ways. The fact that it happened the way it did, yeah, you could say that was an accident."

Jared seemed to be gauging the sincerity of her response. Finally he nodded.

"But you being a cop wasn't an accident," he said.

"No, I suppose not," Sassy agreed. "Anymore than your brother being a killer was an accident."

"Don't call him that," Jared said.

"Why not?" Sassy replied. "That's what he was. He killed."

"So did you," Jared replied. "You've killed two people. Does that make you a killer, too?"

"I killed because I had no choice," Sassy replied. "It wasn't something I wanted to do."

"He had no choice either," Jared replied. "He killed people because they deserved it."

"Is that what you really think?" Sassy asked. "Did Lady Chanel deserve to die?"

Jared opened his mouth slightly, then closed it. He seemed to be struggling with how to respond.

"You can't understand," he said finally. "You weren't there."

"When Chanel was killed?" Sassy asked. "Or when your father was molesting you both?"

Jared didn't respond. He just stared at Sassy sullenly. She decided to keep pressing.

"Here's what I don't understand," she said. "Both of you were molested. How come only one of you became a killer?"

Jared flinched visibly, but again didn't reply.

"I think your brother was a sociopath," Sassy continued, "and that he would have ended up killing no matter what happened in his life. And I think the molestation was just a convenient excuse."

"I don't give a shit what you think," Jared replied angrily.

"Tell me something," Sassy said, ignoring him. "Did you have any pets when you were a kid?"

"What?" Jared replied, though Sassy could see a flicker of apprehensiveness in his eyes.

"Did you have any pets?" Sassy repeated.

Jared nodded slowly.

"And how many of them mysteriously disappeared?" Sassy asked.

"Shut the fuck up!" Jared hissed.

"You're the one who wanted to talk," Sassy replied defiantly.

Jared stood up quickly and started toward the door, then stopped. Sassy could see his shoulders heaving slightly. After nearly a minute, he turned back toward her and wiped tears from his eyes.

"You think that just because you have a degree in psychology, you understand everything," he said in a broken voice. "You don't. Reading about something is not the same as living it. You have no right to judge my brother."

He started to turn away again. Sassy knew that she'd gotten to him, and didn't want to lose the chance to forge a connection. She realized that her life might depend on it.

"I lived it," she said quietly.

Jared froze.

"You asked why I became a cop," Sassy said. "There were lots of reasons. That was one of them. A big one."

Jared slowly turned to face her. He studied her suspiciously.

"My mother's brother," Sassy replied to the unasked question. "Uncle Jimmy."

"When?" Jared asked.

"From the time I was seven until I was ten," Sassy replied.

"And then what happened?" Jared asked.

"I made it stop," Sassy replied.

Jared narrowed his eyes.

"How?"

"I realized it wasn't my fault," Sassy replied. "That gave me the power to say no."

"Just like that?" Jared asked with disbelief.

"Just like that," Sassy replied.

Jared walked toward her and sat on the end of the bed, just out of reach of her feet.

"Did he beat you?" he asked.

"No," Sassy replied. "I never had to worry about that."

"Were you afraid that you'd be abandoned if you told the truth?" Jared asked.

Sassy shook her head.

"Then it was different," Jared replied.

"Yes, my circumstances were different," Sassy replied, "but the shame and the powerlessness I felt weren't."

"Until you were ten," Jared said.

"The shame lasted a bit longer than that," Sassy replied with a rueful smile, "but yeah, the feeling of being powerless was gone then."

Jared looked down and picked some fuzz from the dirty pink blanket. He rolled it into a tiny ball between his thumb and index finger, then flicked it onto the floor.

"Do you think we were weak because we weren't able to stop our father?" he asked without looking up.

"Your brother did stop him," Sassy replied.

"I mean the way you did," Jared replied, looking up.

He suddenly looked much younger and more vulnerable.

"Like you said, I wasn't there," Sassy replied, trying to keep any judgment out of her voice, "but based on my experience, there are usually other ways out besides killing."

"We told Father Cleary," Jared offered without conviction.

"I know, and he didn't do what he should have to protect you," Sassy replied. "That was wrong, and he deserved to be punished. And your parents deserved to be punished, too."

"But not killed," Jared said.

Sassy shook her head.

"No."

They were both quiet for a few moments.

"Drew always thought it was his fault," Jared said finally, his voice distant. "That he should have been able to protect me."

"Your father molested him first?" Sassy asked.

"For almost a year before he started with me," Jared replied with a slow, dazed nod, as though he were reliving the memory.

"How old were you?" Sassy asked.

"Thirteen," Jared replied.

Sassy tried to mask her surprise. In all of the cases of sexual abuse within families that she'd seen over the years, the abuse had always started long before the victims reached puberty.

"Drew thought that if he'd been able to satisfy Daddy, he wouldn't have come for me," Jared continued.

Sassy felt a chill run down her spine and sat up straighter.

"Sexual abuse isn't about satisfaction," she said. "Your father was sick."

"When it first started, Drew and Daddy would lie together afterward and cuddle," Jared said, as though he hadn't heard her, "but then Daddy started coming over to me."

Sassy felt her stomach tense involuntarily.

"You and Drew shared a room?" she asked.

Jared nodded.

"We shared a bed. Always. Right up until you killed him."

He looked at Sassy and gave her a wistful smile.

"That night was the first night in my life I ever slept alone."

There was no recrimination in his tone, just sadness.

"I'm sorry," Sassy said. "I did what I had to do under the circumstances. It wasn't personal."

"I believe you," Jared replied in that same distant voice, then blinked a few times, as though he'd just woken up.

He stood up and looked around the room.

"Is there anything you need?" he asked, his voice focused once again.

"Some toilet paper would be nice," Sassy replied, looking at him curiously.

"I'm sorry. I meant to put some next to the bucket," Jared replied. "I'll bring it right up."

Sassy nodded.

"And I'll bring you some real food later on," he said. "Anything in particular you want?"

Sassy thought about it for a moment. The beignets had only whetted her appetite.

"Some Popeyes?" she replied.

"Three-piece spicy white meat and fries?" Jared replied.

"Wow, you really did do your homework," Sassy replied, trying to sound casual despite the knot she felt tightening in the pit of her stomach.

Jared just smiled enigmatically in response.

Chapter 26

Chance heard a light knock. He jumped from the bed and sprinted to the door. Through the peephole, he could see a uniformed officer who looked both tired and annoyed. Behind the man's right shoulder, Aaron swayed to the beat of unheard music. Chance quickly unlocked the door and pulled it open.

"Sorry to bother you," the officer said without any hint of remorse, "but he was pretty insistent on seeing you. I checked with HQ, and they said he's on the approved visitors' list."

"Yeah, it's fine," Chance replied.

The officer took a step to the side and Aaron breezed past him into the room.

"Thanks a lot," Chance said, offering a sympathetic smile.

"Not a problem," the officer replied. "You have yourself a good night."

Chance closed the door and turned around. Aaron was standing by the foot of the bed, facing the wall. He'd stopped swaying, but his head was still bobbing slightly from side to side. Suddenly he turned sideways and collapsed into a sitting position on the edge of the bed.

"Are you all right?" Chance asked. "You want some water?"

"I want another beer," Aaron replied in a thick voice.

"I don't have any," Chance lied. "Besides, I think you've probably had enough for tonight."

Aaron looked angry for a split second, then it faded and he nodded slowly.

"Yeah, you're probably right."

Chance walked over and sat next to him.

"So where'd you go?" he asked.

"The Bourbon Pub," Aaron replied. "And Oz."

Chance felt an unexpected stab of jealousy, and looked down at the carpet.

"Did you have fun?" he asked, though he wasn't sure he really wanted to know the answer.

"No," Aaron replied flatly.

Chance looked up and tried to hide the small smile of relief that flitted across his lips.

"Why not?" he asked.

"Because I was pissed off," Aaron replied sullenly.

"At me?" Chance asked.

Aaron looked at him curiously.

"Why would I be pissed at you?"

"I don't know," Chance replied. "I was just wondering, since you left here so quickly."

"No. I was pissed at *them*," Aaron replied, jerking his head toward the door.

Chance reflexively looked at it.

"Michel and Joel?" he asked, knowing their room was directly across the hall.

Aaron shook his head more forcefully than necessary.

"The cops," he said. "Those assholes don't think I know what I'm doing."

Chance thought about the earlier conversation with Michel and Lecher. He reached out and took Aaron's left hand.

"That's not what it was about," he said. "They just needed time to check you out."

Aaron blinked at him uncomprehendingly.

"What?"

Chance nodded in reply, and smiled gently. Aaron stared at him blankly for a long moment, then his eyes focused.

"Are you serious?" he asked.

Chance nodded again, and Aaron looked down at their intertwined hands.

"I thought they were trying to get rid of me because they thought I was incompetent," he said.

"Apparently Michel was worried you were too competent," Chance replied.

Aaron looked up at him and smiled.

"I guess I should be insulted," he said with a small laugh.

"Don't be," Chance replied. "He just needed to be sure."

"That's understandable, I guess," Aaron replied.

Then he looked back down at their hands and frowned.

"I think I'm going to go back home tomorrow," he said.

"What? Why?" Chance asked.

"Because I'm not really needed," Aaron replied. "I mean, I'm just a data analyst. Yeah, I can do some computer stuff and I know a little bit about surveillance, but it's not like they don't have anyone here who can do the same things now."

"But Lecher must have brought you in for a reason," Chance protested.

"Yeah, because it wasn't an official investigation yet," Aaron replied. "They couldn't use the police department's resources."

Chance studied him for a few seconds.

"You sound kind of bitter about that," he said finally.

Aaron looked at him with wounded eyes, and shrugged.

"I don't know," he said. "Maybe."

"Are you sure you don't want to leave just because your 'P' hurts?" Chance asked.

"My what?" Aaron asked.

"Your 'P,'" Chance repeated. "Your pussy."

Aaron stared at him uncertainly for a few seconds.

"Are you making fun of me?" he asked finally.

"Duh," Chance replied. "Just because not everyone's kissing your ass, you want to take your toys and go home. Sounds to me like your 'P' hurts."

"Fuck you," Aaron replied indignantly, pulling his hand away. "That's not what it's about."

Chance gave him a teasing smile.

"You're sure about that?" he asked.

Aaron stood and took a few steps toward the door, then turned back. He opened his mouth, but didn't say anything.

"I was in the office yesterday morning," Chance continued in an even tone. "I saw the way you were. You're used to being the center of attention."

"Why are you being mean to me?" Aaron asked, his voice breaking.

"I'm not being mean," Chance replied. "I'm just being honest. Think about it. You got all bummed out tonight because you thought you were being disrespected, and now you want to leave because you say you're not needed. Do you really think you're not needed, or is it just that you're not needed the way you want to be needed?"

Aaron looked down. His momentary anger seemed to have drained away, and he suddenly looked very tired.

"Come on and sit down," Chance said, patting the bed next to him.

Aaron hesitated for a moment, then slowly walked back and sat, though farther from Chance than before.

"Look," Chance said, "the fact is you're probably smarter than anyone on the police force. I think they need your help. But honestly, I don't give a shit if you have to sharpen pencils. If it's going to help find Sassy, I want you to do it."

He reached out and took Aaron's hand again.

"Please. For me."

Aaron looked into his eyes for a moment, then nodded.

"I'm sorry," he said contritely. "I didn't mean to be a dick."

"It's okay," Chance replied with a fast smile. "I can think of a way you can make it up to me."

*****

Joel rolled onto his side and reached for Michel. His hand touched the cool sheet, and he opened his eyes. He could see Michel's naked silhouette, framed in the window.

"Can't sleep?" he asked.

Michel turned to face him.

"I'm surprised you could with the circus going on across the hall. I swear I heard an elephant, two chimps, and a clown."

"I don't hear anything," Joel said, sitting up.

"It stopped about five minutes ago," Michel replied.

"Chance and Aaron?" Joel asked.

"Unless Chance ordered takeout," Michel replied.

Joel made a low murmur.

"Was that a note of disapproval?" Michel asked.

"I just think it's kind of soon," Joel replied. "And really inappropriate given the situation."

"The time-honored rebound fuck," Michel said.

"You're a classy man, Michel Doucette" Joel replied.

"That's why you love me," Michel replied.

He walked to the bed and sat on the edge.

"So are you sure that's all it is?" he asked.

"What do you mean?" Joel asked.

"I thought I sensed a little tension between you and Aaron at the station," Michel replied.

Joel stared at him without responding for a moment, then slid closer and settled back against the headboard.

"It's fine," he said, taking Michel's right hand. "He just said some stuff at the house that I didn't like."

"About me?" Michel asked.

Joel nodded.

"It was no big deal. I just don't be likin' no one talkin' shit about my man," he said, in an exaggerated trailer-park drawl.

Michel smiled appreciatively, and Joel smiled back for a moment. Then his expression turned serious.

"So was the circus the only reason you couldn't sleep?" he asked.

"No, I was already having trouble," Michel admitted, "but

that's what finally woke me up."

Joel squeezed his hand.

"Do you think Sassy's okay?" he asked.

Michel nodded.

"Are you just saying that for my sake, or do you really think so?" Joel asked.

"I really think so," Michel replied with conviction.

"How can you be so sure?" Joel asked.

Michel hesitated before answering.

"Because I think we'd have a body if she were already dead," he replied finally. "And because I don't think killing her is the goal. At least not the main goal."

Joel's eyes grew more anxious.

"So what is the main goal?" he asked.

"It's another game," Michel replied. "But he's upped the stakes. This time if we don't put the pieces together, Sassy's going to die."

He suddenly longed for a cigarette.

"You will," Joel replied.

"But maybe not in time," Michel replied.

He left unsaid his suspicion that the game might be rigged; that no matter when they found Sassy, it would be a few minutes too late.

Joel squeezed his hand again, but didn't say anything. Michel reached out with his left hand and caressed the side of Joel's face.

"I really do love you," he said.

Chapter 27

"You'll never guess who just showed up for work," Al Ribodeau said, walking into Captain DeRoche's office.

"Bouchard?" Michel replied.

"Okay, I guess you will," Ribodeau replied dryly.

"Did you talk to him?" DeRoche asked.

"No," Ribodeau replied. "As soon as his supervisor called, I asked him to escort Bouchard to interrogation."

"Good," DeRoche said.

"I know I have no right to ask this, but would it be all right if I talked with him?" Michel asked.

"Any particular reason?" DeRoche asked.

Michel gave an embarrassed shrug.

"Just a feeling?"

DeRoche studied him for a moment, then nodded.

"Okay, but remember, we'll be right in the next room."

*****

When Michel walked into the interrogation room, Speck's expression changed from worry to surprise, then to fear. He quickly looked at the mirror, as though hoping for a signal that someone else was there.

"You look like shit, Speck," Michel said, noting that Bouchard seemed to have aged five years overnight.

"I could say the same," Speck replied nervously.

Michel gave a small laugh.

"I had trouble sleeping," he replied. "What's your excuse?"

"A dark night of the soul," Speck replied, as much to himself as Michel.

"That's pretty poetic," Michel replied.

"I'm a junkie and a janitor," Speck replied. "That doesn't mean I'm a dumb ass."

"No, it doesn't," Michel agreed, studying Speck carefully.

Bouchard definitely seemed more jittery and unfocused than he had the day before.

"Did you score last night?" Michel asked.

Speck gave him a hard look, then nodded slowly.

"But I didn't use."

"Why not?" Michel asked.

"Like I told Detective Ribodeau yesterday," Speck replied. "I don't want to go back to the way things were. I called my sponsor, and he talked me through it."

"That's good," Michel replied sincerely. "One day at a time."

Speck looked at him with mild surprise.

"You in the program?"

"No, but sometimes I think I should be," Michel replied with a dry chuckle.

"Booze?" Speck asked.

Michel nodded.

"I'm not surprised," Speck replied. "From what I've seen, that seems to be pretty common around here."

Speck reached for his cigarettes, then stopped and gave Michel a questioning look. Michel nodded. Speck fumbled out a cigarette and lit it, then laid the pack and lighter on the table. Michel's eyes locked on them, and his pulse quickened. He could feel a light sweat on his forehead. He took a deep breath, trying to fight the craving, then his resolve crumbled.

"Mind if I bum one?" he asked, already ashamed. "I quit six months ago, but today is just one of those days. You know?"

Speck gave an uneasy smile.

"Help yourself," he said, sliding the pack and lighter across the table.

Michel took out a cigarette and clamped it between his lips, then picked up the lighter. He hesitated just long enough for one last half-hearted debate, then flicked the lighter and inhaled deeply. He held the smoke for a moment, feeling an immediate mild buzz spread through his brain, as his shoulders relaxed. Then he exhaled with a satisfied sigh.

"Thanks," he said, pushing the cigarettes and lighter back across the table.

"No problem," Speck replied.

"So why'd you take off yesterday?" Michel asked. "You were supposed to give a written statement."

Speck looked down at the table, and took another drag on his cigarette.

"I guess I was scared," he replied finally.

"Of what?" Michel asked. "You said you didn't do anything."

"I didn't," Speck replied quickly, looking back at Michel.

Michel turned the palms of his hands up and raised his eyebrows.

"I just...I don't know..." Speck said. "It just seems like no matter what I do, it always ends up the same."

Michel nodded thoughtfully.

"I get it," he said. "You're doing what you're supposed do, working hard, keeping your nose clean, working the program, and then suddenly it feels like you're back in the shit. It's like you can't escape."

Speck only frowned in response.

"Be patient," Michel said. "It'll happen. You're doing all the right things."

Speck laughed bitterly and shook his head.

"You sound just like my sponsor," he said.

Michel smiled and shrugged.

"I told you I should be in the program," he said.

Speck sat back in his chair and seemed to relax a little.

"So I don't suppose you just brought me in here for a pep talk?" he asked.

Michel shook his head.

"I'm afraid not," he said. "Severin Marchand was found dead yesterday."

Speck shot forward in his chair.

"I didn't have anything to do with it!" he exclaimed.

"We know that," Michel replied reassuringly.

Speck stared hard at him, as though trying to gauge whether he was being toyed with, then settled back in his chair again and took a slow drag on his cigarette.

"Who do you think did it?" he asked with awed curiosity.

"Did Marchand ever mention anything about a boy who was living with him?" Michel asked.

"You mean like a *boy* boy?" Speck asked skeptically, holding his left palm three feet above the ground.

"No. A twink," Michel clarified.

"Back when I was dealing to him, yeah, sometimes," Speck replied, "but not since I got out of prison. Why? You think some trick killed him?"

"I'm afraid it's more complicated than that," Michel replied. He studied Speck for a moment, then nodded to himself. "My partner, Miss Jones, is missing. We think she was taken by the same person who killed Marchand."

"Holy shit. I'm sorry," Speck replied with what seemed like genuine sympathy.

"Thanks," Michel replied.

"And you think the guy was living with Marchand?" Speck asked.

"Possibly, though I'm not sure if Marchand really knew what was going on, or if he was just being used," Michel replied. "Based on the fact that he's dead, I'm guessing the latter."

Speck's eyebrows knit together, and he took a long drag.

"So does this have something to do with Marchand wanting me to get your case files?" he asked finally.

"Yeah," Michel replied. "Whoever's behind this has been collecting information on us for at least a year."

"I swear I didn't give him anything," Speck said earnestly.

"I believe you," Michel replied. "But are you sure Marchand didn't mention anyone, or you didn't see anyone with him?"

Speck stared down at the table for a few moments, frowning in concentration. Then he shook his head.

"Not that I can remember," he said. "He definitely didn't mention anyone. I'm not sure if he was with anyone. No one I noticed, anyway."

Michel nodded and took another drag on his own cigarette. It wasn't as satisfying as he'd hoped, and he dropped it into the styrofoam cup of cold coffee on the table to his right.

"I need your help," he said.

For a moment Speck seemed confused, then his expression changed to guarded surprise.

"Okay," he ventured cautiously.

"When I saw Marchand last Saturday, he was clearly still using," Michel said. "Any idea who his connection might be?"

Speck suddenly looked down. From the slight shaking of his shoulders, Michel knew his legs were bouncing nervously under the table.

"Look, we're not going to arrest anyone," Michel said. "We just want to find out if anyone knows anything about the boy. Your name won't even be mentioned. I promise."

Speck still didn't respond.

"Please," Michel said.

Speck stared at the table for a moment longer, then looked up at Michel evenly.

"Can I ask you a question?" he said.

"Sure," Michel replied.

"Am I going to lose my job?"

Michel considered how to respond. He wished he could assure Speck, but knew it would be an empty assurance.

I hope not," he replied instead. "I think you deserve a second chance."

Speck nodded slowly in a way that suggested he appreciated Michel's honesty.

"I've got a couple of names you can try," he said.

*****

"You handled that nicely," DeRoche said, when Michel walked back into the observation room.

"Thanks," Michel replied.

"How was that smoke?" Ribodeau asked.

"Not so great," Michel replied with a wry smile. "So did I miss anything?"

"I heard from my buddy," Ribodeau replied. "He said there hasn't been a graduate from Maryland named Jason Brown over the last five years."

"I'm not surprised," Michel replied with a tired sigh. "One more lead down. What about Marchand's house manager?"

"He just called," Ribodeau replied. "I'm heading over now."

"Mind if I tag along?" Michel asked.

Ribodeau looked at DeRoche.

"Yeah, fine," DeRoche replied. "Just watch your backs. In the meantime, we'll try to track down the leads from Speck."

Ribodeau started to turn away but Michel hesitated.

"Something else?" DeRoche asked.

"What about Speck's job?" Michel asked.

DeRoche furrowed his brow for a moment, then nodded.

"I think I can work something out," he said.

"Good," Michel replied.

*****

Sassy woke up and looked to her right. The narrow crack of light in the wall had returned.

"Hello," she said. "Where'd you get off to? Go home to visit your family?"

She sat up and rolled her head from side to side to loosen up her neck, then took a sip of water. The sour smell of her own body odor wafted into her nostrils, and she made a face.

"I need a shower," she said, looking back at the light. "You think you could arrange that?"

She put the water back on the nightstand, then scooted to her right and stood up.

"This is getting old real fast," she said as she started to undo her pants.

Chapter 28

Ribodeau hit the button outside the gate. There was no response on the intercom, but a few moments later Joseph appeared at the end of the vaulted passageway leading to the townhouse's courtyard. He was dressed in tan linen slacks, a short-sleeved plum shirt, and brown sandals, yet he still conveyed the crispness that Michel remembered from their one meeting at Marchand House.

"Detective Ribodeau?" Joseph asked in a lilting rasp.

"Yes, sir," Ribodeau replied, holding up his badge.

Joseph walked slowly toward them, his footsteps echoing softly off the stone floor and brick walls. He unlocked the gate and stepped to the side. Ribodeau entered first.

"Thank you for agreeing to see us," he said, as he shook the older man's hand. "I know this is a difficult time for you."

"Of course," Joseph said. "Anything I can do to help with your investigation."

Michel stepped into the cool, dark corridor.

"I'm very sorry, Joseph," he said.

"Thank you," Joseph replied, then cocked his head and squinted as he studied Michel's face.

"Mr. Doucette, isn't it?" he asked.

"That's right," Michel replied.

"So you're working with the police now?" Joseph asked.

"Just temporarily," Michel replied.

"Well, I appreciate you trying to help find out who killed Mr. Marchand," Joseph replied sincerely.

Michel tried to hide his surprise. He realized that he'd been so focused on finding Sassy that he'd forgotten they were also searching for Marchand's killer.

Joseph turned and led them to the courtyard. Michel noticed that it was much better tended now than the last time he'd been there. The planters around the edges were all filled with blooming shrubs and flowers, and the stucco walls looked freshly washed.

"Please," Joseph said, gesturing toward a table in the shade to their right. "Can I get you some coffee or iced tea?"

"No, thank you," Ribodeau replied.

"So how can I help?" Joseph asked, as soon as they'd settled in their chairs.

Although the question could have been perfunctory, his tone made it clear it was more than that.

"We're hoping you can give us information about a young man who was living with Mr. Marchand," Ribodeau replied.

"A young man?" Joseph replied.

Ribodeau nodded. "We think he may have been involved in Mr. Marchand's murder, as well as the kidnapping of Mr. Doucette's partner, Miss Jones."

Joseph frowned hard.

"I wasn't aware that Mr. Marchand was living with anyone," he replied, looking down at his glass.

"You weren't?" Ribodeau asked.

"I'm afraid not," Joseph replied, offering an obviously wounded smile.

"What about the rest of the staff?" Michel asked. "Do you think any of them might know something?"

"No," Joseph replied with certainty. "I was the last one to leave the house, and Mr. Marchand was always very discreet about his....friends."

Michel remembered what Scotty McClelland had said about Marchand keeping his sexuality a secret from the staff.

"Didn't you think that was kind of odd?" he asked.

"Mr. Marchand took his responsibility to us very seriously," Joseph replied with a hint of defensiveness.

"Meaning?" Michel asked.

Joseph studied Michel appraisingly for a few seconds.

"This may be hard for you to understand," he said, "but those of us who worked for the Marchands were very proud of it. Mr. Marchand understood that, and wouldn't have done anything to make the situation...uncomfortable... for anyone."

"So the staff really didn't know he was gay?" Michel asked.

A flicker of distaste crossed Joseph's face, and Michel was struck by how much it reminded him of Marchand.

"I'm sure that some of the staff may have had ideas about Mr. Marchand's private life," Joseph said, "but it was certainly not something that was ever discussed, nor something that he ever brought to anyone's attention."

"But you knew," Michel replied.

"I was aware," Joseph replied with a slow nod.

"But you didn't meet any of the men he dated?" Ribodeau asked.

"Mr. Marchand wasn't in the habit of bringing new people by the house," Joseph replied. "I imagine he did most of his entertaining here."

Michel looked around.

"So essentially he lived here to protect the staff?" he asked.

"I suppose you could look at it that way," Joseph replied.

"That's kind of sad," Michel said.

Joseph's posture stiffened and he gave Michel a cold look. Again Michel was reminded of Marchand.

"I don't believe that Mr. Marchand needed anyone's pity," Joseph said.

"I think that's debatable," Michel replied without thinking, then immediately regretted it.

Joseph sat back and folded his arms across his chest.

"I take it you didn't approve of Mr. Marchand?" he asked.

"It's not a question of approval or disapproval," Michel replied quickly, hoping to diffuse the tension. "I just had issues with the way he treated some people. Apparently he was quite different with the staff."

"Apparently," Joseph replied. "The Marchands treated us very well. They were loyal to us, and we reciprocated that loyalty. That didn't stop with Mr. Marchand."

Michel realized that the final statement could be interpreted two ways. He decided that Joseph had intended them both. He wondered how Joseph would feel if he knew that Marchand had actually been a racist.

"Perhaps some of Mr. Marchand's friends might be able to help you," Joseph said abruptly, turning to Ribodeau.

"Perhaps," Ribodeau replied without much conviction. "Mr. Doucette already spoke with Scotty McClelland a few days ago."

"Well, if anyone would know anything, it would be Mr. McClelland," Joseph replied.

There was a finality to his tone that indicated the interview was over. Ribodeau pushed his chair back and stood up.

"Well, we won't take up any more of your time," he said, "but you'll be around in case we have any more questions?"

"Of course," Joseph replied.

"Just one more thing," Ribodeau said. "Did Mr. Marchand have any other properties in the city?"

"Not that I'm aware," Joseph replied. "Just Marchand House, here, and his studio."

"Would it be all right with you if we took a look around the studio?" Ribodeau asked.

Joseph reached into the left pocket of his pants, and took out a large key ring. He quickly located and removed two keys.

"The brass one is for the door, the silver's for the alarm," he said, as he handed them to Ribodeau.

"Thank you," Ribodeau replied. "I'll get these back to you as soon as possible."

"No hurry," Joseph replied.

They walked back to the gate and Joseph unlocked it. Ribodeau shook Joseph's hand and stepped out onto the sidewalk. Michel hesitated for a moment, not wanting to leave things on a sour note.

"I really am sorry about Severin," he said.

Joseph nodded, but didn't extend his hand.

"You should know he told me he considered you family," Michel said.

Joseph stared at Michel for a moment, then nodded again.

"Well, thank you for that," he said stiffly.

*****

"Wow, that charm school really paid off," Ribodeau said as they walked back to the car.

"Sorry about that," Michel replied. "He reminded me too much of Marchand and it just triggered something."

"You think they're related?" Ribodeau asked with surprise.

"I don't know," Michel replied. "I hadn't even thought about that possibility. I just figured Marchand had rubbed off on him over time, the way married couples start to act and look alike after a while."

Ribodeau chuckled.

"My ex and I never made it that long. Probably a good thing. I don't think I would have wanted to be married to balding woman with a pot belly and a hairy back."

Michel laughed. "So where to? The studio?"

"Unless you have another idea," Ribodeau replied.

"May as well start there," Michel replied, "though I was thinking about going to the nursing home again and giving Zelda another shot. Chance said she has good days and bad days. Maybe today will be a good day."

Ribodeau nodded.
"Couldn't hurt to try."

Chapter 29

"Hey," Chance said when Joel opened the door.

"Hey," Joel replied.

"What are you doing?"

"Just watching TV. What about you?"

"Same," Chance replied.

"You want to watch together?" Joel asked.

"Sure," Chance replied.

He walked to the bed and dropped down onto the end.

"This bites," he said. "How come we're the only ones who get stuck here all day?"

"Where's Aaron?" Joel asked as he sat to Chance's left.

Chance shrugged disinterestedly.

"I tuned out as soon as he said the word 'database'."

"Bored already?" Joel asked.

Chance gave him a hard look, then shook his head and smiled tiredly.

"Let's not start again, okay?" he said.

"I'm sorry," Joel replied. "That was a cheap shot. And I'm sorry about last night, too."

"Me, too," Chance replied. "I was just in a pissy mood because of Sassy, and because I didn't know where Aaron was."

"I know," Joel replied.

"Do you think she's okay?" Chance asked.

"Michel thinks so," Joel replied, though his tone suggested he wasn't convinced. "He thinks that if she were dead, we'd know by now."

Chance nodded thoughtfully.

"This is pretty fucked up," he said. "I mean, I'm a vindictive bitch, but I'd never do anything like this."

"Me neither," Joel replied.

He reached over and took Chance's hand. Neither of them spoke for a moment.

"I love you," Chance said finally.

"I love you, too," Joel replied.

*****

"Everything's gone," Michel said, staring at the rows of empty shelves in the back of Severin Marchand's studio.

"What was here?" Ribodeau asked.

"Furniture, art, antiques. Marchand had so much stuff that he'd rotate it in and out of his house."

"Must be nice," Ribodeau replied. "I've been putting off getting a new La-Z-Boy for a year and a half, even though the old one won't recline anymore."

"Splurge, Al," Michel replied sarcastically. "You deserve it."

He looked around the room and frowned.

"So the question is whether Marchand got rid of it himself, or if it was sold without him knowing."

"By Jason Brown?" Ribodeau replied.

Michel nodded.

"I'm really getting the feeling that Marchand was just a pawn in all this," he said.

"And a victim," Ribodeau added.

"Yeah, I keep forgetting that part," Michel replied.

Chapter 30

"Here you go," Jared said, placing the plate on the side table.

Sassy's mouth had begun watering as soon as she smelled the fried chicken. She swallowed again and eagerly sat up.

"I'm going to unlock you," Jared said casually, "but if you try to spork me, I'm going to be really pissed."

Sassy looked at the white plastic spoon-hybrid with its four dwarf tines on the edge of the plate.

"I don't think that'll be a problem," she replied.

Jared moved behind the headboard and knelt down. A few seconds later, Sassy's wrist was free. She looked down at it and rotated her hand in a clockwise circle. It was stiff, but otherwise felt fine.

"Thank you," she said.

Jared came back around to the side of the bed, and sat in the battered green leather chair. Sassy hesitated for a moment before picking up the plate.

"What's the matter?" Jared asked.

Sassy gave an embarrassed half-smile.

"It's just that you may want to move back a little," she said. "I have a feeling this is going to get messy."

*****

"So who started calling you Sassy?" Jared asked, as Sassy finished sucking the grease and butter from her fingers.

"My mother's mother."

198

"Why?"

"Because I was anything but," Sassy replied. "She figured if she started calling me that, maybe eventually I'd grow into it."

"Seems to me it worked," Jared replied.

Sassy momentarily flirted with asking whether Drew Clement had been nicknamed "Psycho."

"So how'd you decide on Jared?" she asked instead.

"I like to stick with J names," Jared replied. "It makes them easier to remember."

"How many names have you had?" Sassy asked.

"A few," Jared replied.

Sassy nodded, knowing that was all she was going to get. She decided to keep pushing for information anyway.

"So, whose body was that in the motel in Tucson?"

"An acquaintance," Jared replied, then frowned slightly.

"An acquaintance?" Sassy repeated.

"A street hustler who happened to look a lot like me."

"And who happened to say he *was* you when he was arrested, then happened to wind up dead, so we just happened to think *you* were dead," Sassy added.

"I already told you I didn't kill anyone," Jared replied.

"So him getting killed was just a happy coincidence?" Sassy replied skeptically.

Jared nodded.

"Do I really look that stupid to you?" Sassy replied.

Jared gave a noncommittal shrug, and Sassy let out a frustrated sigh.

"Why did he say he was you?" she asked.

Jared held up his right hand and rubbed his index and middle fingers against his thumb.

"Thanks, I already figured that part out," Sassy replied dryly, "but *why* did you pay him to do it? What was the point?"

"Because I knew I'd be a suspect, and when you looked for me, I wanted you to think I was a nice safe distance away in

Tucson," Jared replied. "Plus I thought it might be useful to have the wrong face and fingerprints in the police database."

Although there was some logic to it, Sassy felt certain it was a lie. Given how carefully Jared had planned everything else, it seemed unlikely he'd trust such a key element to a casual acquaintance who earned a living hustling on the streets.

"What if they'd decided to try him for killing your parents and the priest?" she asked. "You don't think he would have told the truth then?"

"I knew he wouldn't be tried," Jared replied confidently.

"How?"

"Because I didn't do it. I knew there couldn't be any evidence to charge him."

"Gee, that's putting an awful lot of trust in the legal system," Sassy replied. "Kind of surprising given your history."

"The legal system never fucked me over," Jared replied.

"No, but somehow you've managed to stay a few steps ahead of the cops for seven years," Sassy replied. "I wouldn't think that would inspire a lot of confidence."

"I didn't say I have any confidence in the police," Jared replied pointedly.

Sassy gave him a grudging smile.

"No, I guess you didn't," she replied.

Jared looked at the pile of bones on the plate in her lap.

"Are you done, or did you want to suck the marrow out of those?" he asked.

"I guess I'm done," Sassy replied, though she wasn't ready for the conversation to end yet.

As Jared started to stand, she put the plate on the nightstand and turned to face him.

"So besides Severin, who are you working with?" she asked.

Jared settled back into the chair and smiled playfully.

"What makes you think I'm working with someone else?" he asked.

"You expect me to believe you set up a fake conference website, bugged our computers, drugged me, and got me here all by yourself?" Sassy replied. "And frankly, Severin doesn't strike me as the body-lugging *or* the technology type."

"I already told that I brought you up here in the dumbwaiter," Jared replied.

"But how'd you get me out of my house?" Sassy asked.

"I managed," Jared replied. "You're not *that* fat."

"I'm not fat," Sassy replied with a sour smile. "I'm just big-boned. And the technology part?"

"It's amazing the stuff you can learn how to do on the internet," Jared replied. "And there are all sorts of conspiracy nut jobs out there willing to help out. All I needed was the money for the equipment."

"Which you got from Severin?" Sassy replied.

Jared shrugged coyly in response.

"Using his email was kind of sloppy, don't you think?" Sassy asked. "Unless you were planning to pin it all on him."

"I didn't anticipate Cousin Verle getting accused of murder or dying," Jared replied. "I didn't think anyone would find out about the emails until it was all over."

Sassy nodded.

"So who've *you* been working with?" Jared asked.

"What makes you think I'm working with someone else?" Sassy replied with a mocking smile.

Jared laughed.

"Someone killed my access to Chance's computer," he replied, then smiled teasingly. "And frankly, you and your partner don't strike me as the technology types."

"I guess you're just going to have to figure that one out on your own," Sassy replied.

"It doesn't really matter," Jared replied casually. "I already have everything I need."

Sassy felt a wave of unease, but kept her expression neutral.

"So where's Severin now?" she asked.

"Probably at home curled up in a fetal ball," Jared replied. "He gets that way when I leave him alone for too long. He's really kind of a mess."

"I've noticed," Sassy replied. "So how did you two meet?"

"He was a client when we were living at Zelda's," Jared replied. "He always had a thing for me. Wanted me to be his boyfriend."

"Looks like he finally got his wish," Sassy replied, "though I'm guessing not for much longer."

"He needs to go into rehab and get his shit together," Jared replied with surprising compassion. "I just don't get how someone can be given so much and end up so empty."

"Money doesn't always translate to happiness," Sassy replied. "In fact, it usually seems to go the other way."

"I don't mean money," Jared replied. "I mean his family."

Sassy looked at him questioningly.

"When he's fucked up, he tells me about them," Jared continued. "It sounds like he had an ideal life."

"How would you define ideal?" Sassy asked.

"Parents who love you and protect you," Jared replied. "People who take care of you and support you. Feeling wanted."

Sassy felt a sudden pang of sympathy, but pushed it away. She suspected Jared was trying to manipulate her emotions.

"Well, I wouldn't believe everything I hear, if I were you" she replied dismissively. "He was probably just romanticizing his childhood. People have a tendency to do that. Especially when they have poor mechanisms for coping with reality."

"Do you do that?" Jared asked.

"My mechanisms are just fine, thank you," Sassy replied.

"What about when you lost your baby?" Jared asked. "Were they fine then?"

Sassy felt a surge of anger and looked down at the floor.

"You really did do your homework," she said quietly.

"Do you think your baby would have been a boy or a girl?" Jared asked with obviously feigned innocence.

Sassy felt the blood pumping in her temples.

"I don't think about it," she lied. "That's part of the coping."

"So should I just not think about my dead brother?" Jared asked, leaning forward and watching her intently.

Sassy looked up and locked eyes with him.

"Oh no," she replied slowly and deliberately. "You should think about him every moment of every day. And you should try to imagine what it looked like when that bullet went through the back of his skull and his brains splattered all over the room."

She saw Jared's head jerk involuntarily, but his expression remained calm.

"That wasn't a very nice thing to say," he said.

"And asking me about my baby was?" Sassy replied.

"No," Jared admitted, "but *you're* not the one deciding whether to let *me* live."

"I wouldn't be too sure of that," Sassy replied in a low, threatening voice. "I've never gotten to kill twins before."

Jared was on his feet and moving toward her before she could react. He pulled a pistol from behind his back and pressed it against her forehead.

"I was going to let you use the toilet and take a shower," he said, "but now you can just lie here in your own stink."

Chapter 31

"I wouldn't mind ending up in a place like this," Ribodeau said as they walked toward Zelda's room. "This is pretty nice."

"And I hear the tapioca pudding is great," Michel replied with a smirk.

"I like tapioca," Ribodeau replied.

They stopped outside a partially open door. Through the crack, Michel could see slippered feet on the end of the divan. He knocked on the doorframe.

"Come in," Zelda replied.

Michel pushed the door open. Zelda was reclining by the window, wearing the same housedress she'd been wearing the last time he'd seen her.

"Detective Doucette," she said with a warm smile, her eyes lighting up. "What a pleasant surprise."

"Hi Miss Zelda," Michel replied. "How are you?"

"Very well, thank you," Zelda replied. "And you?"

"Fine, thanks," Michel replied. "This is my friend, Detective Ribodeau."

"Detective," Zelda said with a nod.

"A pleasure," Ribodeau replied.

"Please, sit down," Zelda said, gesturing to two utilitarian wood-framed chairs along the wall to the left of the door.

Michel noticed that they were out of place with the rest of the decor, and guessed they were part of the room's original furnishings. He grabbed a chair and moved it closer to Zelda. Ribodeau did the same.

"So what brings you to my summer cottage?" Zelda asked.

Michel tried to gauge whether it was meant as a joke or if she was simply delusional.

"Well, we wanted to ask you a few questions," he replied.

The smile was gone from Zelda's face in an instant, and Michel saw a flash of the grim, angry creature who'd haunted the bars at Lady Chanel's side for so many years.

"About?" Zelda asked suspiciously.

"Mr. Smith," Michel replied.

Zelda's eyes narrowed.

"Do you remember him?" Michel asked.

"Of course," Zelda replied. "Why?"

"Who was he?" Michel asked.

Zelda blinked at him, then looked down at her housedress and adjusted the hem so that it covered her knees.

"That's a secret," she said in a theatrically hushed voice.

Michel leaned forward and rested his elbows on his knees.

"Zelda, I need your help," he said slowly. "My partner, Miss Jones, is missing. We think Mr. Smith might have something to do with it."

Zelda looked up at him, but her eyes were suddenly distant.

"That's not possible," she said quietly but firmly.

"Why not?" Michel asked.

"Because Mr. Smith is dead," Zelda replied.

Michel exchanged questioning looks with Ribodeau, then looked back at Zelda.

"Was Mr. Smith Severin Marchand?" he asked, wondering how Zelda could already know that Marchand was dead.

Zelda blinked again, and her gaze cleared slightly.

"Is Mr. Marchand dead?" she asked.

"Yes, he is," Michel replied. "He was murdered yesterday."

Zelda shook her head sadly.

"He was such a nice man," she said in an almost girlish voice, then looked out the window and began to quietly hum.

"Zelda," Michel said sharply, but she didn't respond.

Michel looked at Ribodeau and shook his head.

"Fuck," he said. "We were so close."

"Maybe," Ribodeau replied. "My aunt had Alzheimers for ten years. Sometimes you'd be having what seemed like a totally lucid conversation with her, and then suddenly realize she wasn't even talking to you. She'd be reliving a conversation from years earlier. Zelda may have no idea who Smith really is."

"Hunter," Zelda said suddenly.

Michel and Ribodeau both looked at her. She was still staring vacantly out the window.

"What?" Michel asked.

"Hunter," Zelda repeated. "Mr. Smith was Hunter. He told me he'd kill me if I ever told anyone."

Then she turned to Michel and her expression was hard and cold.

"But he's dead now," she said.

Chapter 32

Sassy was just beginning to doze when she heard the door at the bottom of the stairs open, and the light came on. She pushed herself into a sitting position and anxiously watched the doorway. After their last conversation, she half-expected Jared to be carrying his pistol.

After what seemed like minutes, he finally appeared. He was barefoot, dressed in tan cargo shorts and a tight black t-shirt. To Sassy's relief, his hands were empty.

"It's time for you to go," he said flatly.

Sassy noticed he had the same listless expression he'd had when he brought her the beignets, and wondered whether he was bipolar.

"'Go' as in you're going to kill me, or 'go' as in leave?" she asked cautiously.

"Leave," Jared replied.

He walked to the left side of the bed and knelt by the headboard.

"So you've decided not to kill me?" Sassy asked.

Jared didn't respond, but Sassy's wrist was suddenly free. Jared stood up and nodded toward the doorway. Sassy looked at him warily for a moment, then slid to the other side of the bed and stood up. Her heart was beating hard, and her breathing echoed loudly in her ears.

"Go," Jared said without emotion.

Sassy turned toward the door and took a tentative step, then froze as she heard a pistol being racked.

"Just one more thing," Jared said.

Sassy slowly turned to face him.

"You'll have to make it out before you bleed to death or burn," Jared said.

A deafening report filled the room and Sassy collapsed as the bullet shattered the femur of her left leg, just above the kneecap. She screamed and began writhing on the floor as the searing pain shot up her leg and seemed to fill her whole body.

Jared walked slowly around the bed and stood over her.

"I couldn't decide whether you should die or not," he said, "so I'm leaving that up to you. I'm going to give you the chance you didn't give my brother."

He turned and walked to the doorway, then looked back over his right shoulder.

"Personally, I kind of hope you make it," he said, then was gone.

Sassy rolled onto her right side with a loud gasp, and grabbed the side rail of the bed with both hands. Each beat of her racing heart sent a fresh pulse of pain up her thigh and she braced herself, knowing what was about to come. She took a deep breath and held it for three seconds, then jerked herself closer to the bed.

"Fuck!" she screamed through clenched teeth.

She lay still for a moment, breathing hard as she waited for the pain to subside a little. She could feel sweat running down her face, mixing with her tears. Then she rolled onto her back.

She reached up for the sheet and blanket, and began pulling them off the bed. Finally the corner of the pillow appeared. She gave one last tug and it dropped onto the floor beside her.

*****

Sassy pulled the knot tight and sat back against the side of the bed. She let out a loud sigh as she looked down at the makeshift splint she'd made from the sheet and two legs of the nightstand. The pillowcase underneath seemed to have stemmed the bleeding. Only a small circle of red had seeped through the top.

"Now if I can just get up," she said.

She braced her hands on the top of the bed rail and pulled her right leg in, positioning her foot just inside her left thigh, then pushed upward with a loud groan. As her hips cleared the edge of the bed, she fell backwards onto the mattress, sighing with relief.

"Step one," she said with a satisfied smile.

Then a wave of nausea washed over her. She closed her eyes and swallowed hard, trying to will it away. Her thoughts began to drift.

Chapter 33

"Things keep leading back to Joshua Clement," Michel said, as Ribodeau guided the car down the exit ramp.

"I know," Ribodeau replied, "but we know he's dead."

"There's got to be a connection, though," Michel replied.

"Do you suppose whoever's doing this also killed him?" Ribodeau asked.

"Maybe," Michel replied. "He and Marchand were both beaten to death."

"There were other boys living in Zelda's house, weren't there?" Ribodeau asked.

"Yeah, two of them," Michel replied, "but Sassy and I never had any contact with them."

"Still, it may be worth checking out," Ribodeau replied. "Do you know their names?"

Michel shook his head.

"As I recall, all we had were first names, but Chance may know. He lived there with them for a while."

He pulled out his cell phone and flipped it open just as it began to ring. He looked at the display and saw an unfamiliar number. A sudden sense of foreboding washed over him.

"Hello?" he answered anxiously.

"Michel?" a familiar voice replied. "It's Aaron."

Michel exhaled and smiled to himself.

"Oh, hey," he replied. "What's up, Aaron?"

"Well, I know I shouldn't have done this," Aaron replied, "but I've been doing some checking into Jason Brown."

"Oh," Michel replied, not sure how else to respond.

"It's probably nothing," Aaron continued, "and I'm sure the police have already checked it out, but I was looking at property records and found that a Jason Brown bought a place on Fullerton Street in the Marigny district about two years ago."

Michel felt the hairs on the back of his neck prick up and his heart began to race.

"What number Fullerton?" he asked, though he was sure he already knew the answer.

"310," Aaron replied.

"Thanks, Aaron," Michel replied quickly, then hung up.

"What?" Ribodeau asked, staring at Michel curiously.

"Sassy's at Zelda's house," Michel replied.

*****

A sound somewhere in the house broke through the fog, and Sassy opened her eyes. She wondered how long she'd been lying there. The pain in her leg was just a dull throb now, and she realized that shock was overtaking her body.

She lifted her left hand. It seemed impossibly far away, and her skin seemed to shimmer in the light. She drew it back a few inches, then slapped it hard into the headboard. As the tip of her bandaged middle finger struck the wood, she felt a burst of intense pain and her mind suddenly cleared.

She pushed herself up and looked at the door.

"Get moving," she said in a steely voice.

*****

She fell back against the wall of the second-floor landing. It had taken almost five minutes to get that far. Her breathing was ragged and her clothes were soaked through with sweat.

From below she heard a sound like an empty metal barrel being hit with a stick. She pushed herself off the wall and

211

cautiously peered over the railing into the front hallway. She didn't see anything unusual, but the inside of her nostrils began to tingle. She took a deep breath through her nose. The air was rich with the pungent fragrance of gasoline.

With a jolt of adrenaline, she flashed back on what Jared had said just before he shot her: "before you bleed to death or burn."

*****

"Shit," Michel said as he saw the detour sign ahead.

"Don't worry, it's only for a few blocks," Ribodeau said, "and the black and whites are probably already there."

"I hope so," Michel replied.

*****

Sassy reached the newel post at the top of the last flight of stairs and stopped. She could hear sirens in the distance.

"Maybe I can just wait here for them," she thought.

She closed her eyes and listened, trying to determine if they were getting closer. Then she heard movement below. She leaned forward, holding tightly to the post with her left hand. The sound seemed to be coming from the living room, to the left of the stairs. A bare foot appeared just inside the doorway and she quickly pulled her head back.

She wondered if Jared had intended to kill her all along—if letting her go had just been part of a game to give her false hope before he ripped it away.

She looked over her shoulder into the room directly behind her. Both windows were boarded shut.

"Fuck," she whispered.

She leaned forward again. The foot was gone, but she could still hear movement in the living room. She silently stepped onto the top stair, then froze as she heard the unmistakable sound of a match being lit. With a loud whoosh, the entrance to the living room was immediately engulfed in flames.

Sassy fell back against the stairs with a cry of both surprise and pain. Even from a distance, she could already feel the intensity of the heat and knew she didn't have long before the fire spread. She grabbed the railing and pulled herself up.

She braced both forearms on the railing and began a lumbering sideways descent. She could see wallpaper lifting and curling as the flames climbed the wall to the left of the living room, while thick black smoke spread across the ceiling. She winced and lowered her head against the heat. The sweat on her skin seemed to be evaporating as quickly as it poured out of her, and her lungs began to burn with each breath.

Suddenly a shot rang out over the roar of the fire. Sassy dropped down reflexively, slamming her wounded leg into the stairs and cracking the outside brace. She screamed, then gritted her teeth and took several quick sharp breaths. Over the top of the flames she could see Jared on the couch. His head was thrown back and the pistol rested loosely in his right hand by his side. Sassy could see blood running down his neck.

She felt relief but also pity, and quickly crossed herself. Then she pulled herself up and began descending again.

As she reached the bottom stair, she heard an explosion behind her. A blast of scalding air hit her, almost knocking her down. She turned and saw flames erupting out of the kitchen at the far end of the hall.

She stepped down and staggered to the front door, squinting against the smoke. She grabbed the door knob and pulled hard. The door didn't move. She twisted the knob the other way and yanked again. Again, nothing.

Rising panic threatened to overcome her and she closed her eyes for a few seconds, trying to hold it back. When she opened them, the smoke seemed to have thickened impossibly. It stung her eyes, and tears began to well up and run down her cheeks.

She reached up and ran her left hand along the edge of the door and the frame. Two feet above the knob, she felt the angled head of a nail protruding from the frame. A foot below that, she found another protruding from the door.

"You motherfucker!" she screamed in anger and frustration. "You lying motherfucker!"

She turned and looked back down the hall. The flames from the kitchen and living room had merged, and now a thin vein began to creep across the floor toward the side wall of the stairs.

She pulled the collar of her shirt up over her nose and mouth, and started toward the stairs.

*****

Ribodeau brought the car to an abrupt stop.

"We've got a code three at 310 Fullerton Street," he barked into the microphone. "Requesting fire and ambulance."

Michel was already out of the car, sprinting toward the front door. Ribodeau jumped out and followed.

*****

The acrid smoke pressed down on Sassy, choking her, as embers fell all around her. She braced her right leg and grabbed another baluster. The skin on the back of her hand immediately began to blister and she jerked it back with a cry.

She lifted her head. She couldn't tell how far she'd climbed. The top of the stairs was no longer visible. She stared into the swirling darkness for another moment, then lowered her head and closed her eyes. As her body slid down, she was only dimly aware of the door breaking in below her.

Chapter 34

Sassy opened her eyes. She was enveloped in a cocoon of gauzy white. She felt relaxed, peaceful.

"I guess there really is a heaven," she whispered.

She smiled and lifted her right hand, wanting to touch the clouds. The sheet covering her head slipped down, and she could see Michel standing beside the bed, smirking at her.

"Oh, that's funny," she rasped.

"I could tell you were coming around," Michel replied impishly. "And you couldn't possibly believe you'd really end up in heaven, could you?"

Sassy gave him a sour look.

"Well, I'm certainly not worried about running into you there," she replied, then coughed hard.

Her lungs felt as though they'd been spackled with soot. Michel handed her a plastic cup of water and she took a few small sips.

"How do you feel?" Michel asked.

"Crispy," Sassy replied, "and drugged, but otherwise okay."

"They've got you pretty doped up," Michel replied.

Sassy nodded dully and looked around the room. There were three vases of flowers along the window ledge.

"How did I get out of there?" she asked, looking back.

"Al and I pulled you out," Michel replied.

"Thank you," Sassy replied with a grateful smile.

"You have Aaron to thank," Michel replied. "He's the one who figured out where you were."

"How?" Sassy asked.

"He checked the records for the Registrar of Deeds and found out that Jason Brown bought Zelda's house."

"Who's Jason Brown?" Sassy asked.

"Joshua's latest alias," Michel replied.

"Jared," Sassy said.

Michel looked at her quizzically.

"He was calling himself Jared," Sassy clarified. "He said that Joshua died the night his brother killed their parents."

"His brother?" Michel replied skeptically.

Sassy nodded.

"He claimed he didn't have anything to do with it. He said he'd never killed anyone."

"I'm sure Severin would be surprised to hear that," Michel replied.

"He's dead?" Sassy replied.

"Joshua...*Jared*...beat him to death yesterday morning, shortly before he took you," Michel replied.

"I was only there for a day?" Sassy asked with surprise.

Michel nodded.

"About thirty hours."

Sassy let out a weary sigh.

"Well, I've got to tell you, it felt a lot longer," she said.

"No doubt," Michel replied.

Sassy looked down. Her right hand was wrapped in gauze and her left leg was immobilized in a metal brace.

"So how *am* I doing?" she asked.

"You'll live," Michel replied, "but you're going to need reconstructive surgery on your knee. They cleaned it out for now, but wanted to wait until you were stabilized before they put you under."

"Guess I won't be running any races this year," Sassy said.

"I'm sure that's going to be a huge loss for the team," Michel replied.

Sassy smiled at him appreciatively.

"So what was he like?" Michel asked.

Sassy considered it for a long moment.

"A thin veneer of civility masking a seething pit of contempt," she replied finally.

"Wow," Michel marveled.

"Well, I *am* on drugs," Sassy replied, then shook her head. "Honestly, I don't know. At times he seemed perfectly normal, reasonable, but then other times there was something a lot darker going on."

"Manic-depressive?" Michel asked.

"Sure seemed that way," Sassy replied with a shrug. "Especially given the fact that he killed himself. There was definitely some anger lurking just below the surface. I know that much."

"Did he tell you why he kidnapped you?" Michel asked.

"He wanted to get to know me," Sassy replied.

"And a phone call wouldn't have sufficed?" Michel replied.

Sassy let out a laugh that suddenly became a coughing fit. She doubled over, struggling to catch her breath. Finally it began to subside, and she fell back against the pillows with a wheezing sigh.

"Sorry about that," Michel said.

"It's okay," Sassy replied. "I'm sure the more I cough, the faster I can hack up all the crap in my lungs."

"That's a pleasant image," Michel replied dryly.

Sassy took a sip of water, then slowly exhaled.

"Anyway," she said, "he told me he wanted to get to know me so he could decide whether to kill me. I thought he was letting me go. Of course, the whole nailing the door shut and fire thing suggests otherwise."

"But then why didn't he just kill you?" Michel asked.

Sassy cocked her head at him and raised her right eyebrow.

"What have I been telling you?" she asked.

Michel gave her a confused look.

"Because I'm nice to people and they like me," Sassy said.

Now Michel began laughing.

"So when they like you, they just shoot you in the leg and set the house on fire?" he asked.

"Better than shooting me in the head," Sassy replied, then frowned. "I think that was his final 'fuck you.' Making me believe that I was going to get out, then slamming the door shut, so to speak."

She suddenly felt very tired. She looked down at her leg and it seemed to be visibly pulsing. Then the room grew dark, though she could still see her leg clearly. She tried to wiggle her toes and they seemed to sway back and forth, like wildflowers in a gentle breeze.

"You still with me?" Michel asked suddenly.

Sassy's eyes popped back open. Michel was still standing by her side, watching her with amusement.

"I better let you get some sleep," he said. "I don't want to be here when you start drooling again. It's not pretty."

Sassy grunted in protest, but couldn't summon the energy for a reply. She closed her eyes again, and her mind began to drift. She tried to hold on for a moment longer, knowing there was something she needed to tell Michel. Then she gave in and let sleep take her.

*****

Michel walked out into the fading sun and pulled out his cell phone. He hit speed dial and waited.

"Hey," Joel answered after the first ring. "How's Sassy?"

"She's okay," Michel replied. "Resting comfortably at the moment. Where are you?"

"Still at the hotel," Joel replied. "You want to come get me?"

"Well, I was planning to get Blue," Michel replied, "but I could pick you up after that."

Joel hesitated for a moment.

"No, that's okay," he said. "Chance is ready to go now. I'll just walk with him. How about if I meet you at Cabrini Playground? I'm sure she's going to want to run around for a while."

"Okay," Michel replied. "Then we can stop and pick up some dinner on the way home."

"Sounds like a plan," Joel replied. "See you in a little while."

Chapter 35

"Hey, Stan," Al Ribodeau said, looking up from his desk. "You come to say goodbye?"

"I hope so," Lecher replied.

Ribodeau gave him a questioning look.

"I was hoping to take a look at the photos of Clement's body and the fire before I go," Lecher replied. "He already managed to fake his death once. I just want to make sure he's really dead this time."

Ribodeau's expression turned worried.

"You don't think that's really a possibility, do you?"

Lecher shrugged.

"I'd feel a lot better if I could see the photos."

"Okay," Ribodeau replied. "They haven't been sent up yet. Let's go down to the lab."

*****

Michel and Blue had been at the park for almost fifteen minutes. There were no other dogs, so Michel had kept Blue busy playing fetch. As she raced to retrieve the ball for the hundredth time, Michel's phone rang. He took it from his back pocket and saw Stan Lecher's number on the display. He was about to answer when Blue let out a fierce bark.

Michel looked at her. She was standing stock still, her ears and tail up and the fur on her back raised in a ridge, staring behind him. Michel turned and saw someone moving toward him in the shadows under the pavillion near the park's entrance. He recognized the familiar gait and looked back at Blue.

"It's okay," he said. "It's just Joel."

He waved at Joel and Joel waved back. Then someone stepped out from behind the brick column to Joel's left. Joel stopped and turned around.

Michel looked absently at his phone and saw that Lecher had left him a message, then looked back up, wondering who Joel was talking with. Then Joel spun around and began to run. Michel could see terror on his face.

A gunshot ripped the air, and Joel stumbled forward and fell. Jared stood a few feet behind him, the gun still extended in front of him, smiling at Michel.

"No!" Michel cried.

He began running toward Joel. He was aware of Blue racing past him and Jared turning toward the gate.

He reached Joel and dropped to his knees. He could see blood welling from a small hole in the back of Joel's head. Suddenly another shot rang out and Michel heard an anguished squeal. He looked helplessly toward the gate. It was open and Blue was gone.

He punched 911 into his phone.

"I need an ambulance at Cabrini Playground on Dauphine Street," he said. "My boyfriend has been shot."

He dropped the phone as a dry sob wracked his chest. He lay down and wrapped his arms around Joel's still body, cradling him tightly. Then he heard a whimper and looked up. Blue was walking unsteadily toward them, her ears back and her tail down.

She took another three steps, then her front legs buckled. She dropped to the ground and rolled onto her side. Michel could see blood matting the white spot on her chest. She lifted her head and lay it on Joel's right leg, looking up at Michel with pleading eyes.

Michel reached down and began stroking the side of her face. He tried to say something but couldn't. As Blue closed her eyes, the tears came.

Chapter 36

"How did you know it wasn't him?" DeRoche asked, looking down at the photo.

Lecher pointed at a swath of scorched floor leading from the living room entrance to the body.

"That's not natural," he said. "It was caused by an accelerant, and the body was obviously doused, as well. If it were Clement, he would have been a ball of flames by the time he shot himself. This one was dead before the fire touched him. The body position is too relaxed."

"Is that something our guys should have picked up on?" DeRoche asked.

Lecher didn't respond, but his tight expression made his answer clear.

"Fuck," DeRoche replied with a mixture of anger and guilt. "We shouldn't have let them out of protective custody until we were sure it was Clement."

"There's no way you were going to get fingerprints," Lecher replied, pointing at the charred hands in the photo.

DeRoche knew that he was trying to be charitable, and gave him a grateful nod.

"No, but I should have called you in," he said.

"Where's Michel now?" Lecher asked.

"At the hospital," Ribodeau replied.

"What about Chance?" Lecher asked.

"He's on his way there, too," Ribodeau replied.

"Does he know what happened yet?" DeRoche asked.

Ribodeau shook his head.

"Michel wanted to tell him."

*****

It seemed strange that a place so clean, so sterile, could house so much suffering, so much pain, and so much death. The sick and the dying, families and friends, all brought together in this one place with its scrubbed surfaces and improbably shiny floors. But still the smells of sickness—urine, feces, decay—lingered beneath the mask of cleansers and aerosol sprays. As he passed each door, Michel wondered what private hell lay on the other side.

He could see the young officer at the end of the hall watching him nervously as they approached, and for a moment he wished he'd changed his shirt.

"This is Michel Doucette," Michel's escort said to the young officer.

The officer nodded quickly, not making eye contact with Michel, then moved to his right. Michel paused for a moment, then opened the door and stepped inside.

Chance was standing by the waiting room window, looking out at the night sky. When he heard the door open, he turned and took a few steps toward Michel. Michel could see the anxiety on his face.

"Is Sassy okay?" Chance asked, then stopped as he saw the dried blood on Michel's shirt.

His eyes began to widen with panic.

"Chance..." Michel began gently.

"No," Chance cried in a small, wounded voice.

"He's not dead," Michel replied quickly, "but he's in critical condition."

Chance let out a wet gasp, and tears began to well up in his eyes. He suddenly looked so small and frail to Michel. Michel took a few steps toward him, but Chance backed away.

"You were supposed to protect him," he said, his voice trembling as the tears began to spill down his cheeks.

"I'm sorry," Michel said, taking another step.

"No!" Chance wailed, his whole body starting to shake.

Michel heard the door open behind him and looked over his left shoulder. The two officers were looking at him with concern. Michel shook his head and waved them away. As the door closed, he turned back to Chance.

"Chance..."

Before he could finish, Chance suddenly came at him and began throwing wild punches.

"It's your fault!" he screamed.

Michel was able to block most of the blows, though a few connected with his shoulders and chest. He didn't feel them. He looked back at the door expectantly, but it didn't open again.

As the punches began to weaken and slow, he put his right hand on the back of Chance's head and pulled him closer. Chance resisted for another few seconds, then finally collapsed against Michel's chest. As deep sobs wracked his body, Michel held him tightly and stroked the back of his head.

"I know it is," Michel whispered.

Chapter 37

Sassy opened her eyes and saw Michel hunched over in the chair by the side of her bed. His head was down and his hands dangled loosely between his knees. She couldn't tell whether he was awake.

"Hey," she said softly.

Michel looked up. His eyes were red and glassy. Sassy wondered if he'd been crying recently, or if it was just from a lack of sleep.

"What time is it?" she asked.

"Almost six," Michel replied without checking his watch.

"Were you here all night?"

"No, I went back to Joel's room a little after midnight."

"Did you sleep at all?" Sassy asked with concern.

"For about 45 minutes. Until the vet called a while ago," Michel replied.

"And?"

"Blue's awake and drinking," Michel replied. "He said that's a good sign."

"How's her breathing?" Sassy asked.

"Normal so far," Michel replied. "There doesn't seem to be any fluid building up."

"Good," Sassy replied.

"He said she must have been jumping when the bullet hit," Michel said. "It just passed through the lung and out below her right shoulder. It nicked a rib, but no major tissue damage. She should be able to come home in about a week."

He gave a bittersweet smile and Sassy nodded, imagining the conflicting emotions that the prospect of the homecoming must be triggering.

"And what about Joel? Any change?" she asked.

Michel shook his head, then wearily rubbed his eyes with the palm of his hands.

"There won't be any," he said.

Sassy sat up and looked at him with a combination of surprise and worry.

"You can't know that," she replied carefully. "When the swelling in his brain goes down..."

"He has no brain function, Sas," Michel cut her off, though not with any anger. "That's not going to change when the swelling goes down."

Sassy felt at a loss for words. The previous night Michel had been almost manic with optimistic. She wondered what had changed—whether he'd just accepted the grim reality of the situation, or if hope had simply become too painful. She decided that it didn't matter, and that any encouraging words would just be empty, and perhaps cruel.

"Do you know when his grandmother is supposed to arrive?" she asked instead.

"No," Michel replied. "Chance didn't say. He just told me she was coming."

"Have you talked to Al yet today?" Sassy asked.

Michel shook his head.

"I figured I'd wait for him to call me. I'm sure he was up most of the night, too. But if they'd found anything, he would have called by now."

Sassy studied Michel for a moment, trying to get a read on his emotions. He seemed oddly flat.

"What's going on in there?" she asked.

Michel gave her a questioning look, then shrugged.

"I'm just tired. I think I'm just starting to shut down."

"You're sure that's all it is?" Sassy asked.

"Yeah, why?" Michel replied.

"I just want to make sure you're not planning something," Sassy replied seriously. "I don't want you trying to go all vigilante."

"Not like I could if I wanted to," Michel replied, nodding toward the two uniformed officers outside the door. "Mine follows me into the bathroom to make sure I don't try to flush myself out of the building."

Sassy felt her apprehensiveness ease a little, then wondered if that had been Michel's intention.

"I'm serious," she said. "I don't want you doing anything stupid. Let the boys do their job."

"I will," Michel replied, "but it won't matter. They're not going to catch him. He's been planning this for two years. He's not going to fuck up now. And he knows we can't stay hidden forever. Eventually we'll have to come out, and when we do, he'll be waiting. This isn't going to end until at least one of us is dead."

Sassy felt a chill pass over her. While Michel had always been prone to dark impulses, fatalism hadn't been one of them.

"So we'll set him up," she said. "When he goes to strike, the cops will take him down."

"You really think that's going to work given that he seems to have a direct line into the department?" Michel replied. "No. This is inevitable."

"It's not inevitable unless you play into it," Sassy replied sharply. "I know you're tired and angry and heartbroken, but you need to snap out of this."

"Snap out of it?" Michel replied with a bitter laugh. "You mean just get over the fact that my boyfriend's lying in a coma down the hall? That my dog has a bullet hole in her lung? That my best friend almost burned to death? Sorry, but I'm not quite that strong."

"That's not what I meant," Sassy replied. "But this whole fated destiny bullshit isn't you."

"Well, maybe it is now," Michel replied tersely.

Sassy stared at him hard for a moment, fighting the impulse to reach out and slap him.

"Then you need to change back," she said finally, "because this isn't what Joel would have wanted."

Michel jerked back in his chair, and the defiance on his face melted away. Sassy could see him fighting to hold back tears.

"Don't talk about him like he's already dead," he said in a small voice.

"I'm sorry," Sassy replied, "but you needed to hear that."

Suddenly the door opened.

"Mr. Doucette?"

Michel took a deep breath and tried to compose himself before turning around.

"Yeah?" he replied.

"Detective Ribodeau just called, sir," the officer said. "He wants me to bring you down to the station."

"Okay," Michel replied. "I'll be there in a minute."

He stood up and squeezed Sassy's hand.

"Hopefully they'll let me visit you again," he said.

"If not, call," Sassy replied. "I'll be here."

"Thanks," Michel said, then started for the door.

"Michel," Sassy said.

He turned back to face her.

"I love you," she said.

Michel wiped a tear off his cheek and tried to smile.

"I love you, too," he said.

Chapter 38

"You look like hell," Al Ribodeau said, as Michel walked into the squad room.

His tone conveyed sympathy without pity.

"Then I guess I must be looking in a mirror," Michel shot back. "What time did you go home last night?"

"I didn't," Ribodeau replied, "but I got few hours of shut eye in the break room. What about you?"

"Almost an hour," Michel replied with mock enthusiasm.

Ribodeau nodded.

"You want some coffee?"

Michel looked at the dormant coffee maker in the corner. He knew the remainder in the pot would be bitter and cold.

"I think I'd rather be tired," he replied.

"Suit yourself," Ribodeau replied. "The Captain, Stan, and the kid are waiting for us."

*****

DeRoche was seated at his desk, intently studying the contents of a folder. Lecher stood behind his right shoulder.

"What's that?" Michel asked.

"Clement's mug shot," DeRoche replied. "Stan and Aaron ran it through their software."

"And?" Michel asked.

"It's a composite," Lecher replied. "Clement's face was merged over the original photo."

"Which explains why Joel and Chance confirmed it was him," Ribodeau said.

"But not how Clement managed to get the doctored image into the Tucson police database," DeRoche replied, frowning.

He closed the folder and put it on top of a pile to his left. Michel and Ribodeau took the two empty chairs to Aaron's right, while Lecher settled into the one to his left.

"Okay, so where do we stand?" Captain DeRoche asked, looking at Ribodeau.

"Clement paid for the house with a bank check issued in Baltimore," Ribodeau replied. "We checked with the bank and found out that 'Jason Brown' had an account there from October 2004 until January of this year. The address on file was the same chicken and waffle joint he put on his application at the web design company, but his statements were sent to a P.O. box which has since been closed."

"So no mortgage?" DeRoche asked.

Ribodeau shook his head.

"But his property tax bills have been going to a commercial mailbox in Gretna. We haven't been able to get in touch with anyone there yet to get an address for the account."

"Do we know how's he's been paying the taxes?" DeRoche asked.

"I checked with the assessor's office," Ribodeau replied. "According to their records, he's been paying cash."

"Jesus, he's careful," DeRoche said.

"But at least we're starting to put together a trail on him," Ribodeau replied. "We know from Chance that the brothers moved into Zelda's house sometime in 2002, and we know Clement disappeared in September 2004. He opened the bank account in Baltimore in October that year, and worked at the web design company in early 2005. Presumably he went from there to Tucson, then probably back to Baltimore since he kept the bank account there until this January."

"At which point he probably moved into Marchand's house," Lecher added.

"Most likely," Ribodeau replied with a nod.

"There's a three-year gap," Lecher said. "From the time the parents were killed in 1999 until he showed up here in 2002."

"But is it relevant?" DeRoche asked rhetorically.

"I guess we won't know until we know," Lecher replied.

Aaron timidly held up his right hand and waited for DeRoche to acknowledge him before speaking.

"I could try to find out, if you think it would help," he said. "That way you won't be wasting any of your internal resources."

"You wouldn't mind?" DeRoche asked.

Aaron shook his head.

"And I'm sure I'll be able to access the NSA database."

DeRoche considered it a moment, then nodded.

"We'd appreciate that."

"I have a copy of the Maryland driver's license he used for ID when he bought the house," Ribodeau said. "The social security number is bogus, but it may help. Sassy also told us Clement said he always uses names that begin with J because they're easier to remember."

"And, of course, everything he told Sassy was obviously true," Michel muttered with dark sarcasm. "Like, 'I've decided to let you go'."

DeRoche gave him a questioning look.

"Is there a problem?"

"Of course not," Michel replied in a tight voice. "Go on."

DeRoche studied him for a few more seconds, then turned back to Ribodeau.

"What about the house?"

"We searched it from top to bottom," Ribodeau replied. "If he was living there, he took everything out before the fire. It's boarded up now and we have surveillance on the streets in front and behind, though it seems unlikely he's going to go back."

"Do we have an ID on the body yet?" DeRoche asked.

Ribodeau shook his head.

"We know he was about 5' 10", 160 pounds, give or take, approximately 25-years-old, but the fingers were burned too badly for printing. We're going to have to hope someone reported him missing and then match dental records."

"Does it really matter?" Michel snapped angrily.

The sudden silence stretched out uncomfortably as his eyes slowly swept the faces of the others.

"Well, does it?" he demanded. "So what? He's probably just another hustler."

"And also probably someone's son," DeRoche said.

Michel's eyes locked on his former boss.

"Yeah, well not mine," he replied coldly. "The only thing I want to know about that body is why your people didn't realize it wasn't Clement."

DeRoche sat back as though he'd been pushed.

"Michel..." Lecher started.

"No," Michel cut him off. "Don't make excuses for them. You knew it wasn't Clement, and you weren't even at the scene."

Then he turned on Aaron.

"And how did Clement know we were going to be at Cabrini Playground."

Aaron shifted uncomfortably in his seat.

"I don't know," he stammered.

"You checked out my phone, didn't you?" Michel asked, his voice rising. "Was it bugged?"

Aaron's face flushed and he looked helplessly at Lecher.

"I only looked to see why you weren't receiving calls," he pleaded, looking back at Michel.

Michel pulled out his phone and tossed it hard at Aaron. It struck his chest and dropped into his lap.

"Check it *now*," he said, his hooded eyes flashing.

"Enough!" DeRoche barked. "Everyone else, out."

*****

The two men eyed one another in tense silence for nearly a minute after the door closed, then DeRoche exhaled loudly and his expression softened.

"I really am sorry," he said.

Michel nodded in acknowledgment, though his face remained impassive.

"But we're not the enemy, Michel," DeRoche said.

Michel stared at him for a moment, then lowered his eyes.

"I know that," he said softly.

"Look, there's plenty of guilt to go around," DeRoche said. "I feel it. I know the guys on the forensics team feel it. And I suspect you feel it, too, or you wouldn't be lashing out. But Aaron didn't deserve that, and Al sure as hell doesn't deserve it."

"I didn't say anything about Al," Michel replied.

"I know you didn't, but you don't think he feels responsible anyway?" DeRoche asked. "Maybe you've forgotten what it's like. It's all one team. You criticize any part of that team, and Al's going to take it personally."

"I'm sorry," Michel replied. "It's just that..."

He looked back up at DeRoche and shrugged helplessly.

"I know," DeRoche replied. "And I don't blame you, but we can't start turning on each other. I'm sure that's what Clement wants. He knows if we're not working together, he has a better chance of getting you out in the open."

"And you think that's what he wants?" Michel asked, feigning surprise.

DeRoche cocked his left eyebrow skeptically.

"Don't you?"

Michel considered continuing to play coy for a few moments, but nodded instead.

"He wants to finish what he started," he said. "I'm sure he wants me, and maybe Chance, too."

"What about Stan?" DeRoche asked.

"I don't know," Michel replied. "I still can't figure that part out. I don't get the connection to Stan."

"Me neither," DeRoche replied, "but to be safe, I'm putting you all back into protective custody. And I mean full time."

He watched Michel carefully for any sign of protest, but Michel just nodded wearily.

"But we can move you to a different room if that will be more comfortable for you," DeRoche added.

Michel flashed back on the last night he and Joel had spent in the hotel, and wondered if the bed linens had been changed yet. He suddenly wanted to hold Joel's pillow, to smell the traces of Joel's hair on it. He felt his throat tighten and pushed the thought away.

"You don't think he'll look for us there?" he asked.

"It won't matter," DeRoche replied. "The stairwells are secured and we'll have a guard by the elevator in the lobby and another in the hallway outside your rooms."

Michel sensed there was something more, and gave DeRoche a questioning look. DeRoche hesitated for a moment, then sighed.

"We don't think he knew you were there in the first place."

"Why not?" Michel asked.

DeRoche hesitated again, and this time Michel could read the debate going on behind his eyes.

"Why not?" he pressed.

"Because Clement followed you to Cabrini from the hospital," DeRoche replied finally.

Michel blinked uncomprehendingly for a moment, then his face went slack.

"How do you know?" he asked numbly.

"Street cameras," DeRoche replied. "Chance told us he and Joel walked together from the hotel to your office, then Joel cut down to Dauphine. We checked the footage along their route, and there was no one following them."

Michel nodded slowly for him to continue.

"Then we checked tapes from security cameras at the hospital and traffic cams. Clement was parked five spaces away from you in the garage. He followed you from the hospital to the K-9 unit to Cabrini. Then he parked on Esplanade and waited on Ursulines until he saw Joel."

Michel sat back and swallowed hard.

"I should have seen him," he said.

"You can't blame yourself," DeRoche replied. "We all thought he was dead."

Michel took a wet breath and wiped his eyes with the back of his right hand.

"Did you get a plate number on his car?" he asked.

"The car was still there," DeRoche replied. "It belongs to an old woman in Gretna. She didn't even know it was missing from her garage. Said she hasn't driven it in almost a year. We showed her a picture of Clement, but she didn't recognize him. We're canvassing her neighborhood now."

Michel suddenly felt as though all the energy had been drained from his body. He stared listlessly down at his hands for a moment, then looked back up at DeRoche.

"I think I'm ready to go to the hotel," he said.

*****

Aaron and Lecher were sitting by Ribodeau's desk when Michel walked back into the squad room. He faltered for a moment when he saw Aaron, then slowly walked over.

"I'm sorry," he said, holding his hand out.

"That's okay," Aaron replied.

"No, it's not," Michel replied. "Not after everything you've done. Not after you saved Sassy's life. I had no right to treat you like that."

Aaron looked at Michel's hand for a moment longer, then shook it.

"Well, thanks," he said, with equal parts embarrassment and appreciation.

Michel turned to Lecher.

"You ready to go into solitary?"

"Actually I'm going to stop by the hospital to visit Sassy first," Lecher replied. "She called me."

"About what?" Michel asked.

Lecher shrugged.

"I'll find out when I get there."

Chapter 39

Michel and his escort stepped out of the elevator and turned right, then right again at the corner. At the far end of the hall, Michel could see two uniformed officers talking by the door to the stairwell. He recognized the younger one from the hospital the previous night. The other appeared to be in his late forties, and was bouncing up and down on the balls of his feet like a nervous military commander about to launch an attack. Michel thought he looked vaguely familiar.

"Doucette," the older man said as Michel approached. "I was just going over details with Helms here. He'll be taking the next shift."

Michel was immediately annoyed by the assumed camaraderie in his tone, as though they'd been good friends during Michel's time on the force. He made a show of reading the man's nameplate before replying.

"Okay...*Carlson*," he said dully, barely bothering to make eye contact. "Which room is Chance LeDuc in?"

Carlson's eyes narrowed at the obvious slight.

"Five-zero-eight," he replied stiffly.

Michel turned to his escort and gave him a small wave.

"Thanks for the ride."

Then he nodded at Helms and walked to his room. He paused outside his door for a moment. Part of him wanted to check in on Chance, but he knew that would lead to a longer more complicated conversation. He decided talk could wait until he'd had a chance to sleep for a few hours.

He let himself into the room and flipped on the light. His heart fell when he saw that the bed had been made. He knew that the sheets and pillowcases would have been changed in anticipation of some future guests.

He turned away and walked into the bathroom. As he stripped off the surgical scrub top he'd borrowed from the hospital, he saw a small circle of dried blood in the hollow above his right collar bone. Against his pale skin it looked like a bullet wound, and he wondered how he'd missed it earlier. He turned on the tap and let the water run for a few seconds, then changed his mind. He turned the water off and walked back into the other room.

The curtains were closed and the air felt blessedly cool against his bare skin. He stepped out of his shoes and pulled off his socks, then took off his pants and dropped them to the floor. He heard a dull thud against the carpet and reached down to fish his cell phone out of the right front pocket. He turned it off and laid it on the nightstand, then pulled back the quilted comforter and turned off the light.

As he slid between the sheets, he thought he caught a slight scent of Joel, but when he brought one of the pillows to his face, it smelled only of detergent and fabric softener. He rolled onto his left side and pulled the pillow tightly against his chest. His arms still felt empty.

He remembered something he'd read in *A Lover's Discourse* by Roland Barthes, that the first thing one forgets is the amount of space a lover occupied in one's arms. Michel still knew exactly know much space Joel had occupied. He pulled another pillow close and wrapped his arms around both of them. It felt almost right now, familiar.

He suddenly thought of Blue. He wanted to see her, and stroke her face and neck, and tell her that he loved her. He wanted to tell her everything was going to be all right, and make her fear and pain go away.

He felt his throat tighten as a single tear rolled onto the pillow. Then his thoughts drifted to Joel, and he let out a small, wet gasp.

When his mother had died he'd felt a deep sense of loss that had left him uncertain and confused, but it had been a loss tied to the past and the familiar. He'd never mourned for the days his mother would never have, or the time he would never have with her. But now his heart ached for the things that would never be, for the sound of Joel's voice, for the touch of his lips and the feel of his skin, for the time they were supposed to have had as they grew old together.

His chest heaved convulsively and he struggled to catch his breath as a soundless moan escaped his lips. Tears streamed sideways across his cheeks and nose, and he hugged the pillows tighter.

*****

Finally the tears began to slow and his breathing thickened. The images in his mind began to melt and blend into one another as he drifted toward sleep. Then a single vision coalesced. He could feel the texture of the grip against his palm, and the tension of the trigger against his finger as he squeezed it. He could hear the gunshot and see Jared's eyes rolling back into his head as the bullet burrowed into his brain.

Michel smiled as sleep finally overcame him.

Chapter 40

"How are you feeling?" Lecher asked.

"All things considered, not bad," Sassy replied. "At least physically."

Lecher nodded knowingly, then settled into the chair next to the bed.

"So what's up?" he asked.

Sassy hesitated a moment, and Lecher could read the sudden uncertainty in her eyes.

"What?" he prompted.

"How well do you really know Aaron?" Sassy asked.

"Pretty well, I guess," he replied. "We didn't really socialize, but we spent a good amount of time working together outside of class. Why? Where's this coming from?"

"I think Jared is working with someone else," Sassy replied.

"Any particular reason?" Lecher asked.

"A few," Sassy replied, "the main one being that he said he got me to the third floor in a dumbwaiter, then dragged me up to the attic by himself."

Lecher gave her a bemused look.

"If he'd dragged me, I'd have scrapes on my body, but I don't," Sassy explained. "That means I was carried. He's not a very big guy, and in case you haven't noticed, I'm not a small woman. He couldn't have done it alone."

"Okay," Lecher agreed, "but why Aaron?"

"Because of you," Sassy replied.

Lecher blinked in surprise.

"Me?"

Sassy nodded.

"It doesn't make any sense that Jared would have involved you in this because you have no connection to him. But you do have a connection with Aaron."

"Yeah, but that's a pretty big jump from a connection to being an accomplice," Lecher replied doubtfully. "What would be his motive?"

"Ego," Sassy replied. "It could be his way of proving that he's smarter than the master."

Lecher considered it for a moment. He'd certainly seen Aaron's competitive streak with classmates, but he'd never sensed that Aaron viewed him as anything other than a mentor.

"I don't know, Sassy," he replied, shaking his head. "I don't see it. Aaron grew up in Connecticut. He comes from a stable home. How would he even have met Clement?"

"When I asked Jared how he learned to bug Chance's computer, he said he got help from people he'd met online," Sassy replied.

Lecher gave her another skeptical look, and Sassy sensed that he was feeling protective of Aaron.

"Maybe he didn't even know what Jared really had planned," she offered. "Maybe Jared told him it was just some kind of elaborate joke."

"But he knows now," Lecher replied, "and unless I've totally misread him, I can't see him not stepping forward with the truth."

He stared at Sassy's cast for a moment, frowning.

"Have you told Michel about this?" he asked.

"No," Sassy replied. "I drifted off before I could tell him I thought Jared was working with someone, and I didn't come up with the Aaron theory until just before I called you."

"Probably just as well," Lecher replied, thinking about Michel's earlier hostility toward Aaron. "What about Al?"

"I was kind of delirious when he questioned me yesterday," Sassy replied. "

Lecher knew it was an incomplete answer, given that she'd had ample to time rectify the omission. He realized she was extending him a personal courtesy since he'd been the one to bring Aaron into the case.

"Okay, I'll do some more checking," he said with a nod.

"Thank you," Sassy replied.

Lecher started to get up, but stopped. He could see that Sassy had something else on her mind, and raised his eyebrows. Sassy studied him appraisingly for a moment, seemingly debating whether or not to speak.

"Did it give you closure?" she asked finally.

"What?"

"MacDonald's death."

"I already had closure," Lecher replied a bit too quickly.

"I thought I did, too," Sassy replied. "Turned out I was wrong. But I have it now."

Lecher didn't respond. He wondered where she was headed.

"Stan, I have something to ask you," she said.

Lecher nodded.

"MacDonald's heart attack. Was it induced?"

Lecher stared at her impassively for a few seconds.

"Why would you think that?" he asked.

"Because I found a syringe cap in the barn," Sassy replied. "A long one, like for a cardiac needle."

Lecher's expression remained fixed and calm.

"What did you do with it?" he asked.

"I took it home and threw it away," Sassy replied.

It was technically a lie, but substantively true.

"Why?"

"Because I figured MacDonald deserved to die," Sassy replied. "For what he did to Iris and my baby and God knows how many other innocent girls."

Lecher looked away for a few seconds, then back at Sassy.

"That surprises me," he said. "I didn't think you were the type to dispense justice."

"I'm not," Sassy said, "but I was glad someone else was."

Lecher studied her eyes for a moment.

"You know I can't give you an answer," he said.

"Yeah, that's what I figured," Sassy replied. "But did his death give you closure?"

Lecher's eyebrows knit together.

"Why does it matter?" he asked.

"Because Michel is convinced that in the end it's going to come down to him and Jared, and I'm afraid that he might be right," Sassy replied. "I want to know if killing Jared is going to give him closure."

Lecher gave her a small, empathetic smile.

"It may," he replied.

Chapter 41

Michel woke and looked at the clock. It was just after 2 PM. He'd been asleep for almost seven hours. He sat up and rolled his head slowly from side to side, then reflexively looked at the empty space beside him. His momentary respite from thinking about Joel was over.

Oddly he didn't feel like crying again. Instead he laid his palm on the sheet and whispered, "I love you," willing the words through the air to their intended destination.

He threw back the covers and stood up. Though he was still tired, he felt much better. His emotions were level now, and his mind was focused. He felt like himself again...for the first time in a long time.

He walked into the bathroom and flipped on the light. The blood spot above his collarbone was gone. He wondered if it had rubbed off on the sheets, or if he'd just imagined it had been there at all. That morning seemed like a distant memory, or perhaps a dream.

He slipped off his boxer shorts and turned on the shower.

*****

He opened the door and stepped into the hallway. Officer Helms was standing at the far end, facing in the direction of the elevators. Michel looked down at his bare feet and considered putting on his shoes, then decided against it. He was halfway down the hall when Helms turned to face him. Michel was struck by how young he looked, and guessed that Helms was probably a rookie, though his bearing suggested he'd spent some time in the military first.

"Still here, huh?" Michel said.

"Yes, sir," Helms replied.

"Must be nearing the end of your shift," Michel said.

"No, sir," Helms replied. "I'm here until nine."

"Who'd you piss off?" Michel replied with a teasing smile.

Helms' expression remained fixed.

"I volunteered, sir," he replied.

"Any reason?" Michel asked.

For just a moment, Helm's steady gaze faltered.

"Just some issues at home that I'd rather avoid, sir," he said.

"Sorry to hear that," Michel replied. "Anything you want to talk about?"

Helms seemed taken aback by the question, and looked down at the floor nervously.

"At ease," Michel said. "And you can call me Michel. Or Mr. Doucette, if that's more comfortable."

Helms looked up, and an embarrassed smile flitted across his lips.

"Sorry, sir...Mr. Doucette," he said. "Old habits."

"Well, I appreciate your dedication to the job," Michel replied, "but I think you can relax for the moment."

"Thank you," Helms replied with what sounded like genuine gratitude.

"So, what's going on?" Michel prodded gently.

Helms hesitated momentarily, then nodded to himself.

"My wife is pregnant," he said.

Michel almost said "congratulations," but stopped when he saw the conflicted look in Helms' eyes.

"I take it you're not happy about that?" he asked instead.

Helms seemed unsure how to respond.

"Of course I'm happy," he said finally, though his voice

lacked conviction. "I mean, I've wanted to be a father for as long as I can remember. It's just the timing. We'd agreed to wait a few years, but now..."

Michel nodded sympathetically. He suddenly thought about Joel and Blue, and how much pain he could have avoided if they'd never come into his life. Then he thought about all of the happiness he would have missed, too, and for a moment he felt his newly regained armor begin to slip.

No, not now, he thought. Not yet.

He took a deep breath and looked at Helms.

"There's never a perfect time when you're on the job," he said. "You spend the first few years trying to establish yourself on the street. Then you want to get your shield. Then you want to get through your first case, then the next and the next. Before you know it, your career is over and you're left with nothing."

He'd intended the words to be encouraging, but from the shocked look on Helms' face, realized he'd missed the mark.

"I'm sorry," he said. "I didn't mean that to sound so bleak. I just meant that...you shouldn't put off the things that are important to you because..."

you never know how long they'll last

"...you think the timing isn't right."

Helms looked at him with confusion for a moment, then slowly nodded.

"I guess that makes sense," he said.

"You should call your wife and tell her how happy you are," Michel said. "Trust me."

"I'll do that," Helms replied appreciatively. "So was there something you needed?"

"Oh yeah," Michel replied, suddenly remembering why he'd come down the hall in the first place. "I was wondering if I could get a ride to the hospital?"

"I'm afraid not," Helms replied. "Someone called in a bomb threat down at the Riverwalk a few hours ago. All available personnel are down there. It'll probably be a few hours before we can get you any transport."

Michel wondered briefly if Jared had called in the threat to ensure he'd be stuck at the hotel for the day.

"Okay," he said. "Just let me know when I can go."

"I'll do that," Helms replied, then reached into his right shirt pocket. "I forgot to give you this earlier."

He pulled out a card and handed it to Michel. It was a generic NOPD business card, with a phone number handwritten across the top.

"In case you need anything and don't feel like walking down the hall," Helms said. "That will be the number for whoever's on duty here."

"Thanks," Michel said.

He started to turn away, then stopped.

"You wouldn't happen to have a cigarette, would you?"

"Sorry," Helms replied. "I don't smoke."

Chapter 42

Michel heard a soft knock. He turned down the TV and walked to the door, expecting to see Helms through the peephole. Instead he saw an agitated-looking Chance. He braced himself for an argument, and opened the door.

"Hey," he said.

"Hey," Chance replied quickly. "Can I come in?"

"Yeah, sure," Michel replied.

Chance took a few steps past him, then stopped.

"Look, I'm sorry," he said without turning around. "I know it wasn't your fault."

Michel stared at him with shocked surprise.

"I wish I could believe that," he replied.

Chance turned. His expression was serious, determined.

"It wasn't," he said emphatically.

Michel looked down at the floor. He wanted to believe Chance was right, but couldn't.

"I know you think that Joel wouldn't be lying in a hospital bed right now if he'd never met you," Chance said. "Right?"

Michel nodded.

"Well, you're right," Chance replied matter-of-factly. "Because he'd already be dead. Hunter would have killed him two years ago. You didn't get Joel involved with any of this. You got involved with it when you and Sassy saved his life."

Michel wasn't sure how to respond. He realized that he'd been so caught up in what had been happening the last few days that he'd lost sight of where it all began.

"But if I'd picked you both up at the hotel yesterday…" he protested weakly.

"And if I'd never come to New Orleans, or if Joel hadn't been so trusting, or if Jared and Hunter's father hadn't fucked them, blah, blah, blah," Chance replied angrily. "But all that shit did happen, and what happened to Joel isn't my fault or his or yours or Sassy's. It's Jared's fault. Because he's the one who pulled the trigger."

Michel knew he was right, though he was surprised at Chance's emotional clarity. He wondered if it would last, or be replaced soon by another wave of guilt and recrimination.

"Since when did you become the logical one?" he asked.

"Someone has to be while Sassy's in the hospital," Chance replied with a small smile.

Michel nodded.

"Thank you," he said.

"Yeah, well don't get all sappy on me," Chance replied with mock distaste.

"I promise," Michel replied.

"So what do you want to do?" Chance asked.

Michel had been asking himself the same question for the last few hours, though he hadn't expected to hear Chance voice it so directly.

"I'm not sure yet," he replied.

"Well, think of something," Chance said. "I'm really bored."

Michel realized that he'd completely misread the question.

"Oh," he said quickly, trying to cover. "I'm going to the hospital to visit Joel as soon as I can get a ride. Do you want to go with me?"

A mixture of fear and doubt clouded Chance's eyes.

"I'm not sure," he replied.

Michel nodded sympathetically.

"But is it all right if I hang out here until you go?" Chance asked. "I don't really want to be alone right now."

Michel felt his throat tighten.

"Yeah, sure," he managed. "Me, neither."

*****

A loud knocking woke Michel, and for a moment he smiled, happy to have Joel wrapped in his arms again. He hugged him tighter and kissed the side of his neck. Then he heard Chance's anxious voice.

"What are you doing?"

Michel opened his eyes. Chance's blue eyes were staring at him in alarm from just a few inches away.

"Oh, shit," Michel exclaimed, jerking his arm off Chance's chest and rolling onto his back. "I'm sorry. I guess I just..."

He quickly sat up.

"I thought you were Joel," he said, thoroughly flustered.

"Yeah, well, I'm not," Chance replied, pushing himself up against the headboard, "and there's someone at the door."

The knocking began again, and Michel looked at the door. He felt dazed and disoriented. He slowly stood up, trying to regain his bearings.

"I'm coming," he said, as he unsteadily crossed the room.

He unlocked the door and opened it without bothering to see who was there.

"Took you long enough," Stan Lecher said irritably. "What the hell were you doing?"

"Sorry," Michel mumbled. "Chance and I fell asleep."

"Chance and you?" Lecher asked, raising his right eyebrow.

Michel quickly turned away.

"What time is it?" he asked, walking back into the main room.

Chance had moved to one of the chairs by the window, and had his knees drawn up in front of his chest. It struck Michel as a defensive posture.

"Just after six," Lecher replied.

"Where've you been all day?" Michel asked.

251

"At the hospital," Lecher replied.

Michel looked at him curiously.

"You and Sassy must have had a lot to talk about," he said.

"You mean Sleeping Beauty?" Lecher replied with a gentle laugh. "No, I got stuck there when my ride got called to a bomb threat at the Riverwalk."

"Helms told me about it," Michel replied. "Do you know if they found anything?"

Lecher shook his head.

"By the way, Helms said you can go to the hospital now. He said he left a message on your cell phone a half hour ago."

Michel reflexively looked at the phone on the nightstand. He realized he hadn't turned it back on after his morning nap.

"Um, I think I'll wait until morning," he replied quickly.

While he wanted to see Joel, waking up with his arms around Chance had left him feeling oddly unsettled, and he wasn't sure he was up to meeting Joel's grandmother yet.

"But you can go if you want," he said, turning to Chance.

Chance shifted uncomfortably on the chair.

"No, I think I'll wait, too," he replied, then looked away.

Lecher was suddenly aware of the tension in the room. He briefly considered saying something, then decided it was probably none of his business.

"Okay," he said. "Then I guess I'll go to my room now."

"You want to have dinner together?" Michel asked more eagerly than he'd intended.

Lecher considered it for a moment, then shook his head. He decided it would be better to let Michel and Chance work out their issues on their own. He'd also promised Sassy he'd do some checking on Aaron.

"No, thanks," he replied. "It's been a long day and I have work to do. I'll just eat in my room."

"Okay," Michel replied, failing to mask his disappointment. "But if you change your mind, you know where to find me."

"Yes, I do," Lecher replied. "Maybe I'll stop by later."

*****

Michel turned to face Chance as soon as the door closed.

"I really am sorry," he said.

"It's okay," Chance replied. "At least you weren't dry humping me. Not that I could feel, anyway."

He gave a grudging smile, and Michel relaxed a little.

"Do you have cigarettes?" Michel asked.

"I thought you quit," Chance replied.

"I did, but..." Michel trailed off.

Chance nodded understandingly.

"Yeah, but we can't smoke in here," he said. "Helms has to escort us down to the pool area."

"That's okay," Michel replied. "I could use a little fresh air."

He smiled crookedly as he realized the irony.

"Then maybe you want to order some food?" Chance asked.

"Yeah sure," Michel replied. "And I could use a drink."

Chapter 43

Chance had been unusually quiet all during dinner. At first Michel had assumed that it was just lingering unease over what had happened earlier, but as the meal progressed he began to sense that it was something more.

"What is it?" he asked finally, putting down his fork.

Chance kept his eyes fixed on the table, but his posture clearly communicated an internal debate.

"Come on," Michel prompted.

After another few seconds, Chance looked up warily.

"I have something to tell you," he said.

Michel sat back, feeling suddenly apprehensive.

"What?"

"I think Jared is still at Zelda's," Chance replied.

Michel gave him an incredulous look.

"How's that possible?" he asked. "It's boarded up, and the police have it staked out."

"It doesn't matter," Chance replied, then paused a beat before adding, "Unless they know about the tunnel."

"Tunnel?" Michel replied, feeling his anxiety increase.

"It runs from the shed in the backyard to the basement," Chance replied.

"Why would there be a tunnel?" Michel asked skeptically, though he knew he had no reason to doubt Chance.

"It was probably for the Underground Railroad," Chance replied. "There's also a shaft from the basement to the attic."

"What kind of shaft?" Michel asked.

"It looks like it was originally for a dumbwaiter," Chance replied, "because there are old pulley wheels just below the hatch in the attic, but the original doors have been sealed up on the other floors. You can still get into it through hidden panels in the kitchen and bathrooms on the second and third floors, though. That's probably how Jared escaped during the fire."

Michel's eyebrows knit together.

"Are you sure he knew about it?" he asked.

Chance nodded.

"He and Hunter and I found the tunnel behind a bunch of old windows. We figured there had to have been a way to hide the slaves once they got inside the house, so we kept looking around and found the shaft. We fixed the ladder in it so we could get in and out of the house without Zelda knowing."

Michel studied Chance for a moment, trying to gauge where the conversation was headed.

"So why were you hesitant to tell me?" he asked finally.

"Because I was afraid you'd tell the police," Chance replied.

Michel understood the implication immediately.

"Chance..."

"Don't tell me you haven't thought about it," Chance cut him off.

Michel flashed back on the vision of killing Jared he'd had as he was falling asleep that morning.

"Of course I've thought about it," he said quietly.

"And?"

"And I'm willing to wait."

"For what?" Chance asked.

"We both know they're not going to find Jared," Michel replied evenly, "and eventually they're going to have to let us out of here."

"But what if he's not willing to wait?" Chance asked.

"Why wouldn't he?" Michel asked. "He's spent two years planning this. He's not going to let it go now."

255

"Don't you get it?" Chance said. "First he went after Sassy, then Joel. This is when you're most vulnerable."

Michel felt his stomach tighten. He'd assumed that Jared was simply working his way down the list, targeting everyone he felt was responsible for his brother's death. It hadn't occurred to him that the order might have been intended to isolate him.

"All the more reason to wait," he said.

"So he can disappear for another two years, then start all over again?" Chance asked. "Because that's what I'd do. I'd wait until you and Sassy had started to relax, then I'd come back and finish the job."

Though he felt sure Chance was wrong about Jared leaving, Michel knew he was probably right that Jared wouldn't give up, no matter how long it took. He also realized Chance might be right about the need to act quickly, though not the reason: Jared wouldn't be expecting him to make the first move right now.

"But it doesn't really matter," he said. "That guard at the end of the hall isn't just to keep people out."

"But what if there were a way out?" Chance replied. "Would you take it?"

Michel stared down at his plate for a moment. He knew he should just call Ribodeau and tell him to check on Zelda's house, but he couldn't shake the feeling that inevitably it had to come down to Jared and him.

"Yeah," he replied finally. "I'd take it."

As soon as he said it, his reluctance faded. It felt right.

Chapter 44

Lecher clicked on the link. An article from *The Greenwich Crier* dated April 14, 1994, popped up on the screen. It was the results of that year's Pinewood Derby. In the accompanying photo, a ten-year-old Aaron was dressed in a Cub Scout uniform, smiling broadly as he held up his first place trophy. In the background, his parents looked on proudly.

Lecher studied the photo. There was nothing obviously fake about it. From the prominent dot pattern, he knew it was a low resolution scan of a printed page.

"Damn pre-digital era," he thought, knowing the analysis software would be useless on it.

He closed the window and went back to the search results. He scrolled down to a link for an article on the high school track team winning the state championship in 2001, and clicked on it. Another window filled the screen. In the center of the page was a large photo of Aaron crossing a finish line, his arms raised in victory.

"Would it kill you to come in second once in a while?" Lecher asked, then smiled at himself as he realized he was actually jealous.

While he'd always been at the top of his class academically, he'd never had much success in other areas as a teenager. Aaron, on the other hand, had apparently excelled in all areas: academics, sports, and social life. He'd been an honor roll student, track and soccer star, class president, and prom king— all documented with photographic evidence on the internet.

"This is ridiculous," Lecher muttered, sighing with frustration. "Sassy's got me paranoid."

He was about to flip the laptop shut when he remembered what Sassy had said about Aaron's ego. He looked at the small team photo in the bottom right corner of the article, and clicked on it. A larger version popped up in another window.

Lecher searched the faces. They all looked so young, confident, and optimistic.

"I probably would have hated you all," he said.

Finally he found Aaron standing near the left end of the back row, smiling his winning smile as usual, flanked by two identical blonds. Lecher tasted copper as his heart began pumping faster. He quickly looked down at the caption: "Back row: Steve Mason, Jason Brown, Aaron Andrews, Kyle Brown..."

"Fuck!" Lecher exclaimed angrily under his breath.

He picked up his cell phone and punched in Michel's number. After one ring, Michel's recorded greeting began to play. Lecher snapped the phone shut, slipped it into his shirt pocket, and hurried to the door. As he yanked it open, he and Aaron let out simultaneous startled cries.

"Oh, Jesus," Aaron said with a relieved laugh, clutching at his chest. "You scared the shit out of me."

"Same here," Lecher replied, trying to strike a genial note, though his heart and mind were both racing.

"Sorry," Aaron said. "I was just about to knock. Are you okay?"

"Yeah," Lecher replied, with what he hoped would pass for a warm smile. "What's a few less years between friends?"

Aaron smiled back and nodded.

"So, were you going someplace?" he asked.

"Just stretching my legs," Lecher replied.

"I can come back later, if you want," Aaron offered. "I just wanted to fill you in on what I found out about Jason Brown."

Lecher quickly assessed his options. Yelling for Helms or Michel was too risky. The nearest stairwell door was only ten feet away, and Aaron would be able to reach it before either of them could respond. Trying to take Aaron down on his own also seemed risky. Though slighter, Aaron was undoubtedly quicker and in far better condition. His best bet seemed to be to get Aaron into the room, then call for help.

"No, that's fine," he said. "Come on in."

As Aaron passed him, Lecher looked at the open laptop on the table by the window. By the glow on the curtains, he knew the screen was still active.

"Are you hungry?" he asked, stalling for time.

Aaron turned to face him.

"Well, I was going to see if Chance wanted to have dinner," Aaron replied, "but you're welcome to join us."

"I think he and Michel were going to order something about an hour ago," Lecher replied as he closed the door.

Aaron frowned slightly.

"Um, okay," he said. "Sure."

"There's a menu on the nightstand," Lecher replied.

Out of the corner of his eye, he saw the glow on the curtains suddenly fade as the laptop's screen saver kicked in.

"Have whatever you want," he said with theatrical magnanimity. "Courtesy of the NOPD...I hope."

Aaron gave an appreciative laugh as he walked to the nightstand and picked up the menu.

"I'll be right back," Lecher said. "I just have to use the facilities."

"Okay," Aaron replied as he sat on the edge of the bed.

Lecher walked into the bathroom and closed the door. Though his heart was still racing, he felt composed and focused now. He took his cell phone out of his shirt pocket and hit redial. Again Michel's voice mail picked up after the first ring.

"Shit," he whispered.

He hit the disconnect button and took out his wallet, pulling out the card that Helms had given him. He quickly dialed the number and put the phone to his ear. As it began to ring, he heard a muffled synchronized buzzing behind him.

He turned to face the door. The buzzing stopped.

"Hey Professor," Aaron's voice came through the phone.

Then the center of the door splintered and Lecher was knocked back against the cool tile wall. For a second he didn't feel anything, then an excruciating burn began to radiate from the center of his chest. He looked down and saw a crimson stain growing on his shirt.

The door opened. Lecher looked up at Aaron with a combination of anger and bewilderment.

"I was really hoping it wouldn't come to this," Aaron said, with what sounded like genuine remorse. "I was hoping I'd be long gone before you figured things out."

Then he raised the silenced muzzle of the gun and fired twice more.

Chapter 45

"Sorry to bother you," Aaron said. "I'm looking for Chance, but he didn't answer his door."

"He's here," Michel replied. "We just finished dinner. Come on in. There's still some food if you're hungry."

A hint of pique troubled Aaron's face, then was gone.

"That's okay," he said. "I already ate."

"Suit yourself," Michel said, stepping aside.

As Aaron moved past, Michel poked his head into the hallway, then frowned. Helms wasn't at his post. He closed the door and followed Aaron into the main room.

"Where's Helms?" he asked.

"Huh?" Aaron replied, breaking his kiss with Chance.

"Officer Helms?" Michel said. "Big guy with a gun who's supposed to be at the end of the hall?"

"Oh, he said he had to go to the bathroom and asked me to look after things for a few minutes," Aaron replied casually.

He lifted the right side of his t-shirt to reveal a pistol in a black nylon slide holster clipped to his belt.

"Are you even licensed to carry that?" Michel asked.

"Yeah," Aaron replied, looking mildly wounded. "I'm not a field op, but I'm still NSA."

Michel looked at the grip of the pistol. It was dark rosewood, inlaid with Mother of Pearl.

"That's not standard issue," he said.

"No, my parents bought it for me when I finished my training program," Aaron replied.

"I thought you said your parents are hippies?" Chance said.

"They are, but I also told you they're hippies who like to buy nice things," Aaron replied, smiling. "In their minds, this was more like a piece of art."

"A piece of art that can kill people," Chance replied.

"Is it a Walther?" Michel asked, feigning expertise.

Aaron shook his head.

"No. A custom Colt .45 M1911."

Michel eyed the gun for a moment, then looked up at Aaron eagerly.

"May I?" he asked.

"You're not going to try to overpower me and escape, are you?" Aaron asked, his tone only half-kidding.

"If I were, I wouldn't need your gun," Michel replied.

Aaron's mouth twisted in deliberation for a moment, then he unfastened the holster and handed the gun to Michel. Michel held it up and twisted it back and forth, letting the light reflect off the engraved cylinder and barrel.

"It's beautiful," he said.

He brought the gun down and released the magazine to check it, then snapped it back into place and racked the slide.

"Sorry about this," he said, throwing Aaron against the wall.

"What the fuck?" Chance exclaimed.

"I found a way out," Michel replied without looking at him.

"Did you ever consider just asking before you went all Dirty Harry?" Chance replied.

"What are you talking about?" Aaron stammered, nervously eyeing the gun.

Michel stared hard at him for a moment, then lowered it and stepped back.

"Sorry," he said.

"Jesus," Aaron said, indignantly tugging at the bottom of his shirt. "What's wrong with you?"

"We need to get out of here," Chance said.

"Why?" Aaron asked.

"We think Jared is at Zelda's house," Michel replied.

"So why not just tell the police?" Aaron asked.

He looked expectantly from Michel to Chance, then back, but neither replied.

"You can't be serious?" he said, shaking his head.

"We can't?" Michel replied flatly.

Aaron let out a nervous laugh.

"So, *what*? You're just going to waltz out of here with me as a hostage, somehow get to Zelda's house, sneak past the surveillance team, then kill Clement?"

"I hadn't considered the hostage part," Michel replied seriously. "I figured we'd just tie you up and leave you here. I only need your gun."

Aaron looked helplessly at Chance, who just shrugged.

"You have a better idea?"

"Yeah, like letting the police handle it," Aaron replied exasperatedly. "This is ridiculous."

"Probably," Michel replied matter-of-factly, then raised a questioning eyebrow.

Aaron stared at the floor for a moment, and Michel noticed he was nearly panting now, and sweat had broken out on his forehead and upper lip. It was as though his moral struggle were exacting a physical toll on his body.

"Okay, fine," Aaron said abruptly, "but you need to go before Helms gets back. At least that way you'll have a head start."

"Just like that?" Michel replied skeptically.

"I'm an analyst, remember?" Aaron replied, with a touch of anger. "I analyzed the situation. It's obvious you're going to do this whether I help or not, and the only chance you have is if you go right now. If the police know you're out, they're going to stop you and throw you in jail."

Though it made sense, Michel wasn't entirely convinced they could trust him.

"And what about you?" he asked.

"I'll go with you," Aaron replied. "You can hide in my car and I'll drive."

"Then the cops are going to know you're helping us," Chance protested.

"Not if they see me leave alone," Aaron replied. "You go now. I'll wait until Helms comes back, then follow."

"How do we know you're not going to double-cross us?" Michel replied.

"You don't," Aaron replied simply, "but you don't really have a choice."

He reached into his pocket and took out a ring of keys.

"It's a silver Honda Accord, license number 528YWH," he said, handing it to Michel. "It's parked in the lot across the street. But if you ditch me, I swear to God I'll tell them where you're going."

"If we were going to ditch you, I'd just hit you in the head with your gun and leave you here," Michel said. "At least that way you'd have plausible deniability."

"So how do we get out?" Chance asked.

"The stairwell is unlocked from this side," Aaron replied, "but you'll have to find a back way out of the hotel because there's another cop stationed in the lobby."

Michel nodded and looked at Chance.

"You ready?"

Chance looked at Aaron.

"Are you sure you want to do this?"

Aaron hesitated a moment, then nodded.

"Yeah. You should go. Keep my gun, just in case Jared's waiting out there."

"Thank you," Michel said.

He opened the door and peered down the hall.

"Okay, come on," he said, waving Chance ahead of him.

Chance stepped into the hall and nodded at Lecher's door.

"Do you think we should tell him?" he asked.

Michel considered it for a moment, then shook his head.

"I already almost wrecked his life once. I don't want to get him into trouble again."

*****

Ten minutes later Aaron slipped into the front seat of his car and turned around. Michel and Chance were huddled low in the back.

"What took you so long?" Chance asked.

"I was waiting for Helms to get back," Aaron replied. "He decided to go for a smoke after he finished in the bathroom."

Michel's heart suddenly jolted, but he tried to keep his expression neutral.

"So where to?" Aaron asked.

"My house first," Michel replied. "I need to get my car and pick up few things. Then I've got someplace safe we can go."

Chapter 46

"You really think someone's going to break into your car and steal your laptop in a *church* parking lot?" Chance asked.

"Force of habit," Aaron replied, patting the side of his courier bag. "I guess it's a nerd thing."

Chance almost added, "A *hot* nerd thing," but decided it would be inappropiate under the circumstances.

"Wow," Aaron said, as the lights flickered on. He stared at the ceiling in amazement for a moment, then turned to Michel. "So why do you have a key?"

"Joel and I were going to live here," Michel replied quickly.

He set his duffel bag down on the stairs directly in front of the altar, then unzipped it and pulled out a black Kevlar vest.

"Give me 20 minutes, then call Ribodeau," he said, as he slipped it over his t-shirt. "Tell him to come without sirens."

He began tightening and securing the straps.

"What if Jared's not actually there?" Chance asked.

"Then I'm probably going to get locked up until they find him," Michel replied.

He put on a light blue dress shirt, buttoned it, and tucked it loosely into his jeans.

"Too obvious?" he asked, holding his arms out.

"You better wear the jacket, too," Chance replied.

"How can you be sure he won't just shoot you in the head when you walk in the door?" Aaron asked.

"He's been waiting two years for this," Michel replied. "He won't want to make it quick."

He back reached into the bag and took out a holstered pistol. He clipped it to his belt, then put on his jacket.

"Here," he said, taking Aaron's gun from the bag.

Aaron took it and slipped it back into his holster.

"Thanks."

Michel adjusted the position of his own holster and straightened his jacket, then pulled his cell phone out and flipped it open.

"Shit," he muttered.

"What?" Chance asked.

"The battery's dead," Michel replied.

He looked at Aaron.

"Can I borrow yours?"

"Uh, yeah, I guess so," Aaron replied.

He unzipped his bag and did a quick search, then looked up with an apologetic shrug.

"I must have left it at the station."

"So take mine," Chance said.

"You'll need it to call Ribodeau," Michel replied.

He stood there uncertainly for a moment, then dropped his phone into the duffel bag.

"I guess I'll just have to hope I don't need one," he said.

He zipped the bag shut, then turned to Chance, his expression suddenly softening.

"If anything happens to me, you tell Joel I love him," he said. "I know he'll hear you."

Chance blinked involuntarily and swallowed hard.

"I will," he promised.

"And you or Sassy are going to have to take care of Blue."

Chance nodded but didn't reply. The reality of the situation was suddenly settling in on him. He took a few deep breaths to hold back the tears that threatened to come.

"Don't die, okay?" he said.

Michel smiled with what he hoped looked like confidence.

"I'll try," he said, then surprised them both by stepping forward and hugging Chance.

Chance stood with his arms at his sides for a few seconds, then wrapped them tightly around Michel.

"Me, too," Michel whispered.

Chapter 47

"I'm kind of mess," Chance said, wiping his eyes. "I'm going to go wash my face."

"Okay," Aaron said sympathetically.

He waited until Chance passed through the door to the vestry, then quickly went to the first row of pews and reached into his bag. He pulled out his cell phone and hit the speed dial.

"Hey. Michel is on his way," he said quietly. "He should be there in about 20 minutes. And he's wearing a vest."

There was a brief pause.

"His phone's dead, and the transmittor runs on the battery."

Another pause.

"Yeah, I'm sure. He left it here. I can link you into the street camera so you'll know when he gets there."

Another brief pause.

"He's in the bathroom. What should I do with him?"

Another pause.

"Okay. Call me when it's over. In the meantime, I'll start deleting files."

He hung up and slipped the phone back into the bag, then took his gun from its holster and quietly racked it. As he slid it behind his back, Chance walked back into the room.

"You feeling okay?" Aaron asked.

"Yeah," Chance replied with an embarrassed smile. "I just got a little overwhelmed, I guess."

He walked to the pew and flopped down to Aaron's left.

"I just wish this whole thing was over," he said.

"It will be," Aaron replied, as he reached behind his back.

He brought the gun up in one smooth motion and squeezed the trigger. A small, impotent click echoed off the room's stone walls.

Chance's eyes widened and Aaron stared at the gun with disbelief. He tried the trigger again, but it had locked.

"Are you looking for these?" Michel asked.

Aaron and Chance's heads spun in unison toward the vestry entrance, matching expressions of shock on their faces. Michel stood in the doorway, holding up an ammunition magazine.

Chance turned back to Aaron, his face suddenly filled with rage. He swatted Aaron's right hand to the side and lunged at him, grabbing him around the neck and pushing him back onto the hard wood bench. Aaron tried to roll away, but Chance brought his knee up hard into his crotch. Aaron let out an anguished cry, and the pistol clattered onto the floor. Chance locked his left hand around Aaron's throat and began throwing frenzied punches with his right.

"You fucking cunt!" he screamed.

Suddenly Michel's arms were wrapping Chance's shoulders. "Stop!" Michel yelled. "We need him."

Chance continued to struggle for another few seconds, then finally let himself be pulled away, though not before he landed a hard kick to Aaron's rib cage. Aaron winced and rolled off the pew onto the floor.

Michel held Chance tightly for a long moment, both of them breathing hard, then loosened his grip slightly.

"Are you all right?" he asked pointedly.

Chance hesitated, then nodded. Michel let go of him and he immediately spun around to face Michel.

"How the fuck did you know?" he demanded, his face angry and red.

"He said that Helms went for a smoke," Michel replied, "but Helms doesn't smoke. I'm sorry I couldn't tell you, but I was afraid he'd get suspicious if I brought you into the house with me."

Chance glared at him for a moment, his shoulders and chest heaving, then he gave a grudging nod.

Aaron groaned loudly as he pushed himself up onto his hands and knees. Michel grabbed him by the back of the shirt collar and pulled him roughly to his feet, then threw him back against the pew.

"I don't have much time," he said. "Talk."

Aaron stared at him sullenly, slowly and deliberately wiping blood from his lips.

Michel unholstered his gun and chambered a round. He pressed the barrel hard into Aaron's left thigh.

"My boyfriend is lying in a hospital with a bullet in his brain," he said sharply. "He's not going to wake up. I don't give a fuck if you live or die."

With a quick jerk he slid the pistol to the left and pulled the trigger. Aaron's scream was drowned out by the bellow of the report as the bullet splintered the bench just inside his thigh.

"Now, let's try this again," Michel said as soon as the echo had faded. "You said something about street cameras."

Aaron looked at him with a combination of fear and surprise.

"It may be crude," Michel said, tugging an earpiece out of his right ear, "but a microphone in a duffel bag is pretty effective. Now tell me about the street cameras."

Aaron stared at the hole in the bench for a moment.

"I want immunity," he said, looking back up at Michel.

"Fuck you," Michel replied coldly. "I'm not exactly working with the DA right now."

He looked at Aaron expectantly, then tapped the warm barrel of the pistol against Aaron's inner thigh. He could see Aaron calculating how to put himself in the strongest position.

"Guarantee me you'll sign a statement saying I cooperated voluntarily," Aaron said finally.

"Done," Michel replied.

Chance groaned angrily behind him.

"I was going to hook him into the police surveillance system so he could see you coming," Aaron replied.

"And that's the only way he could know where I am?" Michel asked.

"Unless you have Chance's phone with you."

Michel was surprised Aaron had offered up the information so easily, and wondered if he was being played. He decided he had no choice but to trust Aaron.

"Can you set up a five-minute delay on the surveillance feed?" he asked.

Aaron looked at him curiously, then nodded slowly.

"Do it," Michel replied. "And if you even think about trying to send him a message, you'll never walk again."

Chapter 48

Chance watched Michel's taillights disappear around the corner, then closed the door and walked back into the nave. Aaron was sitting on the floor to the left of the altar, his wrists tethered behind his back to the brass footing of a prayer bench. Chance sat on the top step of the sanctuary with his back to Aaron, and opened Aaron's laptop.

"So don't you want to know why I did it?" Aaron asked immediately.

"Shut the fuck up, you piece of shit," Chance replied.

He disabled the wireless connection and started going through folders on the desktop.

"Drew was my best friend," Aaron said. "He and Josh were like my brothers."

"That's nice," Chance replied in a disinterested singsong, as he leaned forward and clicked on a folder labeled, "Video."

"I met Josh in a sex abuse chat room," Aaron said.

"Oh, so now you were abused, too?" Chance asked, with a mocking laugh. "Let me guess. Another priest? Nice transparent play for sympathy."

"By my real father," Aaron replied. "That's why I went into foster care."

Despite himself, Chance's hatred faltered for a split second. He closed his eyes and pictured Joel in his hospital bed.

"Good," he said finally, looking over his right shoulder. "I hope you dream about him every night, and wake up screaming when he starts tearing your ass apart."

He and Aaron locked eyes for a moment, then Aaron nodded slowly.

"I know you don't really mean that," he said.

"No?" Chance replied. "And why's that?"

"Because you have compassion," Aaron replied.

Chance put the laptop to the side, pushed himself up, and walked over to Aaron. He paused for a moment, then kicked Aaron hard in the same spot he'd kicked him earlier. Aaron doubled over, gasping.

"There's your fucking compassion," Chance said, then returned to the laptop and sat down again.

He clicked on the first video file. A window opened, and he saw himself sitting at his desk. The time stamp in the upper right corner read, "9:18 AM 02-03-06." He closed the file and looked for something more recent.

He opened a file dated two weeks earlier and saw himself naked from the waist up. From the movement of his right arm, it was clear what he was doing. He quickly closed the file and dragged it to the trash.

"Fucker," he whispered.

Aaron took several long, labored breaths, then sat back up.

"You would have done the same thing," he said.

Chance ignored him.

"If someone killed Joel, you'd want revenge," Aaron said.

Chance almost replied, "someone did kill him," then immediately felt guilty.

"The only reason you're not dead right now is because you didn't actually pull the trigger," he said instead. "But I'd rather see you in prison, anyway...with a cellmate who can play 'daddy' with you every night."

He focused on the screen again and selected the last file, dated two days earlier. He opened it and saw the open doorway to Michel's and Joel's bathroom.

Suddenly Joel walked into the frame from the left. As he

reached the doorway, a nude Aaron stepped in front of him and kissed him. Joel took a step back. Though his face wasn't visible now, it was clear from his body language and the expression on Aaron's face that Joel was upset. Chance turned up the volume, but there was only a low hum.

"You tried to seduce him?" he asked, looking at Aaron with disbelief and disgust.

"I didn't just try," Aaron replied, smiling smugly.

Chance felt his face burning and looked back at the screen. Aaron took a step toward Joel, but Joel backed away again, then they talked for another few seconds. Then Aaron walked back into the bathroom and disappeared in the direction of the shower as Joel walked out of the frame.

Chance was about to hit STOP when Joel suddenly reappeared. He walked into the bathroom, stripped, and walked toward the shower. Then the screen went black.

Chance stopped the video and narrowed his eyes in concentration. Something wasn't right. He hit rewind, then paused the video just after Aaron started toward the shower. He looked in the upper right corner and saw that the time and date stamp were missing.

He began watching again on half-speed. Joel slowly left the frame, and for four seconds nothing happened. Then the light in the bedroom dimmed slightly just before Joel reappeared.

"Nice try," Chance said, smiling derisively at Aaron.

He snapped the laptop shut and stared at it for a few moments. The camera view had been limited but precise. It hadn't been intended for surveillance. Jared and Aaron had wanted to be able to create the illusion that Joel and Aaron had had sex. But why, and why hadn't they used the video yet?

Chance looked at Aaron and wondered if he could beat the answers out of him. Aaron gave him a taunting smile that made the prospect even more attractive.

"Unfortunately, I don't have time for that," Chance said.

"What?" Aaron replied, the smile fading.

Chance looked at his cell phone. Michel had been gone for almost five minutes.

"Time to fuck up your plans," he said.

He grabbed the laptop and got up.

"Is Jared able to track your phone?" he asked, as he walked to the altar and picked up Aaron's cell phone.

"No, why?" Aaron asked, his expression suddenly anxious.

"Good, that's all I needed to know," Chance replied.

He walked over and threw a hard looping punch that connected squarely with Aaron's nose.

"Oh, and I'll need to borrow your car, too," he added, as Aaron slumped forward.

*****

As soon as he heard the door close, Aaron lifted his head and opened his eyes. Despite the pain of his broken nose, he smiled. So long as the police were out of the loop, there was still a good chance he and Jared could get away. Jared would kill Michel, then call. When he didn't get an answer, he'd come to the church. Chance would probably pass him on the way to Zelda's without even realizing it.

Chapter 49

Michel had parked two blocks away on Decatur. Though it was still almost an hour until sunset, the shadows across Fullerton had grown long, and he stuck to them as he moved quickly down the block. A nondescript brown sedan was parked along the opposite curb on the next block. Even from that distance, Michel could see that it was empty. He wondered if its twin on the block behind Zelda's house was empty, too.

As he neared Zelda's, he could see that the front door had been unboarded, and stood open a few inches. He stopped outside the gate and looked at the sedan again. He suddenly wished he had a phone so he could call Ribodeau. He took a few deep breaths to steady himself, then unholstered his gun and stepped through the gate.

As he reached the porch, he ducked down beside the stairs and closed his eyes, listening for movement. All he could hear was the light rustling of some overgrown lilacs against the porch railing to his left. He opened his eyes and studied the approach to the door. The porch boards were weathered, and most had warped away from the frame. Each step would be a groaning announcement of his arrival.

He sighed and checked his watch. It had been twenty minutes since Aaron had called Jared. He stood and surveyed the whole porch. The boards butting up against the clapboard front of the house were more level, and still bore traces of paint.

He turned and quickly walked around the right corner of the porch, then climbed up over the rail and carefully stepped down. There was barely a sound. He pressed his back against the house and slowly started toward the door.

*****

He pushed the door open another few inches. Mercifully, the hinges didn't protest. He leaned forward and peered through the opening. The walls around the living room entrance had been badly charred, though the floor was relatively unscathed save for water damage. The overwhelming stench of gasoline, smoke, and mildew almost made him dizzy.

He turned his head and took several lung-clearing breaths, then quickly stepped inside and crouched down. As his eyes swept the hallway and stairs, his gun moved along with them.

A sudden scraping noise from above caused him to jerk the barrel of the gun up, but he kept the pressure against the trigger steady. He cocked his head and heard light footsteps. They grew louder for a few seconds, as though approaching the stairs, then receded and finally stopped.

Michel slowly let out his breath and closed the door. He settled on the floor with his back in the corner, and laid his gun beside him. It had taken him longer to get inside than he'd expected, but it would still be another minute or two before he appeared on the surveillance feed. As he looked at the stairs, he realized it didn't matter. Any element of surprise he might have had would be gone as soon as he stepped on them.

He rolled his head from side to side, trying to loosen up his neck and shoulders. Whatever was going to happen was out of his control now. All he could do was try to be ready for it. As he focused on clearing his mind, his eyes settled on two 2 x 4s propping up the outer edge of the staircase. They were obviously new, unscathed by the fire.

"That was awfully considerate of you," he thought.

Chapter 50

Michel stood and dusted off his knees. He leaned forward and looked up to the third floor landing, then took his gun back out of the holster and moved to the foot of the stairs.

He felt silly going through the charade of trying to catch Jared unawares when it was obvious that Jared was expecting him, but knew he had to take his time. He stepped on the first stair and heard a small groan.

"Maybe I should just ride up on a pack of elephants," he thought.

He continued up slowly, staying close to the wall where the structural integrity hadn't been as badly compromised. The balusters and outer edges of the treads were badly charred near the midway point, and he stepped even more gingerly, listening for any sign that the stairs were going to give way. Finally he reached the landing and let out brief sigh.

He quickly checked the room directly opposite the stairs and the bathroom, then moved to the right of the open attic door. He braced his gun with both hands and took a deep breath, then stepped into the doorway. The stairs were clear.

His heart was pounding now, and a loud buzzing seemed to be coming from inside his head as he started to climb. He focused on slowing his breathing to keep from hyperventilating.

As he reached the bend in the stairs, he stopped and leaned forward, keeping his head low. The last time he'd been in the attic, half the room had been crowded with grotesque mannequins in Zelda's clothes and wigs. Now all he could see was a bed and a nightstand to his left. He studied the shadows for a moment, his breathing echoing in his ears, then climbed the last four stairs and stepped through the doorway.

The impact of the first bullet knocked him into the door frame. The impact of the second ripped the breath out of him and forced him to his knees. As he went down, he dropped his gun and it skittered a few feet across the dusty floor boards.

He reflexively reached for it, then gasped as searing pain exploded in the right side of his chest. He collapsed onto his left side and rolled to his back, struggling to breath.

"I wouldn't move too much, if I were you," Jared said, as he reached down and grabbed Michel's left wrist. "From that distance, the bullets probably broke some ribs, and you wouldn't want to puncture a lung."

Then he yanked hard, and Michel screamed as his rib cage lifted and expanded.

Jared dragged him to the side of the bed, then fastened his wrist with a leather cuff and stepped away. Michel could only manage quick panting breaths, and sweat poured down his face. His whole right side felt as though it had been repeatedly bashed by a baseball bat.

"I guess it hurts even with the vest on, huh?" Jared asked.

Michel grimaced as he pushed himself up against the side of the bed.

"How about you put it on and let me shoot you so you can find out for yourself?" he managed. "I promise not to shoot you in the head."

Jared let out an oddly appreciative laugh.

"I can see why Joel liked you," he said. "You've got a good sense of humor. And you're hot. I'd definitely fuck you. In fact, maybe I will before I kill you."

Michel looked down at the leather cuff.

"I think you're going to need more than this for *that* to happen," he said, shaking it.

"Don't worry, I've got plenty more," Jared replied with an easy smile.

Michel was struck by how low key and relaxed he seemed, a stark contrast to his brother's melodramatic intensity. He remembered what Sassy had said, that there was anger lurking just below the surface, and wondered if it would be better to provoke it or let it be.

He pretended to look at the cuff again while he checked his watch, then looked up at Jared.

"So are we going to get to know one other while you decide whether to kill me?" he asked.

Jared smiled.

"Sorry, that was just a one-time deal, and it was only temporary."

"Temporary?" Michel replied, his heartbeat quickening.

Jared nodded.

"I'll let Sassy live for another two years, then I'll come back for her," he replied. "I just want her to feel what I've been feeling for the last two years first."

Michel saw a brief flash of the anger.

"So it's all been about Sassy from the beginning?" he asked. "The rest of us are just collateral damage to punish her?"

"No, the only 'collateral damage' was Lecher," Jared replied. "The rest of you had to...*have* to...die. But it was always going to be you or Sassy last. If Sassy had died in the fire, it would have been you."

Michel was about to respond with a caustic "Lucky me," but stopped when he realized what Jared had said.

"Stan is dead?" he asked instead.

Jared nodded.

"But that had nothing to do with me," he said. "His involvement was all about Aaron. Aaron had to kill him because he figured out the connection between us."

Michel sat in stunned silence for a moment.

"Which is what?" he asked finally, though he no longer cared. He was only stalling for time.

"It doesn't really matter," Jared replied blithely. "But I've got something I want to show you."

He got up from the green leather chair and walked around to the other side of the bed. A few seconds later, he reappeared carrying a laptop. He placed it on the floor a few feet in front of Michel, and opened it, then double-clicked a file in the bottom right corner of the screen.

"These were taken the other morning while you were at the police station," he said.

A photo filled the whole screen. It showed Aaron, naked, standing in the doorway of Michel's and Joel's bathroom. Joel was a few feet in front of him.

Jared hit the space bar and another photo appeared. Joel was standing closer to Aaron now.

"I've already seen the magic you and Aaron can do with photos," Michel replied, shaking his head dismissively, though he suddenly had a sick feeling in the pit of his stomach.

Jared hit the space bar again. A closeup appeared of Joel and Aaron kissing.

Michel turned his head away, trying to appear disinterested.

"I'm not done yet," Jared said. "It's just getting good."

Michel heard him hit the space bar again, and couldn't stop himself from looking at the screen. Aaron had turned away from Joel and was walking toward the shower.

Jared hit the space bar one last time. Now Joel was standing in the bathroom, facing the shower. He was naked.

"I really don't understand why you care about him so much," Jared said. "He wasn't even faithful to you."

*****

Ribodeau rushed into DeRoche's office.

"What's wrong?" DeRoche asked.

"We just got a call from Landreau at the hotel," Ribodeau replied. "He tried to check in with Helms and didn't get a response. He went upstairs and found Helms stuffed in a laundry closet. Stan's been shot, and Michel and Chance are gone. There were no signs of forced entry in either room."

"Fuck!" DeRoche exclaimed. "Did anyone visit them in the last few hours?"

"Aaron Andrews," Ribodeau replied. "He left about 20 minutes before Landreau tried to contact Helms."

"Did you alert the surveillance team at Zelda's house?" DeRoche asked.

Ribodeau nodded gravely.

"No response."

Chapter 51

Jared closed the laptop and studied Michel's face.

"I think we're done here," he said in response to the defeated expression.

He scrambled to his feet and took his gun out of its holster. Suddenly his phone began to ring. He pulled it from his back pocket and looked at the display. Frowning slighty, he turned away from Michel and flipped it open.

"What?...Hello?...Aaron?"

He hung up and took a brief look at Michel, then hit speed dial. A phone began ringing somewhere in the house. After four rings it stopped.

"What the fuck's going on, Aaron?" Jared asked in a tone that made it clear he was talking to voicemail. "This isn't funny."

He snapped the phone shut and looked toward the stairs, then back at Michel.

"I'll deal with you in a minute," he said, though for the first time, Michel thought he could see doubt in his eyes.

Jared slipped the phone back into his pocket and walked to the stairwell, his gun held out in front of him with both hands. He stepped down onto the first step and stopped.

"Changing plans isn't cool, Aaron," he yelled. "What the fuck are you doing?"

Michel saw movement in the shadows along the right outer wall of the stairwell. He quickly looked away in case Jared turned back to him.

"Aaron!" Jared shouted. "You're starting to piss me off!"

Then Chance stepped in behind him.

"Aaron's not here, *bitch*!" he shouted, as he brought Aaron's laptop down hard on the back of Jared's head.

Chapter 52

Chance stood there breathing hard for a few seconds, framed in the doorway, then turned around. Michel was shocked by the barely controlled rage contorting his face.

"Chance," he said in a calming voice. "Bring me my gun."

He nodded toward the middle of the floor. For a moment, Chance didn't seem to comprehend, then he walked to the pistol and picked it up. He stared at it, turning it over in his hands several times, then looked back at Michel.

"I don't think so," he said sharply.

He crossed to the stairs and disappeared. Michel could hear his footsteps moving down, then his voice.

"Get up!"

There was a scuffling sound, followed by a dull thud and a cry of pain. Michel held his breath as footsteps started back up. Jared appeared in the doorway. He was bleeding from an inch-long gash above his right eye, and holding his right arm against his chest. From the odd angle, it was clear his wrist was broken.

Chance shoved him roughly, and Jared staggered a few steps into the room.

"Chance, what are you doing?" Michel asked, trying to keep his voice even.

Chance didn't reply, but kicked Jared behind the left knee.

"Down!" he barked, as Jared dropped with a pained grunt.

Jared looked at Michel, and Michel could see pleading in his eyes. Michel felt both revulsion and sympathy.

"Chance, you don't need to do this," he said.

286

"Yes, I do," Chance replied, his voice breaking.

"No, you *don't*," Michel replied with more authority.

The anger on Chance's face suddenly transformed to anguish, and he wiped at his eyes with the back of left hand. He pressed the muzzle of the gun against the back of Jared's head with a shaking hand.

"Chance, you can't undo this," Michel said.

Chance's shoulders began to shake, and he let out a strangled moan.

"Good," he said, then pulled the trigger and screamed.

As the firing pin clicked on the empty chamber, a circle of wet began spreading down the left leg of Jared's jeans. Chance gaped at Michel, then his whole body began to tremble and he dropped the gun.

Chapter 53

"What's the combination?" Michel asked.

"Zero-one-two-three-four," Jared replied in a flat, barely audible voice.

Michel unlocked the cuff and got to his feet, leaning heavily on the bed for support. He straightened up with a wince, and slowly walked over to Chance. Chance immediately fell against his shoulder and began sobbing.

"It's okay," Michel said, stroking the back of his head.

Chance put his arms around Michel, and Michel squeezed his eyes shut against the pain.

"We better go," he said after a few seconds.

Chance held him a moment longer, then took a step back and dried his eyes and face with the bottom of his t-shirt. Michel picked up his gun and took the magazine from his left coat pocket. He pushed it into the grip, and racked the slide.

"Where's his gun?" he asked.

"Downstairs," Chance replied quietly.

"Go get it for me, please," Michel replied.

While Chance went downstairs, Michel studied Jared. He hadn't moved since Chance had pulled the trigger. Michel wondered what he was thinking.

"Here," Chance said as he came back into the attic, holding Jared's pistol tentatively between his index finger and thumb.

Michel took it put it into his holster.

"Up," he said to Jared.

*****

As they reached the the third floor landing, a rush of loud footsteps came from below. Michel leaned over the railing and saw the balding top of Al Ribodeau's head, surrounded by six men in black tactical gear.

"Al!" Michel called.

Ribodeau's head jerked up.

"We've got him. Stay there," Michel said. "We're bringing him down."

"You sure?" Ribodeau asked.

Michel nodded.

"Any more bodies up here and I think the whole place is going to come down."

"Okay," Ribodeau replied.

"And you should probably move out of the hallway," Michel added. "Just in case."

He waited until the men had moved back, then turned to Jared.

"You first," he said.

"But what if he makes a run for it?" Chance protested.

"To where?" Michel replied.

Chance frowned, but stepped out of the way.

"Go ahead," Michel said, jabbing the gun into Jared's side.

Jared walked to the top of the stairs, then slowly started down. Michel waited until he was on the fourth step, then turned to Chance. Chance couldn't read his expression, and gave him a questioning look.

As Jared took another step, the stairs began to groan, and he froze. Michel smiled softly at Chance. It was the oddest smile Chance had ever seen, full of both sadness and serenity. Then Michel turned and jumped onto the stair above Jared.

A sound like a gunshot rang out as the 2 x 4 supporting the staircase hit the wall of the second floor hallway.

"Al, look out!" Michel shouted.

Jared spun around, his eyes wide with shock. As the stairs began to pull away from the wall, he tried to turn, but Michel grabbed him by the collar and held him in place. They locked eyes for a moment as the sounds of splintering wood and popping nails filled the air. Then Jared smiled.

"No!" Chance screamed.

Michel let go of Jared's shirt and pushed him hard. Jared stumbled backwards and fell, rolling into the wall on the second floor landing. Michel closed his eyes as the stairs dropped away beneath his feet.

Suddenly he felt himself being yanked backward by the belt. Jagged wood jabbed painfully into the backs of his thighs, and he opened his eyes. He looked over his left shoulder and saw Chance, his left hand locked around the newel post at the top of the stairs. The slight muscles in his outstretched arms were quivering, and his face was red with strain.

"Help me, you fucker!" he growled through gritted teeth.

*****

"Are you all right?" Ribodeau called up, peering up around the wreckage of the stairs.

"Yeah," Michel replied, though he felt like he needed a new rib cage after pulling himself up onto the remaining stairs one baluster at a time. "How about everyone down there?"

"No injuries," Ribodeau replied. "Where's Clement?"

"On the landing," Michel replied, nodding straight ahead. "It looks like he's breathing, but unconscious."

Suddenly Jared's left arm twitched.

"Check that. I think he's waking up now," Michel added.

"That's okay," Ribodeau replied. "He's not walking out of here without stairs."

Jared lifted his head and looked around in a daze. Then his eyes fixed on Michel and immediately focused. He sat up and let out a dark laugh.

"Al, is anyone guarding out back?" Michel asked uneasily.

"Yeah, the whole block is surrounded," Ribodeau replied. "Why?"

Michel looked back at Jared.

"Did you hear that? There's no place to go this time."

Jared didn't respond. Instead he grabbed the bannister and pulled himself to his feet. He stood there for a moment, swaying unsteadily, then lifted his right foot onto the short section between the stairs and hallway.

"What the fuck are you doing?" Michel asked, feeling his pulse quicken.

"Jesus Christ!" Ribodeau cried, looking up. "Everybody get back!"

Jared slowly pulled his left foot up onto the banister. He crouched there for a few seconds, holding onto the finial crowning the newel post, then slowly began to rise. Twice he nearly lost his balance, but managed to steady himself until he was standing straight.

"Don't do this," Michel said, though it sounded more like a prayer than an exhortation.

Jared smiled at him and lifted both arms out to his side. The left was straight, but the broken right was bent downward, giving him the appearance of a deformed Christ figure.

"You win," he said, then rocked forward and dove head first into the pile of rubble below.

Michel closed his eyes and took a deep slow breath. As he exhaled, he felt some of the tension he'd been holding for the last few days leaving him. He opened his eyes and looked down at the twisted body.

"Now *that* was more like his brother," he thought.

Chapter 54

Michel and Chance had been silent since they'd left the house. They stood on the sidewalk, bathed in the strobes of a half dozen police cruisers, sharing Chance's last cigarette.

"I tried to kill him," Chance said suddenly, his voice hushed and bewildered.

"We both did," Michel replied quietly.

"But you stopped yourself," Chance said. "I would have done it if the gun had been loaded."

"But you *didn't*," Michel replied with gentle force.

Chance stared down at the pavement, and Michel could see the corners of his mouth twitching. He looked to be on the verge of tears again.

"As soon as I pulled the trigger, I wanted to undo it," he said, his voice trembling slightly. "And when I realized it hadn't gone off, it was like...my life had been spared, too."

He looked up at Michel with an expression that was strangely imploring, almost desperate.

"How did you know I'd try?" he asked.

"I didn't know," Michel replied. "I just wanted to be safe. I didn't want you to have to live with that."

He saw immediately that it wasn't the answer Chance had been hoping for, and sensed he was looking for something more profound, perhaps absolution, or assurance that he didn't bear some telltale mark of a killer. Given Chance's fears of carrying on his family's tainted legacy, Michel decided it was probably the latter.

"Chance, you're not a killer," he said.

"But..."

"But nothing," Michel cut him off. "Under the right circumstances, anyone can kill, but that doesn't mean everyone's a killer. Did you come here planning to shoot him?"

Chance tried to remember exactly what he'd been thinking and feeling on his way to the house. It seemed so long ago now.

"No," he said finally, shaking his head. "I wanted him dead, but I wasn't thinking about killing him. It was just that...when I hit him, I couldn't stop myself. All this anger just came out, and...."

He trailed off and chewed his lower lip.

"That's the difference," Michel said. "You're not a killer. Trust me."

Chance stared at the pavement for a moment, then nodded with what seemed to be grateful acceptance.

"And what about you?" he asked.

"I thought so, but apparently not," Michel replied, his wry smile fading quickly. "No. I wanted to kill him, but when it came down to it, I couldn't do it."

"Kind of ironic, don't you think?" Chance asked. "You wanted to kill him, but couldn't. I didn't want to, but would have if you hadn't taken the bullets out of the gun."

"Yeah, I suppose it is," Michel replied, offering a thin smile.

They lapsed into silence for a few moments, then Chance's eyes grew troubled again.

"How did you know the stairs would collapse?" he asked.

"I unbraced the support holding them up," Michel replied.

"You what?" Chance exclaimed a bit too loudly.

Michel looked around to make sure they hadn't attracted any unwelcome attention, then gave him a warning look.

"It was insurance," he said. "Just in case you didn't make it in time, or something else went wrong. I wanted to make sure he didn't get out of there. Then when the police showed up, I realized it would work out even better. Seven unimpeachable witnesses that he died in an accident."

He shrugged, as if to say, "end of story."

"Then why'd you change your mind?" Chance asked.

Michel took a meditative drag on the cigarette. He didn't fully understand the reason himself, yet. It had all happened too quickly, and he'd simply been reacting in the moment. He exhaled loudly and handed the cigarette back to Chance.

"His smile," he said finally.

Chance looked at him blankly.

"He wanted to kill us, but first he wanted to take away everything that was important to us," Michel said. "When he smiled, I realized I was just giving it all away."

He paused for a moment, weighing what he'd said. It felt right, but incomplete.

"I also didn't want to go out like that," he said. "I became a cop because I believe in justice, but I was about to kill for vengeance. I was betraying my own beliefs. I was supposed to trust the system to do what was right."

He realized the irony of what he'd said, given his history on the force, but still, it felt right, too.

"But you would have been dead," Chance replied. "What would it have mattered?"

"It probably wouldn't have to anyone else," Michel replied, "but I couldn't let that be the last thing I ever did."

Chance nodded, but Michel could see his thoughts suddenly turn inward as he began absently puffing on the cigarette. The rising smoke caught the spinning lights from the cruisers, and Michel found himself being unexpectedly transported back to the night he'd met Joel at Parade. He closed his eyes to savor the memory.

"I thought I'd feel different," Chance said suddenly, breaking the near minute-long silence.

Michel reluctantly let the moment go and opened his eyes.

"In what way?" he asked.

Chance dropped the cigarette and crushed it out.

"I thought I'd be happy he's dead," he said, "but I'm not. I mean, I'm glad he's gone, but it doesn't make me feel good. I just feel kind of...sad. About all of it."

"I'm not sure it's ever right to feel happy that someone's dead," Michel replied, unsure what else to say.

"I'm also glad that you didn't kill him," Chance said. "Even if you hadn't died, too."

"Why's that?" Michel asked.

"Because I don't know how I would have felt about you then," Chance replied. "I'm not sure I entirely get your whole existential drama about not betraying yourself, but I think that if you'd killed him, it would have changed you. Or maybe I'd just feel like it did."

Michel was surprised by Chance's insight and honesty. He also wondered what emotional toll Chance's own attempt to kill Jared would take on him over time.

The flare of a match caught his eye, and he turned to see a young officer lighting a cigarette a few yards away.

"I'm going to see if I can get us another one," he said.

The officer saw Michel approaching, and his body stiffened. He quickly put the cigarette down by his left side.

"It's okay...Flynn," Michel said, glancing quickly at his nameplate. "I was just going to see if I could bum one."

Flynn stared at him unsmilingly for a moment, then pulled a pack from his right pants pocket.

"Thanks," Michel said, taking it.

He studied the young man as he shook out a cigarette. He looked to be about the same age as Helms, and had the same military bearing.

"You wouldn't happen to know Officer Helms, would you?" Michel asked, as he handed back the pack.

"Yes, sir," Flynn replied, his back straightening noticeably.

"Do you know if he's all right?" Michel asked.

"No, sir," Flynn replied stiffly. "He was killed in the line of duty tonight."

Michel felt the energy suddenly drain from his body. Though he'd feared as much, it was still a shock to hear it said.

"I'm sorry," he said reflexively. Then, as much to himself as Flynn, he added, "His wife was pregnant."

"Yes, sir. I'm aware of that," Flynn replied.

Michel stared at the ground for a moment, then looked up at Flynn. Flynn didn't meet his gaze.

"I want to make a donation," Michel said, then immediately regretted it.

The words had sounded hollow and wholly inadequate.

"That won't be necessary, sir," Flynn replied coldly. "We take care of our own."

"I know that," Michel replied. "But I was one of your own."

Flynn looked at him sharply.

"Yes, sir," he said, "but not anymore."

He turned crisply and walked away.

Michel walked slowly back to Chance and handed him the cigarette. Chance lit it and took a long drag, then handed it back to Michel. For a minute they stood in silence, each lost in his own thoughts as they passed the cigarette back and forth.

"They didn't have sex," Chance said abruptly.

"What?" Michel replied, completely caught off-guard.

"Joel and Aaron. They didn't have sex."

Michel looked at Chance with a mixture of hope and doubt.

"How do you know?"

"I saw the video on Aaron's computer," Chance replied. "They tried to make it look like Joel followed him into the shower, but the footage of Joel was shot later."

"But what about the kiss?" Michel asked.

"Joel was walking into the bathroom and Aaron surprised him," Chance replied.

"But why was Aaron naked in our bathroom in the first place?" Michel asked.

Chance shrugged. "I don't know, but when he kissed Joel, Joel backed away. Nothing else happened."

Michel felt a rush of relief and gratitude.

"Thank you," he said, though again his words seemed inadequate to him.

He was about to say more when he noticed Ribodeau walking toward them.

"How are you guys doing?" Ribodeau asked.

"Okay, considering," Michel replied.

"Well, I've got some good news," Ribodeau said. "It looks like Stan's going to make it."

"Stan?" Chance replied. "What happened to him?"

"Aaron shot him," Ribodeau replied. "Three times."

"I knew I should have killed that fucker when I had the chance," Chance said angrily.

Michel and Ribodeau both gave him cautioning looks.

"Jared told me he was already dead," Michel said.

"Guess he was wrong," Ribodeau replied. "Unfortunately, Officer Helms wasn't so lucky."

"I know," Michel replied, frowning. "His wife is pregnant. I want to make sure that she and the baby are taken care of."

"We can arrange that," Ribodeau replied.

"But I'd like to keep it just between us," Michel said.

Ribodeau gave him a curious look, but nodded.

"And what about Aaron?" Michel asked. "Was he still at the church?"

"Yup. He's in custody," Ribodeau replied.

"And in one piece?" Michel asked, cutting a look at Chance.

"So far as I know," Ribodeau replied. "He's also apparently feeling pretty chatty."

Michel nodded.

"I'm not surprised. He probably wants to cut a deal."

"I think he's going to be shit-out-of-luck with that," Ribodeau replied. "With Clement dead, the only one he can testify against is himself."

"And I don't think you'll need that," Michel replied. "His laptop is up in the attic. I'm sure it's got everything on it."

"Good," Ribodeau replied. "We'll send someone up as soon as we're sure it's safe."

"He told me he and Jared and Hunter...Drew...whatever the fuck...were like brothers," Chance said, "and that Hunter was his best friend."

Michel gave him a puzzled look.

"Did he say anything about how they met?"

"He said he met Jared in a chat room for sex abuse victims," Chance replied, "but I couldn't tell if he was telling the truth or just trying to get my sympathy."

"I'm sure we'll find out eventually," Ribodeau said, then yawned loudly.

His expression became sober.

"You'll both need to come down to the station and give statements," he said, "but it can wait until morning. I figured you'd want to go to the hospital first. You should probably get those ribs checked out."

"Thanks," Michel said.

"That's okay," Chance said. "I think I'd rather get it over with now. I can go to the hospital tomorrow morning."

Michel gave him a curious look.

"Are you sure?"

"Yeah," Chance replied. "I just think that would be better."

Michel considered asking Ribodeau to give them a minute alone, but decided to give Chance some space.

"Okay," he said.

Chapter 55

Michel knocked lightly against the door frame, and Sassy opened her eyes.

"I'm guessing it's over," she said.

"No one told you?" Michel asked as he walked over to the bed and sat on the edge.

Sassy shook her head.

"My bodyguard just opened the door, said goodbye, and left. I didn't even have a chance to sing 'I Will Always Love You' to him."

Michel attempted a smile, but didn't quite manage it. Sassy tried to read his expression.

"So did you kill him?" she asked.

"No," Michel replied, "though I tried. He took a header from the second floor landing at Zelda's."

"And you didn't push him?" Sassy asked seriously.

"No," Michel replied.

Sassy knew there was more to the story, but decided not to press. She knew Michel would tell her when he was ready.

"Stan got shot," he said, "but it looks like he's going to be all right."

"By Jared?" Sassy asked.

"By Aaron," Michel replied.

Sassy nodded to herself.

"I had a feeling," she said. "I asked Stan to do some more checking on him. I hope that's not what got him shot."

"I guess we'll find out when he wakes up," Michel replied.

"And how's Chance?" Sassy asked.

"Scared, I think," Michel replied. "He didn't want to come with me. He said he'd come by in the morning."

"You really can't blame him," Sassy replied gently. "Now that Jared's gone, the reality of what happened is probably sinking in. I'm sure he's feeling overwhelmed right now."

"Yeah," Michel replied quietly.

Sassy reached out and took his right hand.

"What about you?" she asked.

Michel didn't reply for a few moments, and Sassy could see the tears welling in his eyes.

"I don't know what I'm going to do," he said finally, as they began to fall. "When I think about waking up...and him not being there..."

"Then don't think about it," Sassy said.

"What?" Michel replied, thinking he'd misheard her.

"Then don't think about it," Sassy repeated.

Michel felt a sudden flash of anger.

"I'm not trying to be callous," Sassy said, reading his eyes. "I understand. But you told me not to talk about him like he's already dead. All I'm saying is don't grieve him while he's still alive either. There'll be plenty of time for that later."

Michel's mouth opened, but he didn't know how to respond. Sassy squeezed his hand.

"Go be with him," she said. "Tell him you love him. Tell him you'll miss him. But don't let go of him yet."

Michel stared at her for a long moment, then sighed and nodded.

"You're right," he said.

He stood up and wiped his eyes, then leaned down and kissed Sassy on the cheek.

"You're welcome," she said.

Chapter 56

Michel heard stirring on the bed and opened his eyes. Joel was watching him. His hair was longer, and he was dressed in a red tank top and tan cargo shorts. He looked exactly as he had the night they'd met.

"Hey," Joel said.

Michel let out a joyful laugh.

"Are you all right?" he asked breathlessly.

"I'm fine," Joel replied. "I'm not in any pain."

Michel tried to stand, but couldn't. He looked down at the chair curiously, then back at Joel and smiled.

"I can't believe it," he said. "The doctors said you'd never wake up."

Joel smiled back at him.

"I had to come back," he said, "but I can't stay long."

"Where are you going?" Michel asked.

"I think you know," Joel replied, "but it'll be okay."

Michel fought back sudden panic.

"But I don't want you to go," he said.

"I know," Joel replied wistfully, "but I don't have any choice. And neither does Mammau."

"Mammau?" Michel replied, looking around the room.

When he looked back, Joel was standing on the other side of the bed. Michel tried to stand again, but his arms and legs wouldn't respond.

"No," he said, as tears began to build.

He watched helplessly as Joel walked to the door.

"Please don't go," he pleaded. "I don't want to be alone."

Joel turned back and looked at him.

"You won't be," he said. "Just remember that I love you."

"I love you, too," Michel replied, choking back a sob.

Then Joel opened the door and was gone.

Michel woke with a start and looked up. Joel was still lying in the hospital bed. Michel let out a wet sigh, and wiped his eyes.

"You slept here all night," a brittle voice said to his right.

Michel turned and saw an older woman standing at the foot of the bed watching him. She was small and slim, with snow white hair pulled back into a tight bun. Her eyes were the same shape as Joel's, but a very pale blue.

"Mammau," Michel said without thinking, as the gateway between dream and reality closed.

The woman nodded and walked slowly toward him. Michel sensed that her pace was deliberate rather than necessary. That she was taking her time to appraise him.

"I'm Estella Gaulthier," she said, holding out her hand.

"Michel Doucette," Michel said, rising and taking it.

Mammau's skin was cool and dry, and her grip firm.

"It's nice to meet you," Michel said.

Mammau nodded politely, but didn't reply. She gave his hand two quick shakes, then released it. Michel couldn't get a read on her expression.

"When Joel and Chance came back home after Chance was stabbed, I knew they weren't telling me the whole truth about what happened," she said. "And when Joel came back here, I figured there must be someone waiting for him. I'm guessing that someone is you."

Michel hesitated for a moment, unsure how to respond, then nodded.

"Do you love him?" Mammau asked immediately.

"I do," Michel replied, his voice breaking slightly.

"Good," Mammau replied. "I'm glad he was loved."

She turned to Joel and caressed his right cheek.

"The doctors say he won't be waking up," she said without looking up. "What do you think I should do?"

"I don't know," Michel replied automatically.

"Then I guess it's a good thing you don't have to decide," Mammau said.

There was nothing harsh or unkind in her tone, yet Michel still felt as though she'd judged him.

"When Joel's momma and daddy had the accident, my Laura lived for almost a month," Mammau said.

"Joel never told me," Michel replied with surprise.

Mammau turned to face him.

"He never knew," she said. "The doctors said there was no chance she was coming back home, so I thought it was better to tell him she was gone and let the healing start. But I couldn't let her go myself, so I asked the doctors to keep her alive. And every day I went to the hospital and sat with her, and prayed for a miracle. Then finally one day it came, and the Lord took her."

Michel knew what was coming next and braced himself.

"I talked with his grandpa, and prayed on it," Mammau said, "and I don't think that God would want for Joel to live like this. I think it would be more merciful to let him go."

Michel couldn't say anything.

"I want to give his friends a chance to say their goodbyes," Mammau continued, "but I can't stay here for long. I need to get back to his grandpa."

Michel nodded numbly.

"You're welcome to be here with me when it's time," Mammau said, "but then I'll be bringing his body back home to be buried, and I'd appreciate it if you'd stay away for that."

Michel swallowed hard and took a ragged breath. Unexpectedly, Mammau reached out and touched his hand.

"Don't let this turn you hard," she said. "I know Joel wouldn't want that."

"I know," Michel managed.

Mammau turned and started toward the door, then stopped and turned back.

"You know, I heard it in his voice when he called," she said. "He was happy here in a way he never was as a boy."

For the first time, she smiled at Michel. It was Joel's smile.

"I'm grateful to you for that," she said.

Chapter 57

"Well, I think we better be heading home," Russ Turner said, looking at his watch. "Corey's got a test in the morning. Come on, Jack. I'll give you a ride to the Gator."

Black Jack Doucette pushed himself up stiffly, and Michel tried to hide his smirk. His father had obviously worn his girdle for the occasion.

"Sassy," Black Jack said, attempting a courtly bow, "it was a pleasure, as always. Thank you for the lovely dinner."

"You're welcome, Jack," Sassy replied with a warm smile.

"Thank you, Miss Sassy," Corey Turner said, holding his hand out with his usual politeness.

"You're welcome, Corey," Sassy replied, ignoring his hand and hugging him instead. "Good luck with your test."

Black Jack and Corey filed out onto the porch, and Russ Turner followed them to the door.

"I'm afraid I'm going to have to get some bigger pants if you keep feeding us like that," he said, smiling at Sassy.

"Hey, I helped," Michel piped in. "I peeled the potatoes."

"More like butchered them," Sassy said, shaking her head.

Michel gave her a comic pout.

"Well, thank you both," Turner said, then stood there awkwardly for a few seconds.

Finally Sassy hobbled over to him, her cast thumping against the hard wood floor, and kissed him on the cheek. Michel noticed the way her left hand lingered on his forearm for a moment.

"You're welcome," she said.

*****

Blue dropped down onto the porch and rolled onto her side with a satisfied groan. Over the last week, her energy and appetite had gradually been returning, though she was still exhausted by the end of each day.

"Well...ain't we a pair...*raggedy man?*" Sassy said.

"Did you just Tina Turner me?" Michel asked, raising an eyebrow.

"You know it," Sassy replied.

They each took a sip of their drinks. Sassy looked at Michel's glass and made a sour face.

"What?" Michel asked.

"I'm just wondering how much longer you're going to be drinking that stuff," Sassy replied.

"Why? Does it bother you?" Michel teased.

"Hell, yeah, it bothers me," Sassy replied. "It makes me feel like an old drunk when I'm guzzling wine and you're sipping soda water."

"You're not *that* old," Michel replied, then took another sip and let out a theatrical "Ah!" of satisfaction.

Sassy shook her head and Michel smiled.

"Don't worry," he said. "I promise I'll go back to the hard stuff one of these days. It just makes the memories a little too real right now."

They were both quiet for a moment, then Michel leaned forward in his chair.

"I finally returned Al's calls today while you were napping," he said.

"And?" Sassy lifted a curious eyebrow.

"Apparently Aaron was telling the truth about being abused by his real father," Michel replied. "The Andrews confirmed it. And he actually did meet Jared in a victims' chat room."

"But how did Jared and Hunter end up in Greenwich?" Sassy asked.

"Aaron's parents invited them," Michel replied.

"They what?" Sassy replied with disbelief.

"They invited them," Michel repeated, "though they obviously didn't know they were psychotic killers at the time. They just thought they were in an abusive home situation and needed a place to go."

"What about Aaron? Did he know?" Sassy asked.

"That part's still unclear," Michel replied. "He claims he didn't, but he's the one who created the Jason and Kyle Brown identities for them. I'm guessing he knew."

"Wow," Sassy said. "So did they actually live with the family?"

"No, the Andrews rented an apartment for them," Michel replied, "but they were treated like part of the family for the two years they were living there."

"But not after?" Sassy asked, catching something in his tone.

Michel shook his head.

"A few days after they graduated, they disappeared. Along with $100,000 from Mr. Andrew's retirement account."

"Courtesy of Aaron, no doubt," Sassy said.

"No doubt," Michel agreed.

"That's cold," Sassy said. "How can you fuck over people who help you like that?"

Michel gave her a deadpan look.

"We're talking about the Clement brothers," he said.

Sassy laughed.

"Good point."

Michel reached into his shirt pocket and took out a pack of cigarettes. Blue raised her head to watch him for a moment, but didn't move farther away. Michel lit a cigarette and took a long, luxuriant drag, then slowly blew the smoke out, watching it curl upward into the darkening sky.

"So, I think it's time for me to go back," he said abruptly.

Sassy gave him a measured look.

"And do what?"

"Well, I'd been hoping to rejoin the force," Michel replied, "but I spoke to the Captain today, too, and apparently escaping protective custody and going after the bad guy on your own are frowned upon."

"Imagine that," Sassy replied sarcastically. "So then what's the hurry? Why not stick around for a while. In fact, why go back at all? Seems to me you could have a pretty nice life here."

Michel gave her an amused smile.

"You sure you're not speaking for yourself?"

"What's that supposed to mean?" Sassy asked, narrowing her eyes at him.

"Oh please," Michel replied. "You and Russ have been eyeing one other like two lovesick 13-year-olds for the past two weeks."

"Excuse me," Sassy replied, sitting forward in her chair. "No we have not."

"Hey, I just calls 'em as I sees 'em," Michel replied, holding his hands up defensively.

Sassy scowled at him, then broke into a shy smile.

"So do you really think he likes me?" she asked.

"Oh my God, I can't believe you just asked me that," Michel replied, shaking his head. "Of course he likes you. And so does Corey."

Sassy couldn't help but smile.

"Well, good," she said in a small, girlish voice.

They each took a sip of their drinks.

"So why *are* you going back?" Sassy asked finally.

"Chance emailed me today," Michel replied. "He's getting back tomorrow. He didn't say anything, of course, but I got the sense he was hoping at least one of us would be there."

Sassy nodded.

"And you're sure you're just doing it for his sake?"

"Meaning?" Michel asked.

"Well, we all loved Joel," Sassy replied, "but it was different for the two of you. You're the only ones who really understand what the other one is going through right now."

Michel considered it for a moment.

"Maybe," he said, "but I don't think we'll be sitting around drinking tea and talking about our feelings any time soon."

"I wouldn't expect so," Sassy replied with an appreciative laugh. "Still, just being there for each other might help."

They were both quiet again for a moment.

"Okay with you if I stick around for a while longer?" Sassy asked finally.

"There's a surprise," Michel replied.

Sassy shot him the evil eye.

"Yeah, it's fine," Michel said. "Give you and Russ a little alone time."

"Alone with your father and Corey," Sassy replied.

"Yeah, you better watch out for my father," Michel said. "And that old codger Cyrus at the market, too. I think they've both got their eyes on you. I saw Cyrus give you a discount on that chicken today."

"I keep telling you," Sassy said. "People just like me because I'm nice to them."

Michel rolled his eyes, then his expression grew serious.

"You are coming back, aren't you?" he asked.

"Of course," Sassy replied. "I've already done my time in the bayou. It's a nice place to visit, but I wouldn't want to live here again. I'll just stay another week or two."

"And if things heat up between you and Russ?" Michel asked.

"Then I guess he and Corey will be moving to New Orleans," Sassy replied breezily.

"Oh, you think you have that kind of power over men, do you?" Michel teased.

"I know I do," Sassy replied.

They were quiet again for a few moments.

"So what's your plan?" Sassy asked finally.

"We've still got a business to run," Michel replied.

"You know you're going to be on your own for a while until this leg heals, don't you?" Sassy asked.

Michel nodded.

"And don't worry, your job will still be there when you're ready to come back."

"I wasn't worried," Sassy replied, then looked down at her wine glass. "And what about the church? You still planning to move there?"

"No, that was for Joel and me," Michel replied without any bitterness. "I think I'm better off staying where I was. Close to the things I know. And the people I love."

Sassy was surprised and pleased that Michel was being so open. She reached out and took his hand.

"So you're leaving tomorrow?" she asked.

Michel nodded.

"You want me to leave Blue with you for protection?"

"No, she should go with you," Sassy replied. "I'll be okay on my own. I'm not planning to go walking in the swamp, plus I've got my gun."

"Not to mention a certain sheriff to look after you," Michel added.

He stared up into the sky, watching the first stars break through the deep blue canvas.

"Wow, I can't believe you're dumping me for another guy," he said after a few moments.

Sassy started to laugh, then her expression grew serious when she saw a touch of genuine hurt in Michel's eyes.

"I'm not dumping you," she said. "I promise, I'll be back."

"It's not going to be the same, though," Michel replied, his voice breaking slightly.

Sassy knew that he meant more than her relationship with Russ, and squeezed his hand.

"No, it won't be," she said. "But we'll get through it. Together."

Available Spring 2013
from

FIERCE

A New Michel Doucette
& Sassy Jones Novel

DAVID LENNON

Prologue

The boy was completely still except for his thumbs, which bounced around like a pair of hyperactive toddlers on sugar highs. The only sounds in the room were the hard tapping of the controller's buttons, and the muted cries of the two warriors on the TV's screen.

A sudden motion to his left caught the boy's eye, and he looked down for a split second. The white kitten gave a feeble, high-pitched meow. The boy looked back at the screen and kept playing. The kitten continued staring at him for a moment, then walked to the foot of the bed and lay down.

The boy executed a series of round house kicks, then moved in for the kill. As his opponent swayed back and forth, the boy quickly punched in an eleven-button sequence, feeling his heart racing. His opponent exploded, leaving only a pile of bloody bones on the screen.

"Yes!" the boy shouted, jerking up into a sitting position.

Suddenly he felt tiny needles in his left foot and looked down. The kitten had wrapped herself around his sock and was trying to gnaw at his big toe.

"Leave me alone, you little shit," the boy said.

He swept his leg sideways over the edge of the bed and shook his foot. The kitten dropped to the floor. She looked around in a daze for a moment, then scrambled clumsily out of the room.

The boy rested the controller in his lap and looked at the clock. It was nearly 5 PM. His parents would be home soon. He grabbed a chocolate chip cookie from the plate on the nightstand and took a bite, then washed it down with some milk. Out of the corner of his eye, he saw the kitten peering at him around the doorframe.

He finished the cookie, put the half-empty glass beside the plate, and lay down. The TV screen was prompting him to start a new game, but he ignored it. Instead he grabbed the bed spread with his left half and lifted it a few inches. He shook it back and forth. The kitten immediately slipped into the room and dropped into a crouch. She began slowly moving forward as she stalked the dancing fabric.

The boy waited until he felt the kitten tugging on the spread, then ripped it upward. The kitten tumbled halfway across the room, and ran toward the door. As the boy made a chucking sound and began to bounce the spread again, she stopped and turned around. She watched curiously for a moment, then crouched again.

The boy closed his eyes and tried to visualize the kitten's approach. He held his breath, and was sure he could hear velvet footsteps He shook the spread more vigorously, feeling the excitement growing inside him.

Then suddenly he sat up and swung his legs over the side of the bed. He brought his feet down hard, and heard a satisfying cry of pain.

He leaned forward and lifted his feet.

"I think your back is broken, kitty," he said, as he watched the kitten's body spasm.

He got down on his knees to watch more closely, and considered crushing its skull, but knew that would be too hard to explain to his parents. Instead he lifted the tiny body and placed it on his pillow. He watched it for a few minutes, waiting for it to stop convulsing, and for its spirit to rise into the air.

Finally it stopped breathing and he placed it on the floor. He sat back on the bed and finished his milk.

Chapter 1

Michel Doucette opened the front door and flipped on the hall light. He hadn't planned on staying out so late, but he'd started chatting with a cute redhead, and before he knew it, one drink had lead to three and it was dark. As usual, Blue was lying in the hallway, waiting for him. After a moment's hesitation to be sure it was him, she jumped up and began skittering excitedly from side to side, then turned and ran a few feet down the hall before stopping suddenly and running back.

"Hey, girl," Michel said. "Did you miss me?"

Blue closed the distance between them, her head down and her ears back, but her tail bouncing. It was the same each time he came home. She was excited at first, then turned shy, as though she needed assurance that he still loved her. He rubbed her neck and kissed her on the top of her head.

"I'm sorry I left you alone for so long," he said.

Blue gave him a quick nibble on the nose, apparently forgiving him. Michel turned to the redhead, standing just inside the door.

"Blue, this is..." he scrunched his face with embarrassment.

"Harlan," the redhead responded.

Of course you are, Michel thought, with a mental eye roll.

"This is Harlan," he said, "and this is Blue."

Harlan squatted down, and Blue walked cautiously toward him. When she was two feet away, she stopped. Harlan held his right hand out, and Blue sniffed his fingers. She quickly backed away. Michel sighed silently.

"I'm sorry," he said, standing up, "but this isn't going to work. I can call you a cab, if you want."

Harlan stood slowly, the disbelief obvious on his face.

"Are you serious?"

"Yeah," Michel replied flatly.

Harlan began to smirk. He suddenly looked much older, and a lot less cute.

"A friend of mine told me you brought him home, then kicked him out because your dog didn't like him," he said, his tone ripe with ridicule. "I figured that was just an excuse when you saw what he looked like with the lights on, but I guess not."

He stared at Michel as though expecting a response. Michel just shrugged.

"And what if I don't want to leave?" Harlan asked.

Michel wasn't sure if he was trying to be playful, or if it had been a threat. He decided it didn't matter. He wanted Harlan gone. He looked down at the floor for a long moment.

In the past, he'd often felt that his attempts to intimidate sounded unconvincing, or even silly. In the two years since the murder of his boyfriend, Joel, however, that hadn't been a problem. Now, even when he was trying to be friendly, people sometimes reacted as though there was something vaguely unsettling about him.

He lifted his eyes and fixed Harlan with a cold stare.

"Do you really think that's an option?" he asked.

Though he'd kept his tone neutral, Harlan's head still jerked back involuntarily.

"Fuck you, freak," Harlan stammered nervously, then turned and hurried out the door.

"That went well," Michel said, watching him fade into the darkness. He knelt down and hugged Blue's neck. "You know, one of these days you're going to have to let Daddy get some."

Blue rested her head on his right knee and looked up at him with her soft brown eyes. Michel let out a resigned sigh.

"Or not," he said.

Blue's tail immediately began wagging. She spun away and ran to the back door.

"Yeah, me, too," Michel said, following her, "but I'll let you go first."

Made in the USA
Charleston, SC
07 April 2012